MARGARET MANCHESTER

Perfect Retribution

First published by Vine House Publishing 2025

Copyright © 2025 by Margaret Manchester

All rights reserved. No part of this publication may be reproduced, stored or transmitted in any form or by any means, electronic, mechanical, photocopying, recording, scanning, or otherwise without written permission from the publisher. It is illegal to copy this book, post it to a website, or distribute it by any other means without permission.

This novel is entirely a work of fiction. The names, characters and incidents portrayed in it are the work of the author's imagination. Any resemblance to actual persons, living or dead, events or localities is entirely coincidental.

Margaret Manchester asserts the moral right to be identified as the author of this work.

Margaret Manchester has no responsibility for the persistence or accuracy of URLs for external or third-party Internet Websites referred to in this publication and does not guarantee that any content on such Websites is, or will remain, accurate or appropriate.

Designations used by companies to distinguish their products are often claimed as trademarks. All brand names and product names used in this book and on its cover are trade names, service marks, trademarks and registered trademarks of their respective owners. The publishers and the book are not associated with any product or vendor mentioned in this book. None of the companies referenced within the book have endorsed the book.

First edition

*This book was professionally typeset on Reedsy.
Find out more at reedsy.com*

Contents

	Acknowledgements	iv
1	The Wrong Costume	1
2	A Sensible Solution	5
3	A Scathing Review	17
4	Orders Dwindling	20
5	Spreading the Word	24
6	Redundancy	27
7	The Quayside	37
8	Lasagne	42
9	The Love of his Life	46
10	Reading between the Lines	50
11	A Depressing Place	53
12	Finding Out	58
13	Spaghetti Bolognese	65
14	A Jog in the Park	69
15	A Walk in the Park	73
16	Dog Shit and Dinner	77
17	A Painful Extraction	82
18	Leaky Milk and a Flat Tyre	91
19	The Kiss	97
20	The Barbecue	102
21	Access All Areas	109
22	Failing Fast	114
23	Anonymous Gift	117

24	Glitter Galore	122
25	Planting Out	132
26	The Electric Company	140
27	Empty Cupboards	145
28	Little Pests	148
29	Impersonating a Neighbour	154
30	Park and Smash	157
31	Another Chance	166
32	In Trouble	170
33	Sympathy and Wine	173
34	Cowboys	178
35	Closing Shop	182
36	Planting Potatoes	185
37	Hot Potato	187
38	Down at the Station	195
39	Abject Failure	197
40	Seafood Paella and Prison	199
41	Coffee with Matt	208
42	Where is my Car?	214
43	A New Car	219
44	Returning The Car	225
45	Reporting Back	229
46	The Foul Smell	232
47	Bad News	235
48	Fire, Fire	240
49	The Yellow Car	243
50	Amanda's Funeral	246
51	Paranoia	252
52	Eviction	259
53	Alone Again	262
54	Homelessness	267

55	Drinking Alone	270
56	A Good Deed	274
57	Stalking Prey	279
58	Retribution	282
59	Identity	287
60	A New Beginning	298
About the Author		300

Acknowledgements

I cannot begin to express my gratitude to my husband, Alec, who has supported me throughout the writing of this book in so many ways, and to my son, Stephen, who has shared many ideas with me over the past six years, some of which I incorporated into this novel.

I would like to extend my sincere thanks to my team of readers, who kindly provided feedback from the first draft to the final version: my sisters, Linda Brown and Dawn Morgan; my brother, Carl Adamson; my niece, Eleanor Adamson; my long-time friend, Jacky Hutchinson; my father-in-law, Leslie Manchester; and finally my friend and author, Phil Mews. Your help was invaluable.

1

The Wrong Costume

July 2019

Dan Howard heard the doorbell chime in his large, detached house in Jesmond, an affluent suburb of Newcastle-upon-Tyne. He leapt up from his armchair to answer the door. A postman had a parcel under his arm and held an electronic signature device to sign. Dan signed his name with a flourish, although it looked nothing like his signature when he'd finished, and took the parcel.

This was so exciting. Dan couldn't wait to try on the costume he'd ordered from Glad Rags for Dave's annual charity bash, which annoyingly coincided with the San Diego Comic-Con event—again! Not that Dan had ever been to Comic-Con, not even the London one, but he loved seeing the photographs of everyone in fancy dress, especially the superheroes.

In anticipation of the parcel's arrival, he'd already propped up two full-length mirrors in the living room, so he could see how he would look from all angles. Glancing in the room as he passed the doorway, he smoothed his short brown hair, pulled in his tummy, and smiled at his reflection.

He then took the parcel into the kitchen and placed it on the oak table. Taking a pair of scissors from the cutlery drawer, he cut along the dotted line so he could reuse the postage bag at a later date; then, rummaging inside, he removed the contents.

Dan took a step back, his eyes wide, and his hand covering his gaping mouth. The costume he removed from the package was not the Spider-Man costume he ordered. The shirt's fabric was blue, but that's where the similarity ended. A red neckerchief, a black leather belt with a holster, a white hat, a black eye mask, and a plastic pistol completed the ensemble. *What the heck was it? And where was Spider-Man?*

He positioned the clothes on the table and looked down at the Lone Ranger. His initial shock turned to anger. His face red, he banged his fists on the table.

'I wanted to be Spider-Man!'

Never in his thirty-two years of life had he been so disappointed.

Under the jacket, Dan spotted the corner of a folded sheet of paper, which he removed. It was a printed receipt for the costume hire, with a handwritten note at the bottom.

Hi Daniel, I tried to call you today, but there was no answer. I'm very sorry, but the Spider-Man costume you ordered has not been returned yet, so we've sent this one instead. I hope it's suitable for your event. Enjoy the party! Best wishes, Amanda.

There was no way on earth that he could go to Dave's party as a glorified cowboy wearing a mask. He would have to cancel. He had absolutely no choice.

The woman at the fancy dress hire shop should have had the sense to send a Batman, a Superman, or even an Iron Man costume as a substitute for Spider-Man. But the Lone

Ranger? How could anyone think the Lone Ranger was a suitable alternative for Spider-Man? *What were they thinking?* The Lone Ranger wasn't even a superhero. *How could they have been so stupid?*

In a fit of fury, he grabbed his laptop to let Glad Rags know exactly what he thought of them for sending such an inappropriate costume. He couldn't bear to see the Lone Ranger lying on the kitchen table any longer, so he took his laptop into the lounge and switched it on. When the screen came to life, he clicked on Google Chrome and opened his email account, where he drafted a message.

Dear Amanda, I am dreadfully upset that you could not supply the Spider-Man costume I ordered from your company in good faith and that you thought the Lone Ranger would be a suitable alternative for a superhero. This shows how little you know about costumes and how little you care about your customers. I would not be seen dead in this outfit, so I will have to make my excuses for the party on Friday night, as there is no way I can attend wearing the Lone Ranger costume. As it's Wednesday today, I don't have time to find anything else to wear. I expect you will refund the £35 hire charge and the £4 postage that I paid. I also expect to receive the cost of the tickets that I can no longer use (which is £60 for two tickets at £30 each), as well as compensation for the distress that this incident has caused me. Yours sincerely, Mr Daniel J Howard.

Dan pressed send and smiled. *That would give them something to think about.* As he closed the laptop, he wondered how long it would be before they replied. With his vast experience of complaining, he knew that most companies caved in to his demands and gave him what he asked for, usually within a matter of hours. It was easy to get what you wanted when you knew how.

Dan sat back in his armchair and chuckled to himself. He hadn't been that bothered about going to the party anyway. Dave's parties were such a bore, and he hardly even knew the guy. Dave had been a friend of Dan's late parents. One year, his mother had insisted that Dan attend the annual fundraising event, saying he needed to get out more, and he had continued to receive the invitations ever since. He'd much rather stay at home, though, and follow what was happening at Comic-Con on social media—that would be much more fun.

2

A Sensible Solution

(The Day Before)

James Webster walked from the dry cleaners in Sandyford to the fancy dress shop in Newcastle City Centre in the drizzling rain. He struggled to unlock the steel door at the back of the shop with one hand, and the fancy dress costumes he held over his arm slithered to the wet ground.

'Shit!'

He gathered them up and took them inside.

'Is that you, James?' asked his colleague from the shop at the front of the building.

'Yes, Matt. It's just me.'

James removed the damp polythene covers and placed them in the bin. Then, he carefully examined each costume and was relieved to see that they hadn't been damaged or soiled when he dropped them on the concrete yard outside.

He weaved in and out between the rows of shiny chrome rails, meticulously placing each outfit in its correct position. When he finished, he pulled a heavy velvet curtain to one side and carried the one remaining costume into the shop.

'The Al Capone suit has a button missing.'

Matt sat in an electric wheelchair behind the counter, doing a crossword in the Daily Mail.

'Leave it here. I'll see to that.'

'Where's Amanda?' asked James, placing the outfit on the counter.

'She's gone to Greggs.'

'Is it that time already?' asked James, checking to see if the sign on the shop door had been turned around to let pedestrians know the shop was closed for lunch.

'Sit yourself down,' said Matt. 'She shouldn't be long. I think she's getting you a ham salad baguette. Hope that's okay?'

'Yeah, that's good. Thanks.'

'I wish they still made those cheese savoury stotties. I used to love them!' said Matt.

'Ham and pease pudding stotties were my favourite.'

James suddenly felt hungry, and his mouth watered at the memory of his favourite sandwich, which had been delicious. He couldn't understand why Greggs had stopped selling them a few years earlier.

The men chatted about the Newcastle United match they'd seen on the telly at the weekend and agreed that the Magpies should have won because, after all, they were the better team. Their opponents had just been lucky to score the only goal of the game in the last five minutes of play.

Amanda breezed through the front door, a bell ringing to announce her arrival, and she placed a large paper bag on the counter.

'I don't know about you two, but I'm starving!'

She handed each of them a sandwich, a packet of crisps and

a soft drink, and they sat in companionable silence as they ate their lunch in the shop. Amanda tapped her foot in time with the 1990s soundtrack playing in the background, and Matt puzzled over the answer to six across.

James smiled to himself. He loved working at Glad Rags, and he loved Matt and Amanda, whom he considered his friends, not just workmates or bosses, which, technically, they were.

Amanda was Amanda. Bright and bubbly. She loved costumes, and with her long, fair hair and petite body, she looked fabulous modelling them. She'd started the fancy dress business after being made redundant from her job as a wardrobe assistant at the local theatre about five years earlier, and she hadn't looked back since opening the shop. There was plenty of demand for costume hire in a city the size of Newcastle upon Tyne to support the shop, but Amanda was ambitious. Once her business was established there, she opened an e-commerce shop online to further expand it, and that's when James joined them. They now provided costumes to customers throughout the country by mail order, and business was booming.

Matt. Matt was something else altogether. He was a soldier and had lost both his legs above the knee in a bomb blast while serving his country in Afghanistan. Still, he never complained. He considered himself lucky to have survived the war and come home; some of his friends had not. Matt was a determined guy and didn't let his disability prevent him from living his life. He helped Amanda in the shop and played wheelchair basketball seriously, training several times a week; he hoped to be selected for the England team to play at the next Paralympics. Amanda was his biggest fan, always going along to cheer him on. Matt still looked like he was in the forces, with his closely cropped hair and muscular body.

Matt and Amanda were made for each other. They were more than just husband and wife. James thought they were each other's crutches in life. He didn't know another couple who supported each other so completely in everything they did.

They had taken him under their wing when he'd needed a job a few years back, and he would always be grateful to them for that.

Although Glad Rags was a small business with only three employees, it had an exceptional reputation, with many customers returning time and time again.

As James crunched on his salt and vinegar crisps, he glanced at the framed certificate hanging on the wall next to a photograph of Amanda shaking hands with the mayor of Newcastle and smiled to himself. He remembered that night well, which was surprising, considering how much he'd had to drink.

They had been invited to a stuffy do with a posh meal and a dance afterwards. It was the kind of dinner where there were so many pieces of cutlery surrounding the plate that James had no idea which to use. He'd waited until everyone else had picked up their cutlery and followed their lead.

At least there had been free wine; the servers topped up their glasses all night, and by the end of the three-course meal, they had been more than a little tipsy and were laughing loudly. The other guests at the table were starting to stare.

And then the speeches began.

James hadn't really been listening to the bloke on the stage prattling on about how many brilliant businesses were based in the city until he heard Amanda's name mentioned, and then he tuned in. The next thing he knew, Amanda was climbing onto the stage in her red, sparkling evening dress and high heels, shaking hands with the mayor while smartphones flashed around the room and people cheered and clapped.

A professional photographer took some photos that night, and one of them, featuring Amanda and the mayor, appeared in *The Chronicle* the next day. Amanda was grinning. She looked so proud that her company had won the *Small Business of the Year* award, and in James's opinion, it was very well-deserved.

Another photo hung on the other side of the certificate. In it, Amanda stood in the centre, proudly holding her award. Matt was on her right, beaming up at her, and James stood to her left, looking tall and lean, wearing a James Bond evening suit he'd borrowed from the shop. His girlfriend, Lisa, had cut his dark brown, untamed hair for the event, and it looked neat for a change.

Matthew broke the silence.

'You'll never guess what the doctor suggested I use for the stump pains I get.'

James saw the corners of Amanda's mouth turn up into a smile.

'No idea.' James shrugged.

'Marijuana!' Matt laughed loudly. 'Apparently, amputees use medical marijuana in the States, and they've had excellent results with it.'

'Are you going to try it?'

'I'll give anything a go if it might help. The doctor wanted me to go to a specialist clinic, but I couldn't be bothered with all that. I bought some cannabis seeds online. Did you know it was legal to buy cannabis seeds? I didn't! Anyway, I *potted* them up last night.'

'Nice one!' James chuckled.

After lunch, Amanda went to her desk in the corner and sat down. She scrolled through the new orders that customers had placed during her break.

'James, we need a Pinocchio to fit a ten-year-old boy, a maid's outfit in a size twelve, and a Spider-Man for a bloke with a thirty-six-inch waist, please.'

Before retrieving the costumes from the back room, James binned the lunch wrappers and cans. He quickly found the Pinocchio and the maid costumes, but there were only Spider-Man costumes in children's sizes on the rails. So, he returned to the shop, carrying the ones he'd found, and gave them to Matt, who wrapped them on the shop counter.

'Amanda, I can't find an extra-large Spider-Man costume back there.'

'Oh! Let me check.' She looked at the computer screen. 'Damn it! It was due back last week, but it hasn't been returned yet. How did I miss that?'

'When does the guy need it?' asked Matt.

'Friday.' Amanda sat back in her chair and thought aloud. 'It's Monday now. Even if I chase it up today, we won't get it back in time to clean it and send it out again in the post to this bloke before Friday. I suppose I'd better call him and see if he'd like us to send an alternative costume.'

She picked up her smartphone and dialled the customer's landline number, but there was no answer. She then called the customer's mobile number.

'He's not answering either of the numbers I've got for him. And he doesn't have a messaging service.' She ended the call and stared into space for a moment. 'If we cancel his order and refund him, he won't have anything to wear for the party on Friday, and it won't give him much time to get sorted with something else. Do you think we should send him a different outfit, anyway? There are a lot of men's costumes out at the minute. We don't have many available in his size.'

'What do we have?' asked Matt.

'Shrek, Zombie, Knights Templar, Hippy, and the Lone Ranger.'

'Out of them, the Lone Ranger is the closest to Spider-Man,' said James.

'If we send him that, at least he'll have something to wear, won't he?' asked Amanda. 'What do you guys think?'

'Sounds like a good plan to me,' said Matt.

James nodded in agreement. He wasn't surprised that Amanda had found a sensible solution to the problem. Solving problems and keeping her customers happy was her forte.

'Great! Let's get him sorted out, and then I need to check what costumes we have for an Alice in Wonderland-themed birthday party. I've got a family with six children arriving soon for a fitting!'

James disappeared into the back room to fetch the extra-large Lone Ranger outfit and passed it to Matt, who took the costume from him and wrapped it neatly while Amanda printed the postage labels and stuck them onto the parcels. James picked up the packages, took them into the back room, and dropped them in a Royal Mail sack. He'd take them and any more orders placed that afternoon to the Post Office on Northumberland Street later. The three of them made a great team.

On Thursday morning, James found Matt and Amanda huddled by the computer and instantly knew something was wrong. After a brief greeting, he went to the kitchen to make coffee: one strong and black for Matt, one with milk and two sugars for Amanda, and a milky one for himself.

'Thanks, love,' said Amanda absent-mindedly when James handed her the steaming mug of sweet coffee.

'What's up?'

'Do you remember that order we got for the Spider-Man costume on Monday?'

James nodded.

'Well, the guy wasn't happy with the Lone Ranger costume we sent him.'

'That's an understatement!' said Matt. 'You won't believe this, James. He doesn't want just a refund. He's asking for compensation for the tickets to the party and—listen to this—compensation for his distress! Can you believe that? If he's so distressed about getting a different fancy-dress costume from the one he ordered, he needs to get a bloody life!'

James noticed Matt's hand move to the stumps of his legs and understood his friend's anger and frustration. Matt had every reason to be distressed, yet he never complained. Not once had James heard him blame the army, the war, or the enemy for what had happened; he had been aware of the risks when he was posted to a war zone. He had accepted his disability and was determined to get on with his life.

Amanda had told him that when Matt was discharged from the army, he received a small payout from the Armed Forces Compensation Scheme, which had enabled them to buy the first batch of stock for the shop and pay a lump sum off their mortgage. Compensation that he was more than entitled to, but in reality, nothing could compensate for losing his legs.

James knew he wouldn't have handled the situation so well if he had been in Matt's position. Matt was a special guy.

'Right! So what are we going to do?' asked Amanda. 'I need

to reply to this bloke.'

'We're not paying him compensation. Full stop!' said her husband.

'What if we offer him a full refund for his order on return of the costume, but tell him he's not entitled to any compensation? Does that sound okay?'

'If you have to,' said Matt through gritted teeth. 'But he doesn't deserve a penny with an attitude like that.'

'What do you think, James?' Amanda swung her office chair around to face him.

'I dunno. I suppose he should get a refund if he's not happy with the costume, and he's not going to wear it, but I don't think you should offer him compensation.'

'Thanks.' Amanda typed away on the keyboard while the men drank their coffees, and after a few minutes, she read her response.

Dear Mr Howard, I'm sorry to hear that you were unhappy with the alternative costume we sent you. Please return it to our shop, using the return label in the package. We will refund the hire and postage costs when we receive the costume back. Unfortunately, we cannot offer compensation for consequential losses. Yours sincerely, Amanda.

The men nodded.

'That sounds good,' said James. 'Very professional.'

'Thank you,' said Amanda, as she hit the send button.

'You were much politer than I would have been!' said Matt grumpily, looking at the wall clock. 'It's ten o'clock already. We've spent an hour discussing and replying to that email. What a bloody waste of time! Now, let's get today's orders out, shall we?'

James gathered the empty mugs, washed them in the kitchen

sink, and left them to dry on the drainer. On his return, Amanda gave him a printout of the costumes they needed to fulfil their orders, and James went to the back room to locate them.

A short time later, he heard Amanda's raised voice and went into the shop to ensure everything was alright, but he could see that something was bothering them: Matt looked furious, and the colour had drained from Amanda's face.

'What's up?' asked James.

'It's that guy again,' said Matt, shaking his head. 'He's trying to blackmail us now. He's threatening to leave a negative review for Glad Rags if we don't reconsider his request for compensation and reimburse him for the tickets.'

'The bastard!' said James under his breath. 'What are you going to do?'

'We're not paying him a damned thing. We'll not give in to blackmail.'

Amanda had been reading an article on her computer screen. She looked up and said, 'Looking at the Consumer Rights Act, he's legally entitled to a refund from us, but nothing else. We don't have to pay him compensation for anything.'

'You had to look that up?' Matt looked surprised. 'Of course, we don't have to give him any compensation. He's threatening us, so we'll give him more money than he's due, but he's picked on the wrong people here!'

A tear rolled down Amanda's cheek. 'I wish we'd cancelled his order when we didn't have the Spider-Man costume in stock. I was only trying to be helpful.'

James didn't know much about consumer rights and stuff like that, but he knew what this guy was doing was wrong. *Wasn't blackmail illegal?* Amanda had tried her best to resolve the problem when she couldn't contact the guy, but her kindness had backfired on her big time. Seeing her cry was unsettling; he'd never seen her cry at work before.

'I think we should call the police,' said Amanda after she'd wiped her face with a tissue and blown her nose.

Matt shrugged his shoulders. 'I'm not sure what they'll be able to do, love.'

'I don't either, but shouldn't we find out at least?'

Amanda picked up her phone and dialled the police non-emergency number. Two minutes later, an operator came on the line and transferred the call, and Amanda waited for another five minutes.

Noticing she hadn't touched the coffee he had made for her earlier, which was now cold, James gathered up the mugs and took them to the kitchen to make fresh ones.

When he returned, he heard Amanda recount the story, and then her face fell as she listened to the response on the line. When she put the phone down, she turned to face the men and picked up her drink.

'He said no crime has been committed,' she said, taking a sip. 'And they can't do anything about what people write on the internet—on review sites and social media and suchlike. He said libel is a civil matter, so if we want anything removed from the internet, we would have to go through a solicitor and prove anything this bloke wrote isn't true.' She shook her head and frowned. 'There's no way we can afford to do that.'

'That's awful, love,' said Matt. 'I'm sorry. Let's hope he doesn't carry out his threat.'

Tears filled Amanda's eyes again, and she faced her computer to hide them.

James took his coffee into the back room and wondered how

the world had become so screwed up that innocent people had to prove their innocence. *Whatever happened to innocent until proven guilty?*

3

A Scathing Review

On Thursday afternoon, Dan sat in an armchair with his laptop open on his knees. He scrolled through his emails, eagerly searching for a reply from the fancy dress hire shop, and smiled with satisfaction when he found one.

He read the message, not quite believing what he saw, and read it again to make sure he'd understood it correctly. The stupid company was refusing to pay for his tickets and compensate him for the distress they had caused. *Hmph! They would regret that!* Just a refund was hardly fair under the circumstances.

His face was stony as he opened the Trustpilot website, and his fingers thumped away as he took out his frustration on the keyboard. When he finished, he read the review with satisfaction and pressed the send button. *That would teach them a lesson!*

Perhaps when they read it, they would reconsider and give him what he'd asked for. He would win this battle, one way or another. Either they would give him what he wanted, or he would make the stupid company suffer.

While waiting for a response, which he hoped would be an apology and a concession, Dan prepared dinner for two: chicken Kyiv served on a bed of wild rice with tender stem broccoli, accompanied by a bottle of Chardonnay, which was chilling in the fridge.

About ten minutes later, his partner, Christopher Smith, arrived home and entered the kitchen.

'Hi Dan, have I got time for a shower before dinner?'

'Yes, it'll be ready in about fifteen minutes.'

When Chris returned downstairs, his hair still damp, he sat at the kitchen table.

'Have you had a good day at work?' asked Dan, taking a tray from the oven.

'Great! Peter didn't come in today. Apparently, he's strained his Achilles tendon, so he might be off for a while. That meant I was in charge! I did some of his office stuff this morning and taught a few classes in the afternoon—Pilates and swimming. It was fun! How about you? What have you been up to?'

'You know. A bit of this and a bit of that.'

Dan plated their meals as though he were competing on MasterChef.

'Come on, spill the beans. I want to know what you do while I'm out at work.'

'Well, this morning, I went to Asda to buy this stuff for dinner,' said Dan, carrying the plates to the table. 'And I complained to that fancy dress company about the costume they sent me. It's disgraceful that they didn't have the one I'd ordered.'

He rolled his eyes.

'At least they sent you something to wear for the party,' said Chris, taking a sip of wine. 'That was thoughtful of them.'

'Oh, Chris!' said Dan melodramatically. 'You don't understand. I can't go to the party as the Lone Ranger. I'd be the laughingstock.'

'I think you'd look fabulous as a cowboy,' said Chris, raising an eyebrow.

'You think I look fabulous in whatever I'm wearing,' said Dan with a suggestive smile, then quickly tucked into his dinner.

Damn it! He shouldn't have flirted with Chris. Not tonight. He hoped he hadn't put any ideas into his head, because he planned to stay up all night. Tonight was the start of Comic-Con in San Diego, and he intended to watch as much of it as he could on Screen Rant, Marvel's YouTube channel, and his Twitter feed.

4

Orders Dwindling

The following Monday, James dressed hurriedly, struggling to find his clothes in the messy bedroom. After eating a bowl of Coco Pops, with milk that was probably on the turn, he grabbed his keys and left the small upstairs flat.

He walked the two miles to work, making his way through the red brick terraces of Heaton to a wide residential road that soon turned into an industrial area with shops and businesses. Then, he passed modern multi-storey buildings on the edge of the city centre before reaching the elegant Georgian streets, where Glad Rags was situated on a quaint side street.

When James entered the shop, he sensed there was a problem. Amanda was sitting at her desk with Matt by her side, his arm draped over the back of her chair.

'Morning, James. Did you have a good weekend?' asked Amanda.

'Not bad, thanks. I took Lisa for a curry on Friday night. It was good. How about you?'

'It could have been better, couldn't it, Matt?'

'Aye, it certainly could.'

James stood in silence, waiting for one of them to explain what was troubling them.

'That Spider-Man guy left an awful review for Glad Rags on Trustpilot,' said Amanda. 'He twisted what happened and made us look completely incompetent. I don't know what we should do now.'

'We need to reply to the review and tell people our side of the story,' said Matt.

'I know we should, but I don't know what to write. Just a thought. Do you think he might take the review down if we give him a payment as a gesture of goodwill? Twenty quid or something like that.'

'No way!' said Matt, shaking his head, his jaw clenched. 'We are not giving him another penny! That's the same as paying compensation. It's blackmail—that's what he's on for, and you would be playing right into his hands. He'll just come back for more.'

James hated seeing his friends like this and wondered how bad the review could be to upset them so much.

'What did the review say?' he asked.

Amanda switched screens on her computer and read out the review, her voice faltering several times. 'Awful Company! Do not use it under any circumstances! My recent experience with Glad Rags was appalling. First, they sent me the wrong costume, and the one I received was totally unsuitable for the event where I intended to wear it. Second, they were less than helpful when I contacted them to put this matter right, and it has still not been rectified to my satisfaction. I would never use this company again, and I would not recommend them to anyone. You have been warned!'

'Wow!' said James, with a sinking feeling in his stomach.

'That is bad.'

He couldn't get his head around what they should do about it, and it wasn't his decision to make, so he went to the kitchen to make coffee, leaving Matt and Amanda to handle the situation. As the kettle boiled, he thought that, in theory, he agreed with Matt and that the company shouldn't be held to ransom. But he understood Amanda's stance, too. She wanted the problem to go away as quickly as possible.

It was hard seeing Amanda so upset. Hearing what that bloke had written about the company he worked for, run by people who were great at what they did, had hit him hard, too. In their shoes, he wasn't sure what he would do. He wished the bloke had never ordered a costume in the first place, and then none of this would have happened. Everything would be as it used to be — happy and fun. But that was not an option. His fists were clenched in his pockets, and he stretched them to relax.

James returned to the shop with three mugs of coffee, and Matt and Amanda took theirs without a word. He could feel the tension in the atmosphere and hated it. Matt had been furious since this guy had complained because he'd upset Amanda, and Amanda was distracted from her work and far from her cheery self. Like Amanda, he hoped the problem would be resolved soon. Glad Rags had always been a pleasant, no-stress kind of place to work.

'Do you have the printout of costumes for today?' asked James.

'Oh! Sorry, James. I haven't even looked at the orders yet,' said Amanda. 'Just give me a minute.'

Amanda pressed a few buttons on her keyboard, printed the list of costumes, and handed the sheet of paper to James.

James glanced at the list. 'There aren't many today.'

Amanda frowned at his remark and shrugged her shoulders. 'I'm sorry. I haven't been able to concentrate on marketing with everything else that's been happening. I don't suppose I'll get any done tonight either, because I'm staying late. A couple of women wanted to come after they finish work to choose some flapper dresses, and I agreed.'

'I'm sure sales will pick up soon,' said Matt, trying to lift the mood. 'But you need to pull yourself together, Amanda. I've never seen you like this before.'

'What! Why do I feel as though you're blaming me for all this?'

'I'm not blaming you, love. It's just that I hate how it's affecting you—us—the business.'

'I can't sleep for thinking about what he wrote about us, Matt. Look! My hands are shaking now, just thinking about it. We know what he wrote is lies, but nobody else reading it will. It's frustrating, annoying, hurtful — I don't know exactly how I feel about it, but it's so unfair. And it's even more unfair that we can't do anything about it!'

Amanda burst into tears, and Matt moved towards her to comfort her.

James slipped into the back room to find the costumes, wishing he'd kept his mouth shut. His offhand comment had caused an argument between Matt and Amanda. *What was going on?* They hardly ever disagreed about anything. It was so out of character.

Was the reason for the orders dropping off because of what the customer wrote in his scathing online review, or because Amanda forgot to do any marketing, as it had distracted her?

Either way, as far as James could see, the Spider-Man bloke was responsible.

5

Spreading the Word

Dan checked his email all weekend, between watching snippets from Comic-Con, but no email from Glad Rags landed in his inbox.

Marvel's announcement on Sunday night, saying that they would produce ten more superhero films, went some way to lift his mood, but he hated to be ignored, and the people at Glad Rags were ignoring him. It was maddening.

As Monday progressed, Dan became increasingly infuriated that he had not got his own way with this poxy little company, and by late afternoon, he was absolutely livid. How was he supposed to concentrate on making Béarnaise sauce when he was so distracted?

After the second failed attempt, he slammed the pan down on the stove with such force that the hot, gooey liquid splashed out of the pan, covering the hob, the cooker hood, the wall cupboards on both sides of the cooker, the chequered tiled floor and his designer clothes.

'Bloody hell!'

Enraged, he ran upstairs and stripped off his clothes. He

changed into a clean set of linen clothes usually reserved for holidays, took the dirty clothes downstairs and put them in the washing machine. Then he wiped down the kitchen in a frenzy, wanting it clean before Chris got home.

The physical exercise helped dissipate his anger, and when he thought more clearly, he decided they could eat the steaks without sauce. Chips and a small salad would do. Chris might even prefer it that way.

Later that evening, after Chris retired to bed, Dan's mind returned to the fancy dress shop, and his anger bubbled up again. There was nothing he hated more than being ignored and losing. He couldn't let Glad Rags get away with treating him this way, so he picked up his laptop.

Where to begin?

He wrote negative reviews for the business on their Google and Facebook pages. *That was just the start.* If they didn't respond to these reviews or his message from the previous week, there was so much more he could do. With a wicked smile, he climbed the stairs.

Dan waited a whole week for a response from Glad Rags, which he thought was very lenient of him, considering the heat wasn't helping his anger or his focus. Even with the house doors and windows open, the heat was oppressive indoors, and he wiped his brow, remembering a news post on Facebook a few days earlier stating that the highest-ever UK temperature had been recorded at Cambridge. He didn't doubt it — it felt hotter in his house right now than it did when he stepped out of the aeroplane in the Canary Islands.

As he hadn't received a reply from Glad Rags, he decided he had no choice but to carry out his threat to discredit the company, and social media was the perfect platform for that.

The challenge ahead thrilled him!

He joined several Facebook groups related to superheroes and fancy dress and then wove his spell. This was something he excelled at, and it gave him immense satisfaction. He told his story in the Facebook groups in an exaggerated fashion, using many emoticons to garner sympathy, and the response to his posts was better than expected.

Within an hour, the post had received likes and replies, and by the following evening, Dan had dozens of messages of support from other Facebook users. A few even offered to leave the company a one-star review to help his cause. Of course, one or two messages supported the company, but he ignored those or reacted with an angry-faced emoticon.

While Dan drummed up hatred against the company, he didn't consider how his actions might affect the owners and the staff at Glad Rags — people whom he had never met. As far as he was concerned, they were getting what they deserved for upsetting him, refusing his request for compensation, and then totally blanking him.

6

Redundancy

August 2019

'I have to go,' said Lisa Evans, rolling out of James's arms and getting out of bed. She grabbed her clothes off the bedroom floor and dressed hurriedly. 'Last night was great!'

With a sexy smile, she leaned over the bed to kiss him goodbye. His arms reached up to pull her back into bed, but she stepped back.

'I need to go, James. I'll be late for work!' she said, rushing for the door. 'See you later!'

James heard the door close as Lisa let herself out of his flat. He looked at his phone. It was just gone seven. He got up and dressed for work, then switched on the telly and sat on the sofa to eat his breakfast: a bowl of Coco Pops swimming in milk and a mug of instant coffee. As he ate, the morning news droned on in the background, but there wasn't much of interest going on in the world. He switched it off, left the empty bowl and mug on the coffee table, and then searched for his keys, which he found on the kitchen worktop.

James walked into the city centre. It was a beautiful Wednesday morning with clear skies, and he couldn't help smiling. Life was pretty good.

Lisa was right. Last night was great! She was spending more time at his place, and she had hinted to him several times about moving in with him. He didn't know why he was hesitating. She was fun, and she was good for him; he had a tendency to dwell on things when he was alone.

When he arrived at work, James entered through the back door because the shop wasn't open yet. Matt and Amanda were sitting at her desk, looking upset. This was becoming a habit. He didn't need to ask. He knew it would have something to do with that Spider-Man customer.

'Morning, James,' said Amanda, faking a smile. 'How are you?'

'Good, thanks. Is there much happening today?'

'Yeah, we have a few orders,' she said, handing him a short list of items to pick from the back room.

As he left, he heard Matt say, 'Why didn't you tell him?'

Tell him what?

It didn't take James long to gather the costumes, and he put them on the shop counter for Matt.

'Everything alright?' he asked.

'Not really,' said Matt. 'That bloke has attacked us online again. This time, he's posted reviews on our Google and Facebook pages.'

'He's lying through his teeth about us,' said Amanda.

James felt his heartbeat quicken at this news. Things had settled down for a while and had almost returned to normal. Amanda had seemed brighter for the last few days, although she still looked tired. He was angry that this bloke was hurting his friends and felt helpless; there was nothing he could do to help.

The following week, James went to work as usual on Friday morning. Matt and Amanda stopped talking when he entered the shop and looked away sheepishly.

'What's up?' asked James.

'I'm afraid there aren't any orders this morning,' said Amanda. 'A few costumes came back in this morning's post, so they need to be taken to the dry cleaners. Perhaps you could start with that.'

'Yeah, no problem,' said James.

James knew that there was a problem—a big problem. For several weeks, the Spider-Man customer's critical reviews of the company had been distracting Matt and Amanda from their work, and more were appearing, from people who weren't even customers. There had been fewer orders every day. Today, there were none. That meant there would be no money coming into the business.

He dropped off the clothes at the dry cleaners and wandered back along the city streets, wondering how to fill the rest of his day. When he returned to the shop, he checked the clothes rails to ensure all the costumes were in the correct place and checked the inventory to confirm clients had returned their costumes.

Around midday, James said, 'I'm finished back here, so I'll go to Greggs today. What do you fancy for lunch?'

He noticed Matt and Amanda looking at each other.

'We're okay, thanks,' said Amanda. 'I brought some sandwiches from home.'

She reached into her tote bag, pulled out a bundle of sandwiches wrapped in cling film, and unwrapped them.

As James left the shop, his heart rate quickened, and he wiped the cold sweat from his brow. Deep in thought, he strolled to the bakery, wondering just how bad things were. Getting lunch from Greggs had been a lunchtime tradition since James's first day at Glad Rags. He guessed money must be getting tight if Matt and Amanda were bringing packed lunches to work.

For the first time, he wondered if things were so bad that he might lose his job. The business had not taken many orders for a while, and there had been little work for him.

What would he do if they made him redundant?

James bought a chicken baguette sandwich at Greggs, not taking advantage of the meal deal offer. Instead, he made himself a mug of instant coffee when he returned to the shop.

Matt and Amanda had already finished eating lunch and were sitting by Amanda's computer, looking at a spreadsheet, and they stopped talking when James returned. Feeling like an intruder, he took his sandwich and coffee into the back room and ate his lunch alone.

When he finished, he stood in the doorway and asked, 'Are there any orders for this afternoon?'

Amanda pursed her lips and shook her head.

'Is there anything else you'd like me to do?'

'Can you come in here for a minute?' asked Matt.

'Aye, of course.' James went into the shop.

'Please take a seat.'

James took a chair from the customer waiting area, carried it across the room, and sat facing Matt and Amanda.

'You know things haven't been going well lately,' said Matt.

James nodded.

'We're very sorry about this, James, but I'm afraid we're

going to have to let you go. We can't afford to keep you on.'

James sat still for a second as he digested Matt's words. He was being fired, which was not surprising under the circumstances, but it still hurt him deeply.

'We're really sorry, James,' said Amanda. 'If there was any other way—'

James nodded again, feeling like the Churchill dog in the television adverts.

'You've been with us for over two years,' said Matt, 'so you're entitled to two weeks' redundancy pay, two weeks' paid notice, and you're owed a week's holiday pay. Hopefully, that will tide you over until you can find another job. If you need a reference, you can use either of us—we'd be glad to help. It's been a pleasure working with you, James. We couldn't have managed without you.'

'This is your P45.' Amanda handed James an envelope. 'You'll need it when you sign on at the Jobcentre.'

James stood up and held the envelope at arm's length as though it were radioactive. 'I'm sorry it's come to this,' he said, struggling to get out the words, and thinking it had been easier just to nod. 'It's been good working here. Thanks for giving me a chance when you did.'

'Good luck, James.' Matt held out his hand and shook James's. 'I'm sure you'll find something soon.'

Amanda stood up and hugged James, and when she pulled away, he saw tears in her eyes.

With yet another nod, James turned away and walked out of the shop. He felt numb when he made his way home and wondered if he might be in shock, although he knew he shouldn't be because the news was hardly unexpected.

At the corner of his street, he saw a black and white kitten watching him from behind a wheelie bin. He liked cats, but as sweet as the kitten was, he was in no mood to pet it, so he walked on by.

When he got home, he turned the key in his front door and climbed the stairs to the upstairs flat. He went straight to the kitchen and took a chilled bottle of San Miguel from the fridge. He couldn't find the bottle opener among the clutter of dirty dishes, empty tins and packets, so in desperation, he put the bottle top against the kitchen worktop and pushed down hard. The lid fell to the tiled floor and rolled under a kitchen cabinet. He did not retrieve it. Instead, he gulped down the cold lager and flinched as it hit a tooth at the back of his mouth.

His phone beeped in his pocket, alerting him to a new message. It was from Lisa. He smiled as he opened his message folder and read her girly text, complete with love hearts and smiley faces, telling him she was on her way over. Lisa lived just a few streets away, so he knew it wouldn't be long before she knocked at his door.

He wondered why he had never given her a key. They'd been seeing each other for over a year, and without actually talking about where their relationship was headed, he suspected she was waiting for him to propose marriage or ask her to move in. *Not much chance of that now!*

Even though he expected the knock at the door, it startled him when it came. He ran down the stairs and opened the door to find Lisa standing there, looking as gorgeous as ever. Her long ash-blonde hair was straightened to perfection. A clingy, low-cut red dress sheathed her curvy body, her dark blue nails were dotted with tiny silver specks, and she wore ridiculously high-heeled sandals.

'Are you going to let me in?'

James stood aside and let Lisa lead the way upstairs to his flat.

'Have you been back long?' she asked, walking into the kitchen and pulling a face when she saw the mess. She began to clean up.

'No, I've just got in.'

Seeing the beer bottle with condensation running down it, she said, 'If you're having a drink, open one for me, would you?'

By the time he'd taken a beer from the fridge, Lisa had uncovered the bottle opener. James opened another bottle and handed it to her.

'Ta. I need a drink after the day I've had,' she said, as she flopped onto the couch and told him about everything that had happened.

James heard only snippets. Something about sitting next to a smelly man on the Metro, not getting the shoes she wanted in the sale because they'd sold out by the time she reached the front of the queue, and dealing with an awkward customer at work.

His mind had been so preoccupied with his day that he'd tuned out, but he switched off completely from her monologue at the mention of a demanding customer. Her demanding customer couldn't be anywhere near as bad as the bastard his company had been dealing with—the one who was responsible for him losing his job.

The problems at work started when he made a complaint.

James had lost his job, yet he had done nothing wrong. He wished he hadn't agreed with Amanda's suggestion to send the Lone Ranger costume. It felt like the right thing to do at the time, but could all this have been avoided if he had disagreed?

Mail order is so impersonal, he thought. It didn't allow relationships between retailers and customers to develop as they would in a traditional store.

Rightly or wrongly, Matt and Amanda had adopted the traditional British stance of not yielding to blackmail and refused to give the customer more than what he was entitled to.

So, what had this bloke gone and done? He'd carried out his threat, that's what. He'd launched a vindictive attack on Glad Rags using the internet and social media to spread his vile lies and entice others to victimise the company too.

When the one-star reviews started appearing on Glad Rags's website, on Trustpilot, Google, and Facebook, the customer's twisted version of events, which painted the company in a terrible light, alarmed Matt and Amanda, but particularly Amanda, who had taken the comments to heart.

Then, one day, Amanda received a phone call from a friend asking if she'd seen the comments about Glad Rags on some internet forum or another, and when Amanda saw what he'd written, she was so upset that she stormed out of the shop. As if the reviews hadn't been bad enough!

And now, because the company's flood of sales had slowed to a trickle and looked likely to dry up completely, Matt and Amanda said they would have to let him go. After two years at the shop, working with people he considered his mates, they had to let him go, just like that, all because of a malicious one-man crusade to damage Glad Rag's reputation when it refused to meet his outrageous demands. *Where was the justice in that?*

He'd had nothing to do with any of it, yet it was he who had lost his job. His heart pounded in his chest, and sweat beaded on his brow. *What on earth was he going to do now?*

James realised that Lisa had stopped talking and was looking at him strangely.

'What?' he asked.

'You haven't heard a word I've said, have you?'

'No, I'm sorry, Lisa,' said James. 'Look, there's something important I need to say.'

Her eyes glowed with anticipation, and a sweet smile appeared on her glossy lips.

I'm sorry, love. It's not what you think.

'I've lost my job. They finished me.'

He watched her face fall as if in slow motion, and it felt like forever before she spoke.

'Aww, no. I'm sorry, James. What did you do?'

'Nothing!' He was shocked that she thought it was his fault. 'They just can't afford to keep me on, that's all.'

Lisa studied his face as she took a swig of her beer.

'I thought they were doing well, with them winning that award and everything.'

'They were—until something happened and everything turned to shit.'

'Will you get any redundancy? Surely, they owe you that much.'

'The redundancy payment is two weeks' wages, and I got two weeks' paid notice and a week's holiday pay.'

'Is that all?' She looked far from impressed.

'Aye, that's the lot.'

'That's only equivalent to five weeks' pay, James. It won't last long.'

'Yeah, I know.' James's eyes were glued to his feet, and he wondered why he felt uncomfortable. It wasn't his fault he'd lost his job.

'I came over to see if you fancy going out tonight. It's been ages since we've been down the Quayside. But I don't suppose you want to, do you?'

James shook his head. 'I'd rather stay in and watch the telly, if you don't mind? There are more beers in the fridge if you want to join me?'

'Nah, the lasses are going out, so I think I'll tag along with them, but thanks anyway.'

Lisa gave him a quick peck on the cheek and a little wave from the door before leaving him alone with his thoughts. She hadn't given him a hug, which was what he really needed.

He grabbed another beer, then switched on the telly.

7

The Quayside

The Quayside in Newcastle was banging when Lisa and her friends, Chloe, Mia and Vicky, arrived in a black taxi, wearing skimpy dresses and strappy high-heeled sandals.

Lisa wished James had come with her—a night out on the town would have done him good. After a hard week at work, she enjoyed having a drink and letting her hair down on a Friday night. Everyone in Newcastle was friendly and out for a good time, except later on, maybe, when the lasses had too much to drink. Arguments would sometimes break out, and the occasional fight, but for now, the atmosphere was just brilliant.

They entered the first pub they came to and made their way towards the crowded bar.

'I'll get the first round in,' said Lisa, pushing her way to the front. 'Four large gin and tonics, please,' she shouted to be heard above the rowdy revellers and the lively music, waving her debit card in the air.

The barman caught her eye and raised his eyebrows. He finished pulling three pints of lager for a guy further along the bar, took payment for them, and then came and stood in front of her.

'Four G and T's, was it, love?' he asked, struggling not to stare at her cleavage in the low-cut dress that left little to the imagination.

'Yeah, make it four large ones, please,' she said.

The barman poured the double measures, looking suggestively over the gin glasses.

'Thanks, pet,' she said as she paid for the order, winking at him with her false eyelashes. Then, turning to her friends, who were giggling behind her, she passed them the drinks and took a sip from her glass. She glanced around the room for empty seats but didn't see any.

'What were you laughing at?' she asked.

'How quickly you got served,' said Chloe. 'That guy couldn't take his eyes off you!'

'Give over,' said Lisa, secretly pleased that they'd noticed. She knew how to attract men's attention when she needed to. 'Oh! I have some news!'

'You're getting married?' asked Mia, almost jumping up and down on the spot. 'Can I be a bridesmaid?'

Lisa shook her head.

'You're not pregnant, are you?' asked Chloe, looking concerned.

'No! Nothing like that. I'm the new Assistant Sales Manager at work. Isn't that great?'

The ladies congratulated Lisa on her promotion.

'Talking of marriage and stuff like that, how are you getting on with that boyfriend of yours?' asked Vicky.

'I dunno,' said Lisa, screwing up her face. 'He's canny enough, and we get on well, but he's taking things too slow.

We've been together for over a year now. I often spend the night at his place, and he spends the odd night at mine, but he seems reluctant to commit. I think he must have trust issues. You'd have thought he'd have made his intentions clear by now, wouldn't you?'

'You'd have thought he'd have made his intentions clear by now!' repeated Chloe in a posh voice. 'Listen to her. She's talking like she's in Pride and Prejudice or something.'

'Where's he at tonight?' asked Mia when the laughter subsided.

'At his place. He lost his job today, so he didn't feel like coming out.'

'What a downer!' said Chloe, who had finished her drink already. 'Everybody should go out on a Friday night—no excuses!'

'I agree,' said Mia. 'He should celebrate your promotion, no matter what's going on in his life. I think he's being selfish.'

'I didn't tell him about my promotion,' said Lisa, taking a sip of her drink. 'How could I when he got made redundant today?'

Lisa wondered why she had wasted more than a year of her life waiting for James to make a commitment. She hoped they would be together by now, either living in the same house or engaged to be married, but after he failed to pick up or act on several very obvious hints that she'd dropped, she realised it wasn't meant to be. Clearly, all he wanted was a casual relationship, so that's what they had. There were no more expectations.

She had a birthday looming—the big three-zero—and the need to find a partner to settle down with was beginning to feel increasingly urgent.

The young ladies finished their drinks and moved on to another bar, waving at the barman as they left. They had one drink in the pubs where there was standing room only and more in those where they found seats.

When they reached the last pub, they were intoxicated and roaring with laughter. Lisa spied an empty table at the back of the room and tottered through the bar in her high heels, with her friends following behind, and nabbed it before anyone else could sit there.

'At least one of you must stay here at all times,' said Lisa, as her friends took a seat. 'No nicking off to the loos together while I'm at the bar, okay? Will one of you come with me to carry the drinks?'

Chloe volunteered and went to the bar with Lisa. Lisa tried every way she knew to attract the barmaid's attention, but everyone seemed to be served before her, even those who had just arrived at the pub.

'Can I help you, ladies?' asked a handsome, dark-haired gentleman wearing a navy suit. He had unfastened the top few buttons of his white shirt, and he looked hot.

'I think the barmaid's blind,' said Lisa. 'I've been waiting ages to get a drink.'

The man raised his arm and clicked his fingers, and the barmaid came running to him like a dog to its owner. His self-confidence and animal magnetism astonished Lisa.

'What can I get you?' The barmaid smiled at the guy, showing a perfect set of teeth.

'Whatever these beautiful young ladies would like.' He turned to face Lisa and winked.

'Four large gin and tonics, please,' said Lisa, who was not smiling. It appeared her charms worked well with barmen, but not barmaids. It was probably the other way around for this guy, she guessed.

When the drinks arrived, he held out his bank card. 'Allow me.'

'Thank you! That's very kind of you.'

When the barman placed the drinks on the bar, Lisa passed two glasses to Chloe, who carried them to their table.

'I'm Harry. May I join you? I think my mates have moved on without me.'

'Yeah, of course you can. I'm Lisa.'

'Nice to meet you, Lisa.' He shook her hand and beamed at her.

Lisa picked up the other two glasses from the bar and carried them to the table, where she introduced Harry to her friends. They looked suitably impressed at her pulling power.

Looking into his sparkling blue eyes, she couldn't believe her luck. He was the best-looking bloke she'd seen out all night, and he was sitting next to her. If James wasn't husband material, maybe this guy was.

They chatted for ages, oblivious to the three women who sat at the table alongside them. They didn't go to any more pubs that evening; they were content where they were, in each other's company, and when the evening ended, she said goodnight to her friends and walked out of the pub on Harry's arm.

8

Lasagne

Dan was sitting at the kitchen table with his laptop open when Chris returned home from work. The smell of the lasagne cooking in the oven filled the house.

'Hiya, Dan. Have I got time for a shower?'

'Yes, dinner will be ready in thirty minutes. I've opened a bottle of wine if you'd like a glass.'

Chris poured himself a small glass of Chilean Merlot, Dan's current favourite as it was on offer at Asda for just £4.50 a bottle. He looked over Dan's shoulder.

'What are you up to?'

'Remember that Spider-Man costume I ordered, and they sent the Lone Ranger one instead, and then they refused to compensate me for the upset it caused me? Well, they're going to wish they had conceded to my demands now.' Dan chuckled maliciously and took a big slug of wine. 'You should see the shitstorm that I've stirred up against them on the internet. Nobody will hire anything from that shop ever again.'

'You're not still going on about that, are you? You shouldn't get so worked up about stuff. The way you go on sometimes, you're like a big kid. Chill out. Stop letting this kind of stuff bother you.'

Dan leaned back in his chair, still smiling from the comments he'd read in the Facebook groups. All he had to do was light the spark, and then sit back and watch. He could always rely on social media for support. Without exception, some of the group members would confirm his spiteful accusations or exaggerate them even further.

One old girl concocted a preposterous story, and he'd laughed out loud at the audacity of it. Of course, she'd fabricated the whole thing, but he knew some people would believe it. *Good on her!*

When Glad Rags replied to the thread, telling their side of the story, the page administrator deleted their comment and blocked the company from the group, having already decided that they were unscrupulous traders—all because of what he, Mr Daniel J. Howard, had written. *Success!*

'I was very upset about it all, Chris, and I won't let them get away with it. They should have sent me the costume I asked for—that's all they had to do.'

'Get real, Dan,' said Chris, putting his empty wine glass on the kitchen top. 'You spent thirty-five quid on a fancy dress costume, and you asked for compensation for loss and damages. No company in its right mind would pay. They refunded you, which is fair enough, in my opinion. Now, let it go, will you?'

As Chris climbed the stairs to shower, Dan defiantly turned his laptop back on. No matter what Chris said, he wouldn't let it go. At the top of the Facebook page, he tapped the tab to change the account and switched to an alias profile to stir up more trouble. He enjoyed nothing more.

After posting a few more comments, Dan went to the kitchen, removed the lasagne from the oven, and dished it out onto two plates. He had cooked it to perfection, but then again, it should be perfect—he'd had all day to prepare it.

Dan thought of himself as lucky. He had never had to work. When his mother died, she'd left a large terraced house in Jesmond, one of Newcastle's most affluent suburbs, and a small fortune in the bank. As Dan was her only child, he'd inherited the lot, which was just as well, he thought, because he didn't fancy going out to work every day until he was sixty-five or sixty-seven or whatever the retirement age was these days.

He was happy with his life, but he disliked how Chris sometimes belittled his accomplishments. For some reason, Chris couldn't appreciate the satisfaction he derived from complaining to businesses and getting them to do what he wanted, or from showing them up online and provoking others to do the same when a company failed to comply with his demands.

Did he still love Chris?

When they first met the previous year, they'd had fun together. Newcastle was great for a night out. Chris moved in with him just after the New Year, but now that they were living together, Dan had to admit that Chris was becoming a bore. After work, he was always tired and didn't want to do anything fun. It was Saturday night, and Chris hadn't mentioned going out, so it would be another night in, watching television, he presumed.

Sometimes, Chris could be annoying, too. Even though he was just four years older, he treated him like a kid. It made him so mad!

But Chris did have his good points. He had a body to die for—working at the gym certainly had its benefits—and his soft green eyes were beautiful when he smiled.

9

The Love of his Life

James hadn't heard from Lisa since Friday night when she'd gone out with her friends, so he texted her to ask if she wanted to come over. He'd been sitting in his flat all weekend, feeling sorry for himself, but there was a football match on the telly later. He hoped she might come over and watch it with him. It was much more fun watching the footie with someone else. They would celebrate if the Magpies won or commiserate if they lost. Whatever happened, they would knock back a few beers together and make a night of it, and if he were lucky, she might stay over again.

His phone beeped, and he checked her reply. *Great!* She was on her way over. James binned the empty curry cartons from the couch and wiped the crumbs onto the floor. When did he last vacuum? He couldn't remember, but the carpet didn't look too bad. The mess and clutter in his flat didn't bother him in the slightest, and he disliked having to clean up before Lisa came over. She always pulled a face when she saw the state of his flat.

When he heard a knock at the door, he went downstairs

to let her in, and as he followed her upstairs, admiring her curvaceous bum, he realised how much he'd missed her.

There it was again—that look of disgust as she entered his living room. It wasn't that bad, really.

'Did you have a good night with the lasses on Friday?' he asked, as they sat on the couch together.

'Aye, it wasn't bad. There were a lot of us out, but I had a stonking headache the next morning,' she said, placing a packet of cigarettes and a lighter on the coffee table. James didn't smoke, so she always brought some with her.

'No surprise there.' James knew how much Lisa liked a drink. 'The match starts in ten minutes. Do you want a beer?'

'Aye, go on then.'

James went to the kitchen, took two bottles of lager from the fridge, removed the caps, and handed one to Lisa.

'Ta!' she said, taking a sip. 'You'll have to sign on tomorrow, won't you?'

'Suppose so.'

James turned the cold beer bottle in his hands, his eyes fixed on it.

'If you don't get another job soon, you'll have to cancel Sky Sports. You'll not be able to afford it on the dole.'

James didn't need to be reminded of his financial insecurity. He knew fine well that his last payment from Glad Rags wouldn't last long. He'd just been on minimum wage when he was working, but it had been enough for him to rent a small flat and live how he wanted. But now, he was concerned about the future and how he would manage; he needed to find another job soon.

'Lisa.' James took her hands in his. 'How would you feel about moving in with me?'

He wasn't sure where that question had come from. His heart was pounding. He didn't know if he wanted her to move in or not, but he heard himself say, 'It would be nice to spend more time together, wouldn't it? And we could share the costs and everything.'

He watched her expression change from one of surprise to anger, and she pulled away from him, rose to her feet and started pacing.

'Well, you certainly know how to pick your moment, don't you, James Webster? Here's me, been waiting months for you to ask me to move in, and then you ask me when you haven't got two pennies to rub together. You're not living off my wages. You can find another bloody job like everybody else.'

Lisa rushed towards the door, leaving her beer, cigarettes, and lighter.

'Wait!' James set his beer bottle on the floor and followed her. 'I didn't mean it like that. I know I should have asked you sooner, and I'm sorry I didn't. Please move in with me, Lisa. I like you being here.'

'I'm sorry, James. You left it too late.'

Lisa left the flat, closing the door behind her.

James rested his head against the door and cried for the first time since he'd lost his job. Being made redundant was bad enough, but having his girlfriend walk out on him because she thought he was a scrounger was something else entirely. His life was rapidly spiralling out of control.

What a fucking weekend!

The match on the telly had started in the background, but James was unaware that he'd missed the kick-off. He wept, feeling totally useless. He didn't know what he should do or how he would cope.

James loved Lisa, or at least he thought he did. He had never been as close to anybody else in his life. Didn't she know that? Her leaving when he felt so low was unbearable. Clearly, she didn't care about him as much as he thought she did.

The first half was almost over by the time James composed himself and moved back to the couch. He stretched out in front of the television, but his mind was not on the game; it was on Lisa.

She would have moved in with him if he hadn't lost his job—he was sure of that. They had been seeing each other for some time and got on great together.

As he watched the rest of the game and drank the opened bottles of beer that they had abandoned earlier, he remembered that the reason he'd lost his job, and now his girlfriend, was not his fault at all.

One person was responsible for everything bad that had happened to him in the last few days—the customer who had ruined Glad Rags's reputation by spreading lies on the internet. He was the reason that James no longer had a job. He was the reason Lisa had left him. He, alone, was responsible for the mess that James was in.

James felt miserable, and he vowed to make that bloke miserable, too. He would enjoy watching him suffer as much as he was now.

The match ended in a victory for the Magpies, and James drank to the team's success.

10

Reading between the Lines

Lisa walked home as fast as her high heels would allow, feeling confused and upset about what had just happened. James asking her to move into his flat had been a total shock, and she had reacted badly.

What crap timing, James!

She'd given up on him making a commitment to her months ago. He had so many opportunities in the past when she'd hinted blatantly, but he had never acted on them. So, she assumed their relationship was a casual affair, with no long-term future.

Then, only two days earlier, she'd met Harry at a pub at the Quayside. She had never believed in love at first sight, but she did now. They had hit it off right away. She went home with him that night, surprising herself, because one-night stands and first-night sex were not something she did, and they spent the entire weekend together.

Lisa had just returned home when James texted her, asking her to come round. That's the kind of relationship she had with James. Casual. If they weren't busy, they spent time together.

James was good company, but he'd always been distant. She knew very little about him and his past, and he never talked about his future—or theirs. He lived firmly in the present.

Harry, on the other hand, was open and an unexpected breath of fresh air after James. He talked freely about himself and his expectations for the future, and he'd already said he wanted her to be a big part of it.

In just two days, she had learned enough about Harry to know she wanted to be part of his future, too. Harry and she were on the same wavelength, and she hadn't laughed so much in months. He was handsome, kind, and thoughtful. His semi-detached house in South Gosforth was comfortable, not too flashy, but nice. However, it wouldn't matter where Harry lived; she knew she would want to be with him. The fact that he had a good job in marketing, a flash car and a pleasant home was a terrific bonus.

When James had texted her that evening, Lisa had gone to his flat, intending to end their relationship gently, but James had surprised her by asking her to move in with him. She knew she had overreacted; how could she do otherwise when she had been so annoyed he'd asked her now, after she'd given up on him? Perhaps it also had something to do with her feeling guilty about spending a fantastic weekend with another man.

James had always been a man of few words, and she'd had to read between the lines with him. Now she wondered if she had read him correctly. Had he asked her to move in because he was feeling insecure after losing his job? Or had he been more invested in their relationship than she'd given him credit for?

Either way, she felt rotten for cheating on him over the weekend and for the way she'd left him. He was a decent guy and deserved better. As she unlocked her door, she considered turning around and going back to apologise, because she hated herself for what she'd said, but decided against it. It was over with James.

There was no doubt in her mind that she wanted to be with Harry now, but if James had stepped up a few months ago, then maybe things would have been different.

11

A Depressing Place

On Monday morning, James woke to the memory of Lisa walking out on him and wanted to crawl back under the duvet and hide, but he couldn't. He needed to go to the Jobcentre to make a claim for Jobseeker's Allowance. From today, he would be on the dole. Could he feel any more miserable?

He threw on some crumpled clothes from the bedroom floor and ate a quick breakfast before heading out.

Rain poured down as he set off for Byker. He didn't own an umbrella, so he pulled up the hood on his hoodie, then folded the P45 and put it in his jeans pocket. By the time he arrived at the Jobcentre fifteen minutes later, he was drenched and dripped water across the tiled floor as he approached the reception desk.

A young woman asked if he had an appointment. He explained that he hadn't made an appointment because he didn't know until Friday afternoon that his employers were going to make him redundant that day, but the woman at the desk found that hard to understand. Because he didn't have an appointment, she told him he would have to sit and wait until somebody was available to see him.

He sat in the waiting area and watched people of all ages and races enter the building and leave again. The one thing they all had in common was the look on their faces—apathy was the best word he could think of to describe it. *What a fucking depressing place!*

Almost two hours passed before a small guy wearing a purple jumper said, 'James Webster! Do we have a James Webster here?'

James stood up, conscious that all eyes had turned towards him, and walked over to the desk where the guy sat. Unlike everyone before him, James smiled at the young man and glanced down at his name badge, which read Josh McIntosh.

'Morning, Mr McIntosh.'

James looked at the clock on the wall to check that it was, in fact, still morning. It was—just.

'What can we do for you, Mr Webster?'

James cringed inwardly, wondering if they could take him back in time. Three weeks was all it would take. He wished he could tell Amanda not to send the Lone Ranger costume, and everything would return to normal.

'I got laid off on Friday. My boss gave me this.'

He handed over the P45 from Amanda and pictured her face as she'd given it to him; her furrowed brow, tight lips, and eyes that avoided his. *Poor Amanda!*

'As you've paid national insurance contributions for the last two years, you're eligible to claim New Style Job Seekers Allowance for six months. You can claim this with or without Universal Credit,' explained Josh.

Filling out the form to apply for Jobseekers Allowance was tedious—page after page of questions. James's mind went blank. He hated filling out forms and never knew what to write.

He was pleased to have Josh McIntosh's help to complete it. Josh guided him through the questions, one by one, and suggested what he should write in each box. James agreed to several declarations at the end, including spending most of his time looking for work, and signed the form.

When Josh placed another form to complete in front of him, James recoiled.

'Do you need to claim Universal Credit?' asked Josh.

'I just need the dole while I'm out of work,' said James, not wanting to admit that he didn't know what Universal Credit was, and eager to leave the place as quickly as possible.

'Okay,' said Josh, not pressing James any further.

He handed James some paperwork.

'To continue your claim for contributions-based Job Seekers Allowance, you must come to the Jobcentre to sign on every two weeks, on Monday at eleven o'clock. If you don't do this, your benefits will be stopped. Right, that's it then. We'll see you in a fortnight.'

With a sigh of relief, James put down the pen, thanked Josh for his help, and walked out of the building with the same expression on his face that he'd seen on all the unemployed people leaving earlier. Apathy.

On his way home, James stopped at McDonald's for lunch. He ordered a Big Mac and sat at a table inside the noisy restaurant. While he ate, he thought about what he needed to do that afternoon.

He decided he would find his laptop first, which must be buried somewhere in his bedroom as that was the only place he ever used it, then set it away to update—it always needed to do updates when it hadn't switched on for a while—and when it had sorted itself out, he would begin his search for the man who was to blame for him losing his job.

It had rained for most of the morning, but the skies cleared while James was eating lunch, and the sun appeared as he walked home to his flat on Claymore Terrace in Heaton. He liked Heaton. It was a decent area of the city, with reasonable rents and an excellent bus service. It was near the Metro route, too, which was handy for travelling into the city, although he usually walked. He preferred to walk because walking helped to keep his head straight.

He hurried along the pavement, oblivious to the shop window displays on his left but aware of the traffic on his right. The road was busy, and he couldn't avoid being sprayed with muddy water thrown up by tyres as vehicles hurtled past. *Sod it!* He didn't have any clean clothes back at the flat. He'd have to do some laundry when he returned, as well.

After his Jobcentre experience, the beer in the fridge was beckoning when he returned home, but he couldn't have a drink yet—he had things to do.

His laptop was poking out from underneath a pile of clothes on the bedroom floor. He grabbed it, placed it on the kitchen worktop, and plugged it in. The screen came to life, and he left it to complete the sixteen updates it needed to do before he could use it. According to the message on the screen, that would take one hour and ten minutes.

James took off his dirty jeans and put them in the washer-dryer, then grabbed a load of clothes off his bedroom floor and shoved them in, too, with a scoopful of powder, some of which spilt onto the tiled floor. He didn't clean it up. Instead, he paced up and down in his flat, checking the progress of the updates every two minutes and becoming frustrated at how long they were taking.

Eventually, when the updates finished, he unplugged the laptop and sat on the couch with it on his lap.

12

Finding Out

James's first stop was Trustpilot. He found the page for Glad Rags and read the one-star review the customer had left for the business. The guy had written the review anonymously as 'A disgruntled customer'. That was not very helpful.

He checked Glad Rags's reviews on Google and Yell, but the reviewer used the same name on those websites.

Why on earth were reviewers allowed to use fake names? Anyone leaving an honest review would surely be happy to use their real name.

Shaking his head, James realised that the entire system for online reviews was ripe for abuse. After this revelation, he knew he'd never look at them in the same way again when deciding what to buy and from where. Not that he'd be buying much until he found another job.

James opened a Facebook account years ago but hadn't used it for ages. He entered the password he used for everything—JW170591, which was his initials and date of birth, and successfully logged into his account on the first attempt.

He looked for the Glad Rags business page. There were so

many businesses named Glad Rags—clothing shops, fancy dress shops, and even cafes. He recognised Amanda's business from the profile picture—Amanda dressed as Little Bo Peep.

In the recommendations and reviews section, he quickly found the one he sought, because it was the only one-star review the business had received. The reviewer's name was Daniel Howard. He'd heard Matt and Amanda talking about the guy at work, and that name rang a bell. He was certain Dan was his man.

James clicked on Daniel's profile page and was surprised to see that his personal information was publicly available. Most people had the sense to hide it, but not Dan. James looked for a piece of paper to make notes, but all he could find was a pizza box. He shrugged and tore off the lid. He could write anything important on that.

Dan lived in Newcastle upon Tyne. Glad Rags had mail-order customers throughout the UK, but this guy was actually in the same city. *What were the chances of that?* He was born on June 4, 1987. He had provided no workplace information, but he was in a relationship. *Lucky him!*

His partner's name was Chris Smith, and when he accessed Chris's account, he saw Chris was a bloke. He worked at Shape Up in Jesmond. *Now, that was a good lead!* He'd heard of Shape Up; it was supposed to be one of the best gyms in Newcastle.

Then James looked for Facebook groups for Superhero fans to learn more about Dan Howard. Dan was a member of the first group he tried. James searched for Daniel Howard in the group and found a thread about favourite and least favourite superheroes.

Dan's reply stated that Spider-Man was his favourite superhero because he could relate to his alter ego in so many ways, and he envied the costume and skills he used as Spider-Man. His least favourite was Aquaman. He couldn't relate to him at all, being unable to swim and being terrified of underwater creatures, and he blamed watching the films Jaws and Piranha as a child for that.

When he found the superhero fan page Amanda mentioned, he searched for the comment that Dan had written about Glad Rags and read it. It was more of a rant than a comment, he thought, and Dan used more emoticons than Lisa did in her girly texts.

The number of replies surprised him. By the time he'd read all the drivel written about Glad Rags, where he'd spent the last two years of his life, James was livid. What Dan had written was blatant lies. James understood why Amanda had been so upset.

Realising he was clenching his fists, James stretched his hands to relieve the tension.

He remembered the group admin had deleted Amanda's post and blocked her, so Amanda reported Dan's post to Facebook. They refused to take it down, though—something to do with it not breaching their community standards, she'd said, and he wondered who set Facebook's community standards and why they had set them so low.

James remembered Amanda and Matt talking about hiring a solicitor to write to Facebook on their behalf, but they didn't have the money. They couldn't afford to clear their names, and yet, they had done nothing wrong.

It was so unfair.

His friends found themselves in an unenviable situation, where they would have to pay to prove the comments on social media were untrue. At the same time, liars got away with writing whatever the hell they wanted, not giving a damn if it was true or not, or who they hurt in the process. They sat behind their keyboards where nobody could touch them, feeling invincible because there were no laws to protect the people on the receiving end of their savage reviews and pathetic lies. *So much for justice!*

James's fingers were twitching. He desperately wanted to post a comment to defend his friends and their business, but he knew the admin was likely to remove the post and block him, just as they had Amanda, so he stopped himself.

Instead, he painstakingly worked through all the comments and replies, clicking on the poster's accounts and checking them out. It was a tedious and painstaking job.

He noticed a guy called Peter Parker had written several responses. That name sounded familiar. Where had he heard it before? It suddenly dawned on him that Peter Parker was the name of the boy in the Spider-Man film. Then, he saw a reply from Anthony Stark. Tony Stark was Iron Man's alter ego. *What the fuck was going on?* He checked both accounts, but there was no public information or profile picture on either.

Another post from Dan Howard appeared at the end of the Facebook thread. James read it carefully, but couldn't make sense of it. Dan agreed with his original post and incited people to share their terrible experiences of using Glad Rags. *Weird.*

As James tried to understand what was happening, Dan's last message disappeared from the thread, and a moment later, the same comment reappeared, but this time, it was posted by Peter Parker.

James sat back and ran his hands through his hair. Two people writing the same remark within a minute of each other—that was no coincidence! Dan Howard and Peter Parker had to be the same person. *Busted!*

To celebrate, James took a beer from the fridge, opened it with the bottle opener that Lisa had put back in the cutlery drawer, and drank a mouthful. His back tooth stung as the cold beer washed over it, but his tooth would have to wait for another day. When he finished the drink, the washer-dryer beeped. It had completed its cycle. He got dressed in his freshly laundered clothes and headed out to Jesmond.

As he left his flat, he spotted the black and white kitten again on his street, hiding behind the wheel of a car.

'Hello, there,' he said, bending down and stroking its head. The kitten meowed and purred as it rubbed around his legs. He noticed it was thin. *Was anyone looking after it?* If so, they weren't doing a very good job of it. He decided to keep an eye on the poor little thing.

When he reached Jesmond, he easily located the exclusive gym. Shape Up was set in well-manicured gardens. Tinted glass covered the front of the building, and James could see his reflection as he tried to peer inside. *I look such a mess.*

Dressed in a pair of old jeans and a black hoodie, James was almost six feet tall and slim. His dark brown hair was overdue for a trim. He didn't mind his hair longer, but Lisa preferred it short and tidy. He wasn't a bad-looking guy, but he didn't have girls running after him, either. His mother had once said he was too serious, and maybe she'd been right. Come to think of it, he couldn't remember the last time he'd had a good laugh.

As much as he would have liked to join the gym, he couldn't afford the subscription, even for a day, so he stood on the opposite side of the road, looking as though he was waiting for someone, and every once in a while, he checked the time on his phone.

About an hour later, his patience was rewarded. James recognised the man leaving the building as Christopher Smith, Dan Howard's partner, and thought his Facebook profile picture didn't do him any favours. He was slightly taller than James, but his body was muscular, and he walked in an effortless manner, which reminded James of lions he'd seen on wildlife documentaries. Majestic was the word he was looking for. Chris moved like a professional athlete.

James pulled up his hood and followed him, walking on the opposite side of the road and keeping a reasonable distance behind so he wouldn't be noticed. It was a busy road, and there were quite a few people about. He was sure Chris hadn't seen him. Then they turned onto a wide street lined with mature trees. The large two-storey terraced houses had small front gardens and large polished doors. Suddenly, there were just the two of them.

Noting the street name on the road sign, Somerset Road, James kept his head down and stopped at a bus stop, furtively watching Chris walk to the end house on the right-hand side of the road. After Chris disappeared inside, James continued to the end of the road and looked at the front of the house. It was number sixty-six, and he chuckled to himself. That was easy to remember—add one more six, and it would be the devil's number. *How appropriate!*

As he turned to leave, he looked back at the house, which he knew must be worth a small fortune; property in Jesmond was expensive. The devil who lived in that house had ruined Glad Rags's reputation over something costing thirty-five quid— thirty-five quid that Amanda had returned to him. *What was thirty-five quid to someone who lived in a house like that?*

It surprised James how easy it had been to find Dan Howard.

But what now? It was over a mile back to Heaton, and he worked out his next move as he walked home.

13

Spaghetti Bolognese

Dan could not believe he'd been so careless, commenting on a Facebook thread without checking which account he was logged into. Luckily, he'd noticed and deleted the post pretty quickly before reposting it under another name. *Phew!*

He didn't want his followers to know that he posted as Peter Parker, Anthony Stark, Bruce Wayne, Clark Kent, and Diana Prince. He didn't use Bruce and Clark very often because they were a bit too conspicuous, but sometimes, he used their initials when leaving reviews.

Dan heard the front door open. Chris was home. He closed the laptop and went into the hallway to greet his partner.

'Hiya, how was your day?'

'Good!' said Chris, taking off his trainers at the bottom of the stairs. 'How about yours?'

'Yeah, alright, I suppose,' said Dan. 'I've made spaghetti bolognese for dinner. It'll be ready in twenty minutes. I just have the pasta and garlic bread to do.'

'Not pasta again!' Chris said, rolling his eyes. 'I'll just have the bolognese sauce tonight. Could you please cook me a roast chicken or grilled steak tomorrow? I keep telling you I need to eat more protein. I don't need carbs.'

Dan put his head down and swore under his breath as he returned to the kitchen and switched on the kettle, thinking, who in their right mind doesn't like spaghetti bolognese?

He heard Chris turn on the shower upstairs, and soon, Chris was singing in his off-key way. Chris could do most things well, but he couldn't sing for toffee. Dan chuckled as he recalled a night out the previous year when the two of them had been so drunk, they'd agreed to have a go at karaoke—Meatloaf's Bat Out of Hell—and they had been so bad that the audience booed them off the stage! Still, it had been a great night. He missed going out on the town and having a good time.

The water stopped running upstairs, and the singing stopped, too. A few minutes later, Chris ran downstairs wearing clean clothes.

'I'm sorry, Dan. I know you work hard shopping and making dinner for us, and I should be more appreciative of what you do.'

'Is that an apology?'

'Yes, it is,' said Chris. 'I didn't mean to upset you.'

'Thank you. You're forgiven. Now, sit down and I'll serve out.'

Dan added one serving spoon of spaghetti and three of bolognese sauce to Chris's plate, and three of each to his own, then put the garlic bread on a plate in the middle of the table to share. He poured two glasses of Merlot, which was the perfect accompaniment for the food.

As they ate, Chris said, 'So, tell me what you've been doing today?'

'Well, I went to Asda this morning. The wine was still on

offer, so I stocked up on that.'

'Anyone would think you were skint the way you shop for bargains.' Chris laughed loudly.

'I might have a bit of money in the bank, Chris, but that doesn't mean I have to spend it! My financial advisor said that if I touch the capital, the interest might not be enough to live on, and then I'd have to find a job to supplement my income.'

'You're a rich miser,' said Chris, teasing him.

'Whatever!' said Dan, not rising to the bait. 'Anyway, this afternoon I ran around the house with the vacuum cleaner—well, you did say I had to get more exercise—and that's about it, really.'

'Oh, my God! Is that all you've done all day?' Chris sighed. 'Your days sound so dull. Why don't you come to the gym on Wednesday? The pool is great. We have an adults-only swimming class for beginners starting, and guess what? I'm teaching it!'

'Do you think I should?' asked Dan, his voice wavering.

'Everyone should learn how to swim. I still find it hard to believe that someone your age can't.'

'And you wouldn't mind me coming to where you work?'

'Of course, I wouldn't mind,' said Chris, grinning. 'I've told everyone at work about you, and they'd love to meet you.'

'Okay, I will. What time does the class start?'

Dan added the swimming lesson to his online planner, unsure whether he would go because he had a fear of water and what might lurk beneath. He recalled a summer trip to Tynemouth when he was thirteen or fourteen—too old to play on the beach, so he strolled along the promenade with his mother, taking in the sea air. After eating fish and chips at a shop on the seafront, she had insisted they visit the aquarium.

Big mistake!

When he saw the enormous tanks filled with Jaws-like fish, he panicked—a full-blown panic attack—and he thought he was going to throw up his lunch all over the concrete floor. Luckily, he didn't, but he hadn't set foot in an aquarium since.

But Dan didn't want to disappoint Chris. He felt conflicted but thought he should make the effort to attend the class.

14

A Jog in the Park

While Dan ate a leisurely breakfast, he was already thinking about that evening's dinner. He was pleased he'd brought the ingredients the previous day, so he didn't need to shop at Asda that morning.

After breakfast, he chopped a couple of onions, fried them in olive oil, and added them to the slow cooker. Then he cubed some casserole steaks, seasoned them, seared them in the frying pan, and added them to the pot. He added chopped carrots, swede, and beef stock, replaced the lid and switched on the slow cooker. The stew would cook all day while he surfed the internet and worked on his social media accounts.

He sat down with his laptop and was disappointed to see that nothing much was happening. Not to worry, he could soon fix that.

Dan began by spreading the word about what the company had done across several more relevant pages on Facebook. He did the same on Twitter and prepared a post for Instagram. He had a wonderful time.

That afternoon, instead of watching sports on television,

Chris persuaded Dan to go for a run. They jogged side by side in Jesmond Dene, an oasis of trees in the urban sprawl of the city. Dan liked autumn. He admired the beautiful leaves, which were a vibrant mix of red, gold, and green. Then, once he'd had that thought, he couldn't get Karma Chameleon out of his head. He loved Boy George. As he ran, his feet pounded the ground to the beat of the song.

Chris moved ahead of him, and they continued in a single file, as a young woman approached them on a bicycle. She waved in thanks as she passed.

Dan was panting and covered in sweat. He thought he must look a complete mess. Admiring Chris from behind, he wondered how he could look so good when exercising. Unlike him, Chris loved to jog. He loved all sports and forms of exercise, for that matter—and his body showed it. Dan was embarrassed that he carried more weight around his waist than he cared to admit. That's what happens when you like food so much, he thought. He quickened his stride to catch up with Chris.

'The steak casserole will be ready when we get back,' said Dan, between deep breaths. 'I can't wait. You can't beat a good casserole with creamy mashed potatoes, and a glass of red wine.'

'Sounds great—but I'll give the potatoes a miss,' said Chris. 'Too many carbs for me.'

'You don't need to watch your weight. Just look at you!'

'It's taken me years to get a body like this, and now that I'm getting older, I need to be more careful about what I eat.'

'Come off it!' said Dan. 'You're just thirty-five. The way you're going on, you'd think you were ancient!'

'I'm thirty-six.'

Dan went quiet. *Was Chris thirty-six?* He knew his date of birth and worked it out in his head, and yes, he must be. *How bad was that? Getting his partner's age wrong!* He hoped he hadn't forgotten Chris's birthday. *When was his birthday?* He tried to remember the date for a while and then gave up. It didn't matter anyway because he knew he'd saved the date on his phone and set a reminder for two weeks before, so he couldn't have missed it.

They slowed down as they reached the park gates and walked the few streets back to Somerset Road in silence, each wondering what the other was thinking.

When they reached the house, Chris went upstairs to shower first, and Dan opened a bottle of wine to allow it time to breathe before dinner. He turned on a gas ring and set the pan of potatoes, which he'd peeled and chopped earlier, to boil.

Then he entered the lounge, sat in his armchair, and opened his laptop to find twelve notifications on Facebook. He scrolled down the list, clicking on one that he thought looked promising, and laughed when he saw the comments posted on a thread he'd created earlier, most of them supporting his condemnation of Glad Rags, and his cronies had shouted down anyone who had the audacity to side with the business. He was delighted with his accomplishment.

Chris walked into the room.

'What were you laughing at? More videos of pets doing stupid stuff?'

'Yeah, something like that.' Dan closed the laptop to hide what he was doing on Facebook.

Then he dragged his tired, aching body upstairs for a shower. He felt much fresher when he returned downstairs to finish making dinner. Glancing in the lounge on his way to the kitchen, he saw Chris relaxing in an armchair, reading a sporting magazine; that's all he ever read.

Dan mashed the boiled potatoes with a large knob of butter and then plated the meal. 'Dinner is served,' he shouted.

Chris joined him in the kitchen, and they sat at the table. As Dan admired his mountain of potatoes surrounded by a sea of stew, his mouth watered. He couldn't wait to dive in.

'It's no wonder you're getting podgy,' said Chris. 'Eating stuff like that and not getting much exercise.'

'What do you mean, podgy?' Dan's face reddened.

Chris grabbed Dan's side and pinched a roll of fat. 'That's what I mean. You must have put on five kilos since I moved in. You're not comfort-eating, are you? Are you happy?'

'I'd be happier if you didn't call me podgy.' Dan shovelled a forkful of mash coated in rich beef gravy into his mouth.

'Okay. I won't mention it again. But promise me you'll look after yourself. You know I worry about you.'

'I'm fine, Chris,' he said, filling his fork again. 'And I'll try to exercise more if that will make you feel better.'

Chris stood up, took two wine glasses from the wall cupboard, and placed them on the table, and Dan poured the Merlot from the bottle he'd opened earlier.

'Teamwork!' laughed Dan. 'See! We do make a great couple.'

15

A Walk in the Park

Sitting around his flat, dwelling on the fact that he'd lost his job and his girlfriend was not doing James any good. It would drag him down into a deep depression, and he didn't want to go there. He must think about something else to take his mind off his troubles, and conveniently, Dan Howard was lurking there in the background.

James couldn't stand being in his flat alone any longer. He had to get out. He grabbed his wallet and keys and picked up a polythene carrier bag from the living room floor, which he shoved in his jacket pocket with a mischievous smile.

The sun blazed down from a cloudless sky, and a slight breeze helped to alleviate the oppressive heat. It was a glorious day for a walk in the park. James took the path through Heaton Park to Jesmond Dene, enjoying the shade of the mature woodland trees and the sound of birds singing in the treetops. He didn't have far to go before he found what he was looking for—an enormous pile of fresh dog poo.

Shaking his head, he wondered why so many people still didn't clean up after their pets, even though they could buy bags for that purpose, and the council supplied bins along the paths to dump them in. It couldn't be any easier.

James took the plastic bag from his pocket, turned it inside out, and then collected the faeces with the bag, being careful not to get any on his hands. He left the park and headed for Somerset Road. When he reached the end of the street, he looked around to see if anyone was watching. Nobody was in sight.

He walked up the short path, bordered on either side by shrubs, to the front door of number sixty-six and dumped the bag's contents on the doorstep. Then, he threw the empty bag in a neighbour's waste bin around the back of the house. Returning to the front, he stood at the bus stop on the opposite side of the road from where he could see Dan Howard's house.

James hoped nobody had seen him go to Dan's door. As it was warm, he wore a T-shirt and jeans. He realised he should have put on his hoodie to conceal his face. He kicked himself for being so reckless. The next time he ventured to Somerset Road, he would have to be more careful.

Pretending to speak on his phone, James stood at the bus stop for ages. When a double-decker bus slowed down to stop, James walked further down the road and returned to the bus stop after the bus disappeared around the corner.

A woman passed him with a yellow Labrador on a leash; the dog pulling so hard that the woman was almost dragged along the pavement. She apologised when the dog ran to James and greeted him by jumping up and licking his arms. Eventually, she dragged the dog away and continued their walk.

So much for trying to be inconspicuous.

Then James heard a door open. He glanced towards the house. The man standing in the open doorway was Dan

Howard. James was sure of it. Dan was about five feet nine, plump, with short, light brown hair receding at his temples. He was carrying a sports bag in one hand and his car keys in the other.

James fought to contain his excitement, longing for Dan to step in the dog poo and mess up his shoes.

As Dan stepped out of the door, his foot slipped in the dog shit. Waving his arms in the air, trying to regain his balance, both of his feet slid forward as if in slow-motion, and he landed on his backside with a thud, right on top of the dog shit.

Absolute comedy!

James struggled not to double up laughing and tried so hard to look as though his eyes were fixed on his phone's screen. He watched Dan out of the corner of his eye.

Dan struggled to get up, looking around, as people do whenever they fall over, and then he turned to go back inside the house.

James saw that Dan's trousers were covered in dog poo, and it looked like he'd messed himself. As the front door closed, James couldn't control himself any longer. He creased up and howled with hysterical laughter.

After that magnificent fall, he didn't expect to see any more of Dan, so he put his phone in his pocket and walked home wearing a massive grin. He imagined Dan cleaning up the mess and trying to remove the disgusting smell from his posh house. There was nothing worse than the smell of dog shit, and it would be worse than ever in the current heatwave.

James's day had certainly improved; he hadn't felt this good since before he'd lost his job, and it had stopped him thinking about how much he missed Lisa for a little while.

When he entered his street, the kitten ran to James and

meowed. He picked it up and noticed how light it felt.

'Is nobody feeding you?' he asked.

James carried the kitten into his flat and checked the date on the milk carton before pouring some into a saucer for the kitten. It lapped it up and then sat and gazed up at him expectantly.

'Okay, I know you're hungry. I guess you want more than just milk.'

He opened a tin of tuna, scraped a little onto the empty saucer and made himself a sandwich with the rest.

After they had eaten, James returned the kitten to where he'd found it. Because it was thin, he thought it unlikely that it belonged to anybody, but despite his reservations, he took it back outside in case somebody was looking for it.

16

Dog Shit and Dinner

Dan picked himself up, looked around to check if anybody had seen him fall, sighed with relief when nobody had, and then rushed back inside the house, clutching his sports bag and car keys. He slammed the door, hung his keys on the wall hook by the door, checked that his bag was clean, and threw it into the hallway.

Then, assessing the situation, he registered that his clothes and trainers were filthy, and the smell coming from him was atrocious, but at least nobody had seen him fall or, worse, recorded a video that could end up on Harry Hill's television show.

Dan had landed heavily on the concrete. His bum felt bruised, so he rubbed it, immediately withdrawing his hands when they came into contact with the sticky dog shit on his trousers. He held his hands out in front of him and stared at them in horror, making a guttural sound when he saw the filth coating them. Germs dominated his thoughts, and he wondered how many were on his hands.

Thousands? Tens of thousands? Millions?

His heart pounded, and his breathing quickened. Removing his trainers, he carried them upstairs to the bathroom, where he turned on the shower, stepped into the flow of hot water without undressing, and placed the offending shoes by his feet.

Once his clothes were well-rinsed, he held his shoes under the shower head until they looked clean, and then he undressed and concentrated on cleaning himself. He was in the shower for almost an hour, washing himself several times with his Gucci shower gel before he felt clean and sweet-smelling again. The television advertisement for the product that claimed to kill ninety-nine per cent of germs was at the front of his mind. Even as a child, he had feared the one per cent that was lurking somewhere, ready to strike.

In the bedroom, he put on a pair of jeans and a navy polo shirt and doused himself in Hugo Boss aftershave—but he could still smell the dog shit.

He went downstairs, took a pair of yellow rubber gloves from the kitchen cupboard and put them on. He then retrieved his sodden clothes from the shower, carried them downstairs, put them in the washing machine, selecting the hottest setting, and added two laundry tablets and sanitiser.

Checking the soles of his trainers, he found that despite the long soak in the shower, bits of dirt were still stuck between the treads. He took a knife from the cutlery drawer and levered the muck into the kitchen bin. Then he rinsed them under the cold tap. Eventually, when he was sure the shit had gone, he dropped the soiled knife into the waste bin. He couldn't use it again after that.

He'd had a shower, his clothes were in the washing machine, and his shoes were spotless. He wrinkled his nose. *Why was there still a smell?*

Dan wandered around, sniffing the air. The smell was worst in the hall, and he discovered two brown footprints on the red carpet. *Oh, no!* Out came a bucket containing equal proportions of water and bleach, and with a scrubbing brush, he scrubbed the pile until the water turned pink. *Pink!*

He stood up and surveyed his handiwork, his mouth agape and eyes wide. The bleach, which he'd added to kill the germs, had removed the dye from the carpet, turning the patches that he'd cleaned from red to pink.

Dan didn't want to spend money replacing the hall carpet, which also covered the stairs and landing. It was a huge area, and a carpet that size would cost a fortune. He'd buy a mat to cover the faded patches; he couldn't think how else to hide them.

He opened the front door to get rid of the dreadful smell in the hallway, thinking the draught might help to dry the carpet, and then he cleaned the doorstep with the remaining bleach mixture. After spraying air freshener liberally around the house, he went to the kitchen and poured himself a well-earned glass of Merlot.

When Chris came in after work, he found Dan sitting in an armchair with a wine glass in his hand, staring into space.

'It stinks in here,' said Chris, opening the window.

'It does *not* smell in here,' argued Dan.

'It does, Dan. It smells like farts covered up with air freshener. Have you got the shits again?'

'No, I haven't!'

'Anyway, I thought you were coming to the pool today,' said Chris, trying not to sound petulant.

'I tried to, Chris. Honestly, I did. You'll never believe what happened!'

'Go on, try me.'

'A dog shit on our doorstep. I slipped in it and fell over. I was covered in dog shit! It was too awful for words. It got absolutely everywhere. I've had the most horrendous afternoon cleaning it up.'

'Pull the other one,' said Chris. 'If you didn't want to come to the gym and meet my colleagues, you should have told me. I was so disappointed when you didn't show up. I'd told everybody you were coming, and they were looking forward to meeting you.'

'But it's true, Chris. It is. Honest. That's what the smell is.'

'You said there wasn't a smell,' said Chris, looking away and shaking his head.

'The carpet is still wet from when I washed it,' said Dan. 'Come and have a look. You can see that it's faded by the door where I cleaned it.'

Dan got up and went into the hall to show him, but Chris didn't follow. Instead, he went into the kitchen.

'There's nothing in the oven,' said Chris. 'So I guess we must be having steak tonight.'

'Oh, Chris. I'm sorry. I haven't had time to think about dinner.'

'You haven't had time to think about dinner!' Chris shook his head in disbelief. 'What have you been doing all day?'

'I've already told you what I've been doing.' Dan rolled his eyes. 'I spent all afternoon cleaning up dog shit.'

Chris looked at Dan and shrugged. Then he went upstairs for a shower, as he did every evening after finishing work at the gym.

When he returned downstairs, Dan said, 'I'm sorry I didn't make you anything for dinner, but what I said about the dog shit is true. I did intend to go to the pool and meet the people you work with. Look! My bag is still there on the floor.'

Dan pointed to the discarded sports bag at the end of the hallway.

Chris ignored the comment, no longer interested in Dan's excuses.

'We should go to the Steakhouse for dinner,' said Dan. 'Then you can have whatever you want to eat.'

'That's a good idea,' said Chris, perking up at the thought of a healthy, protein-packed meal. 'The food there is superb.'

Dan still wasn't sure Chris believed his story, but he was pleased with himself for suggesting going out to eat. It had cheered Chris up and given him a night off from cooking. *Win, win!*

17

A Painful Extraction

Putting his bowl of cereal down on the kitchen worktop, James reached for a box of paracetamol from the top shelf of the cupboard. His tooth hurt every time he ate or drank anything, and the cold milk on his Coco Pops had set it off again. He needed to see a dentist. He had been putting it off, but he couldn't any longer.

He wasn't registered with a dental surgery in Newcastle, but he had seen one on Chilton Road, which was only a five-minute walk from his flat.

At nine o'clock, he phoned to book an appointment, but nobody answered, so he grabbed his mobile, wallet, and house key and left his flat.

When he entered the reception of the dental surgery, a plump middle-aged woman with straight blonde hair and long nails asked if he had an appointment. He wondered if Lisa might look like her in twenty years' time.

After he explained that his tooth hurt and needed to see a dentist as soon as possible, she asked him to take a seat in the waiting room. She then disappeared into a room at the back of the building.

While he waited, James took out his phone and scrolled through his Facebook feed. Before long, he couldn't resist looking at Lisa Evans's profile. She looked stunning in her profile picture, and he felt gutted that she was no longer a part of his life.

He cringed when he saw that her relationship status was 'It's complicated'. *That's one way to put it!*

She had not changed her status to single, and he wondered if that meant he might still have a chance.

The most recent post on her page was a photo that Vicky Henderson, one of her friends, had tagged her in from their night out at the Quayside. It showed a few lasses sitting around a table in a bar, looking worse for wear, and Lisa at the end of the table, facing slightly away from the camera. She was talking to a well-dressed bloke, and the smiles on their faces told James that they were interested in each other. *Is that what she meant when she said he'd left it too late? Had she met another guy?*

The receptionist returned and showed James into the dental surgery, where he saw a young woman standing by the reclining chair.

'Morning. I'm Anika,' she said with a faultless smile. She took his medical history and then said, 'Please take a seat, Mr Webster, and we'll see what the problem is.'

James sat in the reclining chair and opened his mouth wide. The dentist leaning over him didn't look any older than he was. He hoped she knew what she was doing. His hands shook, and he placed them on the padded arms of the chair to still them; he'd always had a fear of dentists.

'You need a filling in your back molar,' she said. 'I'd

recommend a local anaesthetic. Is that alright?'

'I don't like injections. Do you have to numb it?'

Looking at the troublesome tooth again, she pursed her lips and said, 'It's not a deep hole. I could fill it without anaesthetic, but it may hurt for a short time while I'm working on it. On the plus side, it won't take as long because we won't need to wait for the anaesthetic to work. It's up to you.'

'Without anaesthetic, please,' he said, sounding braver than he felt.

James was tense sitting in the dentist's chair and took a few deep breaths to help him relax.

'Are you alright there?' asked Anika.

'Yeah, I'm okay.'

'Right, we'll get started then.'

James thought about Lisa while the dentist drilled and filled his tooth. He'd heard somewhere about going to your happy place in times of stress and anxiety, and, until a week ago, Lisa had been his happy place. He'd had a few girlfriends in the past, but she was the only one he'd ever been serious about, and he thought they would end up together. Why had he waited so long before asking her to move in?

'We're all done here, Mr Webster. I hope that didn't hurt too much?'

'No, it was fine, thank you,' said James, who expected the pain to be much worse.

'You shouldn't have any bother with that tooth now,' she said. 'But if you do, you're welcome to come back and see me.'

'Thank you.'

James darted for the door. At the reception desk, he took his wallet out of his jeans pocket and waited for the woman to check her computer screen to determine the cost of the treatment.

'Amalgam filling, no anaesthetic, that'll be £120, please.'

'One hundred and twenty!' he said. 'But I'm unemployed. Isn't dental treatment reduced or free when you're unemployed?'

'I believe it's free on the NHS if you get Income-based Jobseeker's Allowance, Mr Webster. But this is a private clinic. We don't see NHS patients here.'

Shit!

That was a sizeable chunk of his redundancy pay gone already; it wouldn't last as long as he'd hoped. James felt his whole body slump as he handed over his debit card. He should have realised it was a private clinic when he saw a dentist right away.

His hands fisted in his pockets; Dan Howard had a lot to answer for. After leaving the reception, James went home and found the mail lying on the floor as he entered the hallway. He sorted the letters into two piles, left one by the door of the downstairs flat and carried the other upstairs.

He opened the first envelope. A reminder to pay his overdue electric bill, which he added to a pile of bills on the kitchen worktop. Next was a flyer for a bargain booze shop opening soon on the neighbouring street. It went into the bin. The brown envelope at the bottom contained a letter from the Jobcentre, reminding him to attend and to bring evidence that he'd been looking for work. That would be difficult, he thought. He had been so preoccupied with losing his job, losing Lisa, and thinking of ways to get back at Dan Howard that he hadn't begun to look for a job yet.

Exactly two weeks after his first visit, James walked to the Jobcentre in Byker. During those weeks, he knew he should have been searching for jobs, but he had been preoccupied with his frightful situation and bent on seeking revenge.

James wandered into the building, took a seat, and waited for his turn.

'Mr Webster, what evidence of your job search have you brought for us today?' asked Josh MacIntosh.

'What do you mean by evidence?'

'Have you completed the job search book I gave you? Or brought any job advertisements you've applied for? Or any letters or emails you've received from the companies you've applied to?'

James shook his head.

'Have you applied for any jobs since you made your claim, Mr Webster?'

'I've asked around,' lied James, 'but there's nothing going.'

'Well, we're in a bit of a pickle here. I'm not supposed to let you sign on without seeing evidence that you've actively been seeking work. As this is your first time signing on, I'll let it go, but the next time you come in, you must have something to show me, or your benefits will be stopped. Do you understand?'

James nodded and signed the form.

'Thank you, Mr MacIntosh.'

James stood up to leave. He couldn't wait to get out of the place. The despair that he'd been holding off was threatening to return, and the only way he knew to stop it was by walking and keeping his mind off his miserable excuse for a life.

'Before you go, let's have a look for some jobs now, shall we?'

James hoped his face didn't show how he was feeling. 'Okay, why not?'

Josh led the way to a touchscreen kiosk and asked, 'What

sort of job are you looking for?'

'I dunno, really.'

'Well, what did you do in your last job?'

'I worked at Glad Rags,' said James proudly. 'It's a small fancy dress place in the town. I did all sorts of things: picking costumes for orders, checking the inventory, taking clothes to the dry cleaners and taking the post to the post office. I did a bit of cleaning, bought lunches for the staff, and made coffee. Whatever needed to be done, really.'

'So, would you say you were a shop assistant?'

'Nah. I never served customers or worked at the till or anything like that. I just helped the owners.'

'Do you have any qualifications or training?'

'No.' James shook his head.

'There's not much here for unskilled workers,' said Josh. 'Do you drive? There's a taxi firm needing drivers, and a delivery company is hiring people who have their own vans.'

'I don't have a driving licence.'

Josh continued his search.

'The Freeman Hospital has a vacancy for a porter. The salary is just above the minimum wage. Perhaps you could apply for that.'

'That sounds good.'

He waited for Josh to print out the job description.

'You need to apply for at least two jobs each week until you find one,' said Josh as he handed James the sheet of paper. 'Have you considered working at a fast food place? You would start as an apprentice and get training on the job. KFC has a vacancy at its city centre store.'

'I'll be honest with you. I'll take anything that'll pay the rent.'

'Scrap that then. Apprentices don't get enough to pay rent. The only other position that might be suitable is an assistant at a privately owned care home for the elderly.'

'Where is the care home?' asked James.

'It's in Heaton.'

'That would be handy. I live in Heaton,' he said. 'I'll take the info for that one as well, thanks.'

When he got home, James fired up the laptop, spent two hours filling in the forms for the vacancies that Josh had found, and sent off the applications. That was his mandatory job-seeking done for the week.

He put on his hoodie, took a Swiss army knife from a drawer in the kitchen, and then walked the two miles to Jesmond, knowing the walk would do him good.

James needed to know more about this Dan Howard guy, and he reckoned that watching him would be the best way. Just along the road from number sixty-six was a house with a low stone wall around the front garden and a view of Dan's house. The wall was a comfortable height to sit on. The owners were out—James had seen them get into a white Audi A3 and drive away—so he sat there, scrolling through his phone.

While he waited, he checked out Dan Howard on Google, entering a search for his name. Photos of many men named Dan Howard from all around the world appeared in the results, but none of them matched the Dan Howard in question. Maybe he needed to be more specific.

Next, he searched for 'Daniel Howard Jesmond'. Only one search result was a match—an obituary in *The Newcastle Journal*.

November 23, 2016. HOWARD, Marjorie, nee Westwood, of Jesmond, aged 59, widow of the late John, mother of Daniel John, died peacefully at St. Hilda's Hospice, Newcastle-upon-Tyne. Donations for Cancer Research in lieu of flowers.

Wow! With just one search, he'd discovered Dan's middle name was John, his mother's maiden name was Westwood, that both his parents were dead, and he didn't have any siblings. More information to store away until it becomes useful, he thought.

Finally, he looked up '66 Somerset Road, Jesmond' and sighed when the results appeared. There was not much of interest there. A planning application for a conservatory, which sounded boring, but James followed the link to the council's website. Mr John Backworth had submitted a letter of objection to Dan's proposal. He was a resident of number sixty-four, next door to Dan Howard. Two years ago, the council granted permission for the development, with some minor amendments to the plans.

He was on the point of leaving Somerset Road when a silver Mercedes pulled up outside number sixty-six, and Dan stepped out of the driver's side. The boot lid opened, and Dan removed several shopping bags before walking to the house and letting himself in.

James smiled. Now, he knew which car belonged to Dan and that he shopped at Asda. He was learning more about the man all the time.

He glanced up and down the street, and couldn't see anyone, so he crossed the road and knelt on the pavement beside the rear wheel of Dan's car. Looking again to ensure he wasn't being watched, he unscrewed the cap off the valve stem, took the Swiss army knife from his pocket, opened the Phillips screwdriver, and pressed the pin. The air hissed as it passed through the valve.

James watched the tyre deflate, and when it was almost flat, he put the cap back on and walked away, trying his best to look inconspicuous.

18

Leaky Milk and a Flat Tyre

Dan heard the front door opening over the sound of Billie Eilish's latest single.

'Is that you, Chris?'

'Yes, it's me!'

A moment later, Chris stepped into the kitchen where Dan was preparing dinner and turned down the music.

'That smells good. What are you making?' he asked.

'Cajun chicken, rice with coriander and lime, and I'll stir-fry some sweet peppers and onions to go with it.'

'Wowsers!' said Chris. 'That sounds delish. I'll have a quick shower, and I'll be right back.'

'Don't be long. It'll be ready in ten minutes.'

When Chris returned, Dan set the table for two and stirred some brightly coloured strips of peppers and red onions in a frying pan. When the peppers were cooked, he served the food onto plates and carried them to the table.

'Could you open the Prosecco, please? It's in the fridge.'

Chris opened the bottle with a pop and poured the sparkling wine into the champagne flutes already on the table. He put the bottle back in the fridge to keep it chilled before he sat down.

'Are we celebrating something?'

'No,' said Dan. 'The Prosecco was on offer today at only £4.25 a bottle. I've never seen it that low before, so I had to get some.'

Chewing the first mouthful, Chris made sounds of appreciation, and when he finished, he said, 'You can't half cook, Dan. This is very good. Restaurant quality, even. You could have been a chef!'

'Thank you!' Dan was delighted with the compliment. 'It's not bad, is it?'

'So, what's your day been like?' asked Chris.

'It could have been better,' said Dan. 'I went to Asda this morning, and you'll never guess what happened. I got to the checkout and loaded everything onto the conveyor belt, and then I noticed the milk container was leaking. It had spilled all over the place. It was on the vegetables and the tins and even the toilet roll packet. The girl behind the counter asked someone to wipe everything down. You know me. I told them what I thought in no uncertain terms. They should seal the milk bottle tops securely so that the milk can't leak out and contaminate people's shopping. Milk stinks when it goes off, and if they hadn't cleaned the shopping properly, it would make my house and fridge smell awful.'

He wrinkled his nose in distaste.

Chris nodded as he savoured his dinner and listened to Dan's story.

'Well, at that point, I couldn't decide if I wanted the shopping or not, and I considered asking them to get me some clean stuff off the shelves, but that would have been even more inconvenient because it would have taken them ages. I'm sure I could do it quicker myself. Anyway, they offered me a small discount as an apology for the hassle. Wasn't that nice of them?'

'If you say so.' Chris was enjoying his meal too much to interact more fully.

'You should have seen the girl's face,' said Dan, taking a sip of the fizz. 'The one at the checkout. It was bright red! But really, people should do their jobs properly, shouldn't they? It's not too much to ask.'

Chris rolled his eyes, but Dan ignored it. He didn't want to argue with Chris, not tonight when he'd praised his cooking skills.

After dinner, they took their drinks into the lounge, sat on the sofa, and Dan turned on the large-screen television.

'What do you fancy watching tonight?' asked Dan.

'I'm not fussed. You choose something.'

They watched EastEnders, followed by a new top-rated action movie on Netflix, and then they had an early night.

The following morning, Dan cleared the breakfast dishes and filled the dishwasher after Chris left for work. He was startled when he heard the front door open and went into the hallway to see who was there. Chris was heading towards him, looking solemn.

'Have you forgotten something?' asked Dan.

'Just thought I should let you know that you've got a flat tyre. The rear one on the driver's side.'

'Not again!'

'The last time that happened, you drove away and ruined the tyre and the rim,' said Chris. 'Promise me you'll get someone to fix it before you go anywhere. Okay?'

Dan didn't like being told what to do, but he knew Chris was right, so he shrugged his shoulders and reluctantly agreed.

'I'm running late. I must run.'

Chris rushed out of the house, and Dan followed him down the path, watching him jog up the street. He could see the back tyre of his car; it was very flat. Even he would have noticed that before he'd driven anywhere.

Dan went inside, filled the dishwasher, cleaned the kitchen, and then used his laptop to search for garages in the Jesmond area, but he became distracted by a Facebook notification and visited his social media accounts, where he became engrossed in the discussions and lost track of time.

When his stomach rumbled, he got up to make a sandwich with smoked salmon and cream cheese with chives for lunch and suddenly remembered about the flat tyre. He ate one sandwich to satisfy his hunger, wiped the crumbs from his lips, and then searched for a garage online.

He recognised one nearby, so he called the number and asked if they could send someone out to fix his tyre. The man on the phone said somebody would come out that afternoon.

Dan finished his lunch and drank a can of cola, wondering what to do while he waited for the mechanic to arrive. Going shopping was out of the question because he couldn't use his car. The house was clean, so he picked up his laptop and surfed the internet.

When he heard a knock at the door, he opened it to see a middle-aged man wearing a hand-knitted hat and holding a toolbox.

'Mr Howard? Is this your Merc out here?' he asked, nodding towards Dan's car.

'Yes. The tyre was fine yesterday, so it must have gone down overnight. Can you fix it?'

'Yeah, no worries. I'll pump it up and check it for damage.'

'I didn't drive it with a flat tyre,' said Dan defensively.

'I didn't think you had. What I meant was, I'll check if the tyre has a puncture that needs repairing. There might be a nail or something stuck in it.'

'Oh! Okay.'

Dan left the man to do his work and went inside, where he watched from the front window. He saw the tyre inflate, and the man looked like he was listening to the tyre, which Dan thought was rather funny. *Why would he listen to a tyre?* Then, he turned towards the house and approached the door.

Dan opened it.

'Did you work out what was wrong with it?' he asked.

'There's nothing wrong with the tyre,' said the mechanic.

'So why did it go flat?'

'Your guess is as good as mine.' The man shrugged his shoulders.

'Huh! You're supposed to be the expert here,' said Dan.

'That'll be £75 for the call-out, please.'

'How much?' screeched Dan. 'But all you did was blow up the tyre.'

'Maybe, but this morning, you had a car you couldn't drive, and now you have a car that you can drive.'

Dan slunk off to find his wallet and returned with four brand new twenty-pound notes straight from the cashpoint machine, which he handed to the man and waited for his change.

The mechanic pulled a crumpled, greasy five-pound note from his back pocket and handed it to Dan, who recoiled from the dirt.

'Keep the change,' said Dan, closing the door. He didn't want a filthy bank note contaminating his beautiful Louis Vuitton leather wallet.

Disgusted at the charge for blowing up a tyre, Dan picked up his laptop, found the garage's page on Google, and wrote a one-star review.

This garage will fleece you. I live less than half a mile from this garage. My car had a flat tyre this morning, so I called them. They sent a mechanic to my house to blow up the tyre. He couldn't find a puncture and couldn't tell me why the tyre had gone flat, and then he had the cheek to charge me £75, which was a complete rip-off. I wouldn't recommend anyone to use this garage under any circumstances.

Checking the time, he realised he didn't have time to shop before Chris came home from work, so he looked in the freezer. Burgers, chicken dippers, fish fingers, peas, and pepperoni pizza. Nothing inspired him, but he removed the fish fingers and peas, thinking Chris would prefer those to the other options, and peeled some potatoes to make chips. The meal wouldn't be up to his usual standards, but it would have to do under the circumstances.

19

The Kiss

It was Monday again. James was thankful it was not a signing-on day. Instead, he had a lie-in and then spent the afternoon wandering around Heaton Park. The grass was freshly mown, and the sweet smell hung in the air. He admired the ancient ruins, imagining what the building would have looked like and who would have lived there in years gone by.

On his way home, he approached the ornate park gate and spotted a navy baseball cap on a seat. Nobody was nearby, so he picked it up and put it on his head. It kept the sun out of his eyes, but it could be useful to hide his face, too, he thought.

Just a few streets away from home, he saw a car pull up outside Lisa's house. He stood and watched in trepidation as he saw a figure he knew well, intimately in fact, in the passenger seat. She leaned across and kissed the driver before getting out and taking a load of carrier bags emblazoned with the names of high street stores from the back seat. Lisa waved at the driver as the car pulled away from the kerb and then let herself into her flat. She hadn't seen him standing at the corner of the street watching her.

He stood frozen on the spot, shocked by what he'd seen. Lisa had kissed a man and got out of his car. It might be innocent, he told himself. She might have accepted a lift from a friend or a colleague. But James didn't think so. Not with a kiss like that. *Was it the man in the photo at the Quayside?*

It looked like they'd been shopping together. *Had he bought her all that stuff?*

James had never had the money to spoil Lisa. His budget just about stretched to a curry or a pizza at the weekend and a few beers. Lisa didn't seem to mind; sometimes she picked up the bill. He suspected that she earned more than he did at Glad Rags, but salaries weren't something they'd ever discussed.

He thought back to Lisa's comment when she'd left him. She'd said he'd left it too late to ask her to move in, and clearly, he had. She had found another bloke already.

Or had she been cheating on him?

Well, that was that. End of. Over. No more Lisa in his life.

He'd suspected their relationship had ended when she walked out on him that day, but he'd hoped he was mistaken. Anger and jealousy flooded his veins, and he wanted to punch the guy for stealing his woman, but he'd missed that opportunity. The car had turned the corner and was out of sight.

Without thinking about what he was doing, he marched to Lisa's house, his hands fisted in his pockets, his jaw clenched, and when he reached it, he banged on the door.

Lisa opened it; her smile quickly disappeared when she saw the look on his face.

'Who was that bloke?' asked James through gritted teeth.

'What's that got to do with you?'

'Are you seeing him?' James asked, but didn't know if he

wanted to hear the answer.

'I'm sorry you're upset, James, but it's none of your business if I'm seeing somebody. We're not together any more.'

'Were you seeing him when we were together?' asked James, staring into her eyes.

'God, no! How could you think that? I've just met him.'

James felt tears stinging his eyes. He needed to get away from Lisa; he couldn't let her know how much seeing her with that bloke had affected him. Turning away, he drifted home, his head lowered, his cap hiding his tears from passers-by.

On entering his flat, he slammed the door behind him. He went straight into the bedroom, lay down on his bed and sobbed, clutching his pillow in his arms.

Several hours later, his stomach was grumbling. He tried to remember if he'd had anything to eat that day, but couldn't. When he couldn't ignore his hunger any longer, he got up, washed his face and went for a takeaway.

Several food places were nearby, and he walked along the street before stopping at a pizza shop. He placed his order and waited outside while they made it, leaning against the shop front. While he was there, he saw a large rat run across the road and get hit by a car. When the car passed, the rat was lying by the kerb, not moving, and he presumed it must be dead. He envied the rat because it couldn't feel anything any more. No more hurt. No more pain. But he shouldn't think like that.

A guy behind the shop counter called him. His pizza was ready. James went inside to pay and then took it home to eat. He usually loved pizza, but he struggled to eat that night. It seemed to stick in his throat.

His mind was still on Lisa. Thinking about her with another man made his blood boil. She was meant to be with him.

Leaving the partially eaten food in a box on the sofa, James went back outside. He needed to walk off the negativity that threatened to engulf him.

Dashing back to the shopping street, he entered the first shop he came to, which was a greengrocer's.

'Could I have a carrier bag, please?' James asked the guy behind the counter.

'Of course you can,' said the shopkeeper. 'They're five pence. I'll add it to your bill when you've chosen what you want.'

'No, sir. You don't understand. I just want a carrier bag.'

The man's eyes shone with mirth, thinking this was a trick of some sort.

'Really! You just want a plastic carrier bag?'

'Yes.'

James fished in his jeans pocket and found a five-pence piece. The shopkeeper took the change and handed him a bag, unable to hide his amusement.

James left the shop and walked further down the road, where he'd seen the rat run over, and was grateful that its partially flattened body was still there. He lifted it by its tail and placed it in the plastic bag he'd bought from the shop.

Then he carried the dead rat to Somerset Road in Jesmond and went to the back street at the rear of Dan's house. Dan's garden had a central lawn edged with bushes, a flower bed in front of the conservatory, and an area of wooden decking with outdoor seating and a gas barbecue. He smiled. *Perfect!*

He looked up and down the street and double-checked that nobody was in the garden. It was empty. Then, he saw a movement and ducked down, hiding behind the wall, frozen in fear of being discovered.

Peering through a tall shrub, James watched the conservatory door open, and Dan entered the garden. He turned on the tap that was fixed to the house wall and had a hosepipe attached, and he used it to water the flowers and shrubs around the lawn. It seemed to take him an age, but James was in hiding for less than five minutes.

The conservatory door closed, and the coast was clear.

He waited a few more minutes to ensure Dan didn't return to the garden. When there were no more sounds, he stood up to get a better look and couldn't detect any movement in the house or garden. Now was the perfect opportunity.

He climbed over the waist-high wall and ran over to the decking area. A plastic ventilation strip ran along the base of the conservatory on either side of the patio doors. He lifted a strip, threw the dead rat under the wooden planks, and pushed the strip back into place.

Then he ran, vaulting the wall, and not slowing down until he was several streets away. Walking home, he was satisfied with his achievement and relieved that he hadn't been caught.

20

The Barbecue

Looking at the clock at the bottom of his screen, Dan realised he didn't have time to go to Asda to buy ingredients for dinner. He had been so engrossed in surfing the internet and wading through his social media feeds that he'd completely lost track of time. Closing the laptop, he put it on the side table.

Driving to the nearest shopping street, which was just around the corner, he parked outside the butcher's shop, where he bought three organic fillet steaks, three free-range chicken breasts, and half a dozen of the butcher's best pork sausages. The extra pieces were for Chris, who had the appetite of two.

When Chris came home that day, hungry as usual after a physical day at work, he asked, 'What are we having for dinner?'

'It's Friday, and it's a lovely evening,' said Dan. 'So, I thought we could have a barbecue alfresco with a few drinks.'

'That sounds great! I'll just have a shower and get changed, and then I'll help you with the cooking.'

When Chris came downstairs, he was wearing a clean sports

shirt and shorts. Dan had already lit the barbecue and opened a bottle of Merlot. He poured two glasses, handed one to Chris, and sipped the other.

About ten minutes later, when the barbecue was hot, Dan removed the meat from the fridge, carried it outside on a plastic tray, and arranged the pieces on the grill.

The garden faced southwest, and Dan and Chris sat at the patio table in the warm evening sun, enjoying the wine while they waited for the food to cook.

'Are you sure that meat's fresh?' asked Chris, wrinkling his nose.

'Yes, I got it from the butcher's this afternoon.' Dan sniffed the air. 'It doesn't smell good, though, does it?'

'It smells rank. I'm not eating that. Put it in the bin, would you?'

Annoyed at having wasted almost £25 on supposedly fresh meat that was off, Dan photographed the offending food, which was now cooked, before bagging it up in a clean zip-lock bag and putting it in the fridge.

Tomorrow morning, he would go back to the shop and tell the butcher what he thought of him for selling rotten meat to unsuspecting customers. The butcher would regret spoiling Dan Howard's plans for the evening.

Dan would have to find something else for dinner, so he rummaged around in the freezer until he found the chicken dippers. He had barbecue sauce, mayonnaise and tomato ketchup for dips. That would be okay.

The following morning, armed with the bag of barbecued meat, Dan returned to the butcher's shop. He impatiently tapped his foot, clicked his tongue, and sighed loudly while waiting in line until he reached the counter.

'I came in here yesterday and bought some steaks, chicken and sausages for a barbecue last night,' said Dan. 'The meat was off! The stink from it when it was cooking was atrocious. Here! See for yourself.'

Dan thrust the bag toward the butcher, feeling proud that a couple had left the shop after hearing what he'd said.

The butcher untied the bag and sniffed loudly.

'It smells perfectly alright to me,' he said, shrugging and handing the bag back to Dan.

Dan sniffed the meat. It smelled just like barbecued meat—very nice, actually. Puzzled, he sniffed it again.

'It didn't smell like this last night.'

'There's nowt wrong with that meat. Now, if you're not buying anything, please move aside so I can serve these customers.'

Dan stormed out of the shop, dived into his car, and drove home. When he parked up, he sniffed the meat again, and it still smelled good. He thought he might have the chicken for lunch. Once inside, he put the meat in the fridge, except for one chicken breast. He filled a bread roll with the sliced chicken and some shredded iceberg lettuce, adding a large dollop of garlic mayonnaise.

While eating his delicious sandwich, Dan remembered his thwarted attempt at a barbecue and was annoyed that the meat had spoiled his evening. Not only that, the butcher's treatment of him when he went to the shop today had been shocking—he'd practically thrown him out!

Once he'd finished the sandwich, he picked up his laptop and found the shop's contact details online. He drafted a complaint, which he emailed to the shop, and then left a one-star review on Trustpilot, along with a report about the rotten meat he'd bought there. He didn't care that it was untrue and that the meat was perfectly edible. It was scrumptious, in fact. The butcher had upset him, and he deserved to be punished for what he'd done.

Putting down his laptop, Dan went to Asda to buy the ingredients for dinner that evening. He planned to make beef bourguignon, one of his favourite dishes.

'Have you been up to much today?' asked Chris as he and Dan sat down to eat that evening.

'Not a lot.'

Dan explained what had happened at the butcher's that morning and told Chris about the complaint and the review that he'd written.

Chris nodded, looking distracted.

'It took hours to make this food, though,' said Dan, pointing at his plate with his fork. 'When I asked where the shallots were in Asda, a young fella took me to the spring onions. Can you believe he didn't know the difference? And you should try getting lardons around here. Nobody seems to know what they are. I ended up going to Sainsbury's for them.'

'I wish all I had to worry about was where to buy food.'

'Why? What's up with you?'

'Peter, the manager at the gym, is leaving. Turns out he hadn't injured his ankle. He was taking time off work to attend job interviews. Anyway, he's been offered a job at a gym in Leeds, and he suggested I should apply for his job as manager.'

'Wow! That's exciting. Are you going to apply?'

'I don't know,' said Chris. 'I've been at the gym as long as anybody, so I might stand a chance of getting the job, but I enjoy the teaching and training side of things. I'm not sure I want to sit in an office for most of the day, scheduling staff rotas and ordering supplies and doing stuff like that.'

'Is the pay better?'

Dan picked up his glass and took a sip of Merlot, which went incredibly well with the beef dish.

'Yes, it's almost five grand more per year.'

'You should go for it,' said Dan. 'That's enough for a couple of super holidays. We could go all-inclusive.'

Chris looked at Dan and said, 'You have plenty of money to go on holiday whenever you want, and you can easily afford to go all-inclusive. All-inclusive at a hotel usually works out cheaper than going to restaurants and bars in the resort, anyway.'

'Huh!' said Dan. 'I was just trying to be supportive, and then you throw it back in my face.'

'Well, if you really cared about me, you'd want me to be happy, and I'm happy doing what I'm doing—the training side of things.'

'Oh, Chris! Stay in the job you have, then. I don't really care any more.'

'Thanks a lot!' Chris left the table without finishing his meal and without touching his wine. He poured a glass of tap water and drank it by the kitchen sink. When he'd finished, he said, 'I'm going for a run.'

Dan refilled his wine glass, took it into the garden and sat in a rattan chair, facing the evening sun. It was another lovely evening for September. His mother would have called it an Indian summer. It was very pleasant—except for that dreadful smell.

He sniffed the air and pulled a face. The smell of the rotten meat still lingered. He put down his glass and went to the kitchen, where he found a pair of rubber gloves, the oven cleaner and a cloth. He scrubbed the barbecue until the grill looked as good as new, rinsed it and then sat down again to finish his drink in the sunshine.

The barbecue gleamed in the sunlight, but the putrid smell still lingered in the air. If anything, it was worse than the previous night.

When Chris returned from his run, he came out into the garden carrying a glass of water and apologised for being snappy about the job earlier, but before he finished, he said, 'It still stinks out here. Maybe it wasn't the meat that smelled bad last night.'

'I've just cleaned the barbecue. It's absolutely spotless.'

'Where's the smell coming from?' asked Chris. 'It's not the bins, is it?'

'No, it's worse over here.'

'I wonder if there could be something under this decking,' said Chris. Pulling his phone from his back pocket, he switched on the torch and peered through the gaps in the decking to the ground below. 'Ah-ha!'

'What is it?' asked Dan, standing over him.

'There's a dead rat down there.'

'A rat! Are you sure?'

'Yes, I'm sure. So, it definitely wasn't the meat to blame last night. You should apologise to the butcher and remove the review you wrote while you're on.'

Dan pressed his lips together and folded his arms. Chris had no right to boss him around. He would never apologise to the man who had literally thrown him out for complaining. He deserved the negative review for that, in Dan's opinion.

'I'll have to take the side off the decking to get it out,' said Chris. 'I'll do it on my day off.'

'When is that?'

'Thursday.'

'Oh, Chris! I can't put up with that smell until Thursday. Can't you do it now, please?'

'I'm shattered,' said Chris. 'I worked nine hours today, and I've just got back from a ten-mile run. I'm desperate for something to eat and a rest.'

Dan's eyes pleaded with him to remove the dead rat right there and then.

'Okay. Fetch me a screwdriver.'

21

Access All Areas

September 2019

James hadn't slept. He had tossed and turned all night; his mind was too active, thinking about Dan Howard and how he had destroyed his life.

As he poured Coco Pops into a bowl, he felt something on his foot and looked down to see a fat mouse run under the kitchen cupboards. It wasn't the first mouse he'd seen in his flat. They didn't bother him, so he didn't bother them.

He sat in front of the television and watched a morning news program while he ate his breakfast. The new theory that the Loch Ness Monster sightings were actually giant eels rather than some prehistoric monster interested him, but the following item was about the economy, and he tuned out.

When he heard the letterbox rattle downstairs, he collected his post and took it to his flat, where he leafed through the pile.

Junk mail. More junk mail. A bank statement. Flyer.

He opened the bank statement and looked through the transactions. It showed a large payment from Glad Rags credited to his account on the second day of August, his last day at work, and his monthly bills going out—rent, council tax, electricity, and gas. The payment for the dental surgery had hurt him more than the toothache or the filling. Then, various grocery shops and a few takeaways—not extravagant costs by any means, but they added up. Even though he'd received his first Jobseeker's Allowance payment, the final balance was lower than expected.

He would have to cut back his spending until he found another job. He hadn't worried too much about his finances in the past. His salary went in, his bills came out, and there was nothing left at the end of the month—but he had got by.

Thinking about his current situation—no job, money declining rapidly, and loneliness—made him angry. He had never been so lonely in his life. He missed his lovely Lisa, and he missed Matt and Amanda from work. They were the only people he socialised with, apart from Mrs Green downstairs when he chanced to see her.

He took the junk mail into the kitchen and dropped it in the bin, and he remembered the mouse he had seen earlier, which gave him an idea. He put on his hoodie, picked up his wallet, and went outside.

Walking up Chilton Road, he stopped at a hardware shop and went inside. Shelves lined the shop's walls from floor to ceiling, and several aisles of shelving filled the floor space. He didn't know where to look.

'Do you sell mousetraps?' he asked an assistant who was stacking shelves.

'Yes. We have the traditional ones that kill them and the

humane ones to trap them so you can release them somewhere safe. Which would you like?'

'I'll take a humane one, thanks.'

The assistant smiled as she turned away to fetch the device, and James thought she looked relieved that he didn't want to kill his little intruder.

She grabbed a box off a shelf and took it to the shop counter.

'Is there anything else you'd like today?'

James looked around the shop and saw that the navy decorator overalls were heavily discounted.

'Is there something wrong with these?' he asked, reaching for a pair of overalls and checking the size.

'No, we have too many in stock, so we're selling them off at cost price to clear the space.'

'I'll take these as well, please.'

James paid for his purchases, and when he returned home, he followed the instructions to set the mousetrap and placed it on the kitchen floor.

He went out to buy a few groceries, hoping that by the time he returned, the mouse would be inside the trap, eating the last of the cheese that he'd used as bait.

When he got home, carrying a bag of groceries, the mouse was there, eating the cheese, just as he'd hoped. He grinned and picked up the trap, realising the mouse wasn't fat, but heavily pregnant. *Perfect!*

After eating a Pot Noodle, in a hot curry flavour called a Bombay Bad Boy, he dressed in the cheap blue overalls he'd bought from the hardware shop and put on the navy baseball cap he'd found abandoned in the park. He fished the junk mail out of the bin, folded the letters in half so that the plain side was to the outside, and hooked a ballpoint pen over them.

Then, he double-checked he had everything he needed in his pockets and left the flat, wishing he had a pair of boots. He hoped his scruffy trainers weren't too obvious under the wide-legged trousers.

On the walk to Jesmond, James almost turned back several times. He felt paranoid, thinking everyone was looking at him suspiciously, and a trickle of sweat ran down his spine. The plan was bold, and he hoped his nerve would hold. If it was so risky, perhaps he should abort the plan and go home. Could he get away with it?

He kept on walking. When he reached Somerset Road, James pulled down the cap and knocked at the door of number sixty-six, which Dan opened.

'Meter reader,' said James in a monotone voice, looking down at his papers to hide his face. His heart was pounding in his chest, and sweat beaded on his brow. It felt like ages before Dan responded. He pointed to the cupboard under the stairs and barely glanced at James.

'It's in there.'

Dan's phone rang, and he wandered into the garden. James guessed he was speaking to Chris from the snippet of conversation he heard.

Knowing that Dan couldn't see him from outside, James glanced furtively around the ground floor. He noticed an open laptop on a sideboard in the hall and edged towards it, listening keenly for Dan's return to the house. As long as he could hear Dan talking outside, he would be safe.

James hit a button on the keypad, and the screen lit up, showing a snippet of Dan's Facebook feed. He checked the icons at the bottom. Google Chrome. *Great!*

He quickly accessed the Google Password Manager and saw

that most of the stored passwords were the same three words, all relating to superheroes. Dan was predictable. With his phone, he took a photo of the computer screen and then another of the router's passwords.

He was acutely aware he'd been in the house longer than intended, so he went to the under-stairs cupboard, removed the pregnant mouse from his pocket and placed it gently on the floor. It shuffled to the back of the closet and climbed clumsily into a walking boot.

His job done, James sneaked out of the house, leaving the door ajar, not wanting to alert Dan to how long he had been there. As he walked away, he expected Dan to shout from the doorway or run after him, but he didn't.

When he turned the corner at the end of the street, James stopped, leaned his back against the wall, and exhaled. He took off the baseball cap and wiped the sweat from his brow. He had done it!

Grinning, he punched the air. The plan was more successful than expected. He had accomplished his mission, which was to re-home the mouse in Dan's house. Accessing his laptop and passwords had been an unexpected bonus.

He walked back to his flat through the parks, and as he turned the key in his lock, James heard a meow. The kitten jumped out from behind a large plant pot and rubbed around his ankles, purring loudly.

'Hello. Have you come to have dinner with me again?'

22

Failing Fast

Amanda sat and stared at her laptop screen, her face impassive.

'Are there any orders this morning, love?' asked Matt.

'Just the one. Mrs Robson has ordered Antony and Cleopatra for herself and her husband. Apparently, the Newcastle Rotary Club is having a Roman-themed party this weekend, so hopefully, we might get a few orders for that. Mrs Robson was one of our first customers—maybe even the first! I'm pleased she hasn't deserted us.'

'Just one order on a Monday morning?'

'Yeah, I know. We used to be so busy on Mondays, and James was always run off his feet—the poor lad.'

'I'm sure this will all blow over,' said Matt, preparing the packing materials on the counter. 'Business will pick up again soon, and we'll be laughing about it in years to come. You'll see.'

'God, I hope you're right. We took only £140 last week. That's nowhere near enough to pay the rent and rates, never mind our wages.'

'We can manage without our wages for a month or two,

love. It's more important to pay the rent and rates to keep the business going.'

'Okay,' she said, heading towards the back room. 'I'll just grab these costumes for you to pack, and then I'll look at the bills that need to be paid.'

A delivery van pulled up outside. The driver climbed out, opened the rear doors, and removed a large box, which he carried into the shop.

'I have a delivery for you.'

The driver placed the parcel on the floor in front of the counter and held out a clipboard.

'Can you sign here, please?'

Matt signed the paperwork, watched the driver leave the shop, get back in his van, and drive away.

Amanda returned with the two costumes and gave them to Matt.

'A delivery just arrived,' said Matt. 'Any idea what it is?'

'Oh, no!' Amanda rushed to the box. She checked the label and screwed up her face. 'I thought as much. It's more costumes from the wholesalers. It must be over six weeks since I placed the order. There's been a huge delay. The owners were away for a month—in the Caribbean, I think.'

'A month in the sun. Nice for some,' said Matt as he packed the Roman costumes.

'With the way business has been lately, I should have cancelled the order, but to tell you the truth, I'd forgotten all about them. That's another bill I'll need to pay.'

'Can't you return them?' asked Matt.

Amanda shook her head, sat at her desk, and ran her hands through her hair. 'I ordered them in the sale and got them at a good price, but they don't allow discounted items to be returned.'

'That's a shame.'

'I'm not surprised I forgot about the order,' said Amanda. 'They usually email a despatch notification. I must have missed that as well. I can't concentrate with all this review stuff going on. It's awful seeing my company's name being dragged through the mud, and I don't think I've done anything to deserve it. That horrible, vindictive man. His online reviews and comments were bad enough, filled with slander and lies, but the other reviews weren't even from actual customers. How can people be so cruel? Our Google rating has dropped from 4.8 to 1.3, and on Facebook now, only 5% of reviewers recommend us. It used to be 100%. How can they do this, Matt? They've ruined my business!'

She buried her head in her folded arms on the desk and cried.

As Matt comforted her, he couldn't disagree. He also feared for the company's future. He could strangle that blackmailing bastard for the damage he'd done.

23

Anonymous Gift

James finished a bowl of tinned spaghetti bolognese, picked up the remote control, and turned off the telly. He hated daytime television, but sometimes he would switch it on when eating lunch, just for the company.

He opened his phone and checked the photo gallery for the photo of Dan's passwords. Looking through the list of websites, he spotted several of interest: Google, email, his planner, Facebook, and Trustpilot.

He accessed Dan's planner and frowned when he saw the sparse entries for the coming month or so. A swimming lesson for August 14 at Shape Up, the gym where his partner worked. An appointment with a hairdresser. A one-week holiday in Tenerife. His birthday. And that was it.

James realised Dan must have been on his way to the pool the day he'd slipped in the dog shit. James had expected him to tread in it and curse a lot, not to fall over like he did. He chuckled to himself as he remembered how hilarious it had been when Dan turned around, showing his backside covered in shit.

Scrolling down, he saw Chris's birthday was on October 16. Chuckling to himself, he deleted the entry and added it on November 16.

The email account was more interesting than the planner. It gave James access to Dan's contacts and their messages. It would take ages to read them. Cynically, he wondered how many of the contacts were fake identities, like those Dan used on Facebook. He studied the account holder's details and memorised Dan's phone number.

He entered the Trustpilot website first, using Dan's password, and was tempted to change Dan's review on Glad Rags, but decided not to. It could draw attention to the fact that someone had accessed his account.

James shook his head and sighed. He knew a lot about Dan, and now he could access much of his data, but he couldn't think how to use it.

Needing a break, he grabbed his keys and put on his baseball cap. He walked to Heaton Park to clear his head. The sun was shining, and the park was busy. He dodged a few cyclists and joggers and passed a young couple strolling along the path, holding hands. Seeing them laugh and smile at each other made him miss Lisa even more. He wondered what she was doing. Was she with the man James had seen her with at her flat?

As James thought about the two of them together, Lisa and her new bloke, his melancholy veered towards rage, and his mind returned to Dan Howard, the man he held responsible for Lisa leaving him. Before he knew it, James had left the park and found himself walking through the back streets near the city centre.

He passed a sleazy-looking pub with two men standing by

the door smoking. He paused before going inside. The room was dark and grimy, and his shoes stuck to the carpet as he walked to the bar. He pulled down the cap to hide his face.

'Do you have a phone I could use, please?'

'Over there, mate.'

The barman pointed to a recess at the rear of the room.

Few customers were in the pub in the mid-afternoon, and they paid no attention to him. The payphone hung on the back wall of the recess, and business cards were pinned to the surrounding walls, advertising anything a drunken punter might want: taxis, takeaways, The Samaritans, sexual health clinics and sex workers. On the floor was a little blue pen that somebody had borrowed from a betting shop.

James unpinned a business card, picked up the pen, and wrote on the back: *Good-looking gay guy wanting a good time, Jesmond*, followed by Dan's mobile number. He then pinned it at eye level above the phone, the most prominent position where it couldn't be overlooked.

On his way out of the building, he saw a recycling bin filled with various-sized cardboard boxes, flattened so they would fit in the bin. He lifted a few out and found a square one, which was clean and plain, measuring about forty centimetres. *Perfect!*

He went to a nearby shopping arcade and entered a small craft shop, where a middle-aged shop assistant was cleaning the shelves.

'Hello. What can I get you, love?' she asked.

'Hi, I'd like some polystyrene packing material, the tiny polystyrene balls, and some glitter, please. The colour doesn't matter, but the smaller the pieces, the better.'

'You're in luck. We have some minute-sized glitter in silver or gold, like the kind you use on birthday cards.'

'Great! I'll take one in silver.'

She selected a small container of glitter from the shelf behind her and put it on the counter. Then, she went through a door at the back of the shop and returned with a plastic bag filled with tiny white balls, tied with clear tape.

'Three millimetres is the smallest we have. Is that okay?'

'Yes, thanks,' he said, handing over cash to pay for the products. 'If I pack this box now, could you spare me a bit of tape to fasten it, please?'

'Of course I can, love. Help yourself.'

The shop assistant handed him a heavy tape dispenser filled with a roll of clear tape and left him at the counter to assist another customer in selecting some oil paints.

James taped the bottom of the box, filled it to the brim with the polystyrene balls and sprinkled the whole tube of glitter over them. He then sealed the box. A marker pen lay on a shelf behind the counter. He reached for it and wrote Dan's address on the top.

He thanked the assistant, left the shop and carried the box to the post office on Northumberland Street, which he had visited two or three times a day to despatch fancy dress costumes when he worked for Glad Rags. After queuing for about ten minutes, he handed the box to the post office worker and paid for first-class postage to ensure the parcel arrived on the correct day.

Then he went home, wondering if he should have disguised himself in the pub, the craft shop and the post office. They would all have CCTV. Anxious about what he had done, James fretted about his handwriting being visible on the card in the pub and on the box, and worried about whether the police could lift fingerprints from cardboard. Why hadn't he paid more attention when watching crime programmes on the telly?

Just relax, he told himself, taking some deep breaths. It's not a crime to post a box of craft materials.

24

Glitter Galore

Even though it was Dan's birthday, and Chris had given him a lovely gift of silver cufflinks that morning, Dan felt down. He'd had a run of bad luck lately, with the dog shitting on the doorstep, the flat tyre, and a rat dying under the decking in the garden. *Could life get any worse?*

Bad luck was supposed to come in threes—that's what his mother used to say, anyway—so he'd had his fair share now. Hopefully, that would be it, and things would improve.

Dan spent the morning browsing the internet, and just before noon, the postman knocked at the door, disturbing him. Dan opened the door and signed for a parcel—a medium-sized cardboard box, and he wondered what it might contain.

He took the box inside and set it on the lounge table, thrilled to have received another birthday present. It could only be a surprise gift from Chris because, since his mother died, nobody else had bought him anything for his birthday.

The box was plain—no shop logo to hint at its contents, and no return address to confirm who sent it. Puzzled about what it could be, he cut through the tape and opened the flaps.

Inside, he saw millions of polystyrene balls. Thinking it must be something fragile, he gently lowered both hands into the packaging to feel for the surprise concealed inside, but there didn't appear to be anything there. *It must be something very small.*

Dan rummaged around a bit more, inadvertently pushing the polystyrene balls over the edges of the box and the tiny pieces of silver glitter along with them. Someone had gone to great lengths with the presentation, he thought. The packaging looked fantastic. Now, he just needed to find the elusive birthday gift in the box.

Finally, in desperation to retrieve it, he tipped the contents of the box onto the table and then stood back in amazement with his hands on his hips.

How annoying!

The box contained nothing except the polystyrene balls and the glitter, which were now all over the table, the chairs and the carpet. Dan was horrified. Not only did he feel deprived of a lovely surprise, but now he had the room to clean, which was a complete mess.

With his arm, he swept what was on the table into the empty box and did the same with the chair seats. Then, on his hands and knees, he cupped his hands to pick up the worst of it.

When he stood up, he was sweating profusely and wiped his brow with his sleeve. *What was going on?* The tiny white balls clung to his clothes, and he frantically tried to remove them, but they immediately stuck to him again. He couldn't get them off.

Dan took the vacuum cleaner from the under-stairs cupboard, plugged it in, and ran the nozzle over his clothes before cleaning the floor. He went around the room several times, but when he finished, he could still see specks of silver on the carpet. He vacuumed the floor again, but the glitter was still there, embedded in the deep pile.

He wondered why Chris had sent him a box with just packaging and glitter inside. Was he so stupid that he'd forgotten to enclose a gift?

Dan hadn't given dinner a thought yet—he hadn't had time—but he was ravenous after spending most of the afternoon cleaning the lounge. Chris would be home from work in about twenty minutes—that was hardly time to make cheese on toast, never mind the sort of food that Chris demanded. Dan could have murdered a plate of sausages and mashed potatoes with thick onion gravy, but Chris would turn up his nose at that.

Craving comfort food, Dan decided on fish and chips from the takeaway just a few streets away. He took his car keys off the hook by the door, went to his Mercedes and drove the short distance.

A car that was parked right in front of the fish and chip shop door pulled out and drove away, and Dan grinned when he spotted the empty parking space, thinking his luck must be changing at last. He indicated to pull in and put his foot down, but another car darted into the space. A silver Ford Fiesta.

Dan pulled up alongside it, double parking, his face red as he climbed out of the car and glared at the young woman who had stolen his space. He watched her lift a small boy from a child seat in the back, lock the car and enter the takeaway.

Dan followed her inside the shop, still glowering at her.

'What's your problem?' she asked.

'You parked in my parking space,' said Dan. 'You saw me indicating to park there, and you took it anyway. That's what my problem is.'

'It's a public road. Anyone can park there, and I got there first,' said the woman, turning away and talking to her child.

'You'll regret taking that tone with me,' said Dan under his breath.

'Did you say something?' she asked, turning around.

'No, not a word.' Dan smirked.

The woman picked up her order and left the shop, carrying her little boy in one arm and the bag of food in the other.

The smell of fish and chips made Dan's stomach growl. He was starving and couldn't wait to eat. He placed his order, watched the shop owner expertly fold sheets of white paper around the food and put the wrapped parcels in a thin plastic bag.

'Thank you,' he said, handing over a twenty-pound note. After collecting his change, he went to his car, opened one of the parcels, and stuffed a few chips in his mouth.

The woman in the Fiesta was waving her arms at him, urging him to move his car. Dan ignored her and continued eating his chips. She got out of her car, went to his driver's door and knocked on the window. He stuck two fingers up at her and then totally blanked her, continuing to eat his chips. They were so delicious.

She returned to her car, dialled a number on her phone, and gesticulated wildly as she spoke to the person on the other end.

A few minutes later, a police car pulled up behind Dan's car. A police officer got out, walked to Dan's door, and knocked on the window. Dan had been so intent on eating his food that he hadn't seen the police officer arrive and assumed it was the Fiesta lady knocking again, so he stuck up his fingers, but this time, the knocking continued.

He glanced up, saw a police uniform, and pressed the button to lower his window.

'I'm Police Constable Rob Marshall. Do you know why I'm here, sir?'

'No.'

'You're double parked, and your car is causing an obstruction.'

'I'm sorry, I didn't realise,' said Dan. 'I'll go now.'

'No, you won't. Pull the car forward, let this lady out, and then reverse into the space. We're not done here.'

Dan was fuming as he begrudgingly started his car, moved it forward, and watched the Fiesta drive away, the woman laughing at him as she left.

That stupid woman had called the police, and now he was in trouble. It was all her fault. If she hadn't pinched his parking space in the first place, he wouldn't have had to block her car in, would he?

When Dan parked by the kerb, the police officer returned to the open car window. 'Double parking is an offence, and the penalty is £70,' he said. 'If you pay within fourteen days, it will be reduced to thirty-five. What's your name and address?'

Dan provided him with the information he requested.

'Can I see your driver's licence?' asked the policeman.

Dan removed his wallet from his trouser pocket, took out his licence and handed it over.

PC Marshall studied Dan's face for a few seconds to check whether the licence belonged to him, recorded the driver's number, and returned it.

'I must remind you again that double-parking is an offence, and so is obstructing other vehicles on the road. Don't let us catch you doing it again.'

After giving Dan a stern look, the police officer returned to his car.

While driving home, Dan was fuming. Thirty-five quid was what he'd got back from that stupid fancy dress company, and now he was going to lose it all over again because of another stupid woman. When he returned home with his carrier bag of fish and chips, Chris was already there.

'I was worried when you weren't here,' said Chris. 'You're always at home when I get in from work.'

'Sorry, Chris. I got held up. I've had a rotten day.'

'Is that fish and chips I smell?'

'Yes, don't they smell delish? My stomach's been rumbling all the way back from the shop.'

'Oh, Dan! How could you?' asked Chris. 'You know I don't eat chips.'

Dan's face fell. That's all he needed. He plonked the bag on the table, took two plates out of the cupboard and shared the meal between them, not accounting for the fact he'd already eaten half a portion of chips in the car.

Chris sat down, pushed his chips onto Dan's plate with a knife, and removed the crispy batter from the cod.

'Can I have your batter if you don't want it?' asked Dan.

'Yes, you can have it if you want it,' said Chris.

Dan grabbed the pieces of fatty batter from Chris's plate.

'You need to think about eating more healthily,' said Chris. 'If you don't look after yourself, you'll have a heart attack when you're in your forties like your dad did.'

Dan looked at the greasy food on his plate and put down his fork, suddenly losing his appetite. His father had just been forty-six when he'd had a massive attack, which killed him outright. He knew he had his father's build and liked the same foods. *How can something so tasty be bad for you?*

'Why have you got glitter in your hair?' asked Chris, realising he'd upset Dan and trying to lighten the mood.

'No! I haven't, have I?'

Dan ran his hands through his hair and rushed to the mirror in the hall.

'It's all over my clothes as well. What must that policeman have thought of me?'

'What policeman?' asked Chris.

'It was nothing, really.'

'Tell me.'

Dan recounted what took place outside the fish and chip shop, and Chris shook his head in bewilderment at Dan's antics.

'So, how did you get glitter all over you?'

'It was from the parcel you sent in the post,' said Dan, sitting back at the table. 'By the way, was there supposed to be a gift inside? I couldn't find one.'

'I know nothing about a parcel,' said Chris. 'Why would I send you something in the post when I live here? Anyway, I gave you the cufflinks I bought for you this morning.'

'As a surprise, maybe? I don't know. I just assumed it was from you.'

Dan's mobile beeped, indicating he had a message. He picked up his phone and read: *I'm up for some fun. Tonite? Rick.*

Dan's eyebrows furrowed as he tried to make sense of the message.

'What is it?' asked Chris, who had finished the fried cod and was breaking some eggs into a bowl to make himself an omelette.

'I don't know. I don't know anyone called Rick.'

Chris took Dan's phone, and his face hardened. 'What's there to understand? Rick wants to meet you tonight for some fun. I thought you'd taken your profile off all the dating websites when I moved in here.'

'I did.'

'Yeah, it looks like it,' said Chris, pouring the egg mixture into a frying pan.

'I did, Chris. Honest. I don't know how this Rick guy got my number.'

Dan picked up his phone and reread the message, wondering who Rick was and how he'd got his contact details.

After Chris ate the omelette, the couple moved into the lounge.

'There's glitter all over the floor in here,' said Chris.

'Yes, I know. I've hoovered the carpet umpteen times already, and it won't budge. I'll try again tomorrow.'

If Chris hadn't sent him the parcel, Dan wondered who had. *Could it have been Rick, the guy who sent the message?* Dan had no idea who Rick was.

'I won't be a minute,' said Dan. He went through the conservatory and out the back door, retrieved the box from the recycling bin, and looked at the handwritten address. It was not Chris's writing on the box. Why hadn't he noticed that before?

He put the box back in the bin and returned to the house, wondering whose writing it was.

'What was that?' asked Chris, pointing to the bottom of the internal door.

'What was what?'

Dan sat down, picked up his wine glass, and took a sip.

'Something just ran across the floor. It went under the door and into the hall.'

'What was it?' asked Dan.

'I think it was a mouse, but it could have been a rat.'

'No! It can't be,' said Dan. 'I keep a spotless house. We can't possibly have vermin in here.'

'Believe what you want, but I know what I saw.'

'It doesn't sound like you do. You didn't know if it was a mouse or a rat.'

'Either way, it was vermin, and you should get a trap,' said Chris, and then switched on the television.

They watched Emmerdale, followed by a Harlan Coben thriller on Netflix, and didn't speak a word to each other all evening. They were both preoccupied with the message on Dan's phone and the anonymous gift he'd received, and Dan was stewing on the fact that he had mice in his house and rats in his garden.

At ten thirty, they went to bed, and as Dan plugged his phone into the charger on his bedside table, it beeped again. He picked it up and read the text message: *No strings. No limits. Call me. Dave.*

Chris leaned over and checked the screen.

'Another one! Promise me you'll take your dating profile down tomorrow, Dan, or I'll think you're not happy with me any more. Was it one of these guys who sent you that present?'

'Of course, it wasn't,' said Dan, more confidently than he felt. 'I don't know who they are, and there wasn't a present in the box anyway. It was just an empty box.'

Chris grunted before turning over and lying with his back to Dan.

Dan switched off the lamp and lay in the dark for a long time, thinking what a shit birthday it had been. He wondered who had sent him the parcel, and why he'd received two messages from potential hook-ups. He was sure he'd removed his details from the dating websites ages ago, around the time Chris moved in, but he'd check in the morning to make sure.

Chris was a catch for a guy like him, and Dan didn't want to lose him over something so trivial.

25

Planting Out

It was Monday, and signing-on day again. As James had no plans for the day, he decided he might as well go to the Jobcentre and get it over and done with. He needed more money; his bank balance was dwindling.

He left the flat and almost collided with Lisa at the corner of the street.

'James, I didn't expect to see you!' she said, stepping back.

'Really! You know I live on this street.'

'How are you doing?' she asked.

'I'm fine. Why wouldn't I be?'

'Oh, James. Don't be like that. I know how much that job meant to you.'

But do you know how much you meant to me?

James couldn't stand seeing what he thought was sympathy in her eyes. Yes, it had broken his heart to lose his job at Glad Rags, but this woman had broken his heart all over again when she walked out on him a few days later. It felt like she had ripped it out of his chest, crushed it and then stamped on it.

'I'm fine,' he muttered and walked away.

Was he fine? No, far from it, but he didn't want Lisa to know that.

James went into a newsagent's shop, bought a copy of the local newspaper, *The Chronicle*, and sat on a bench overlooking the road. He glanced through the 'Situations Vacant' pages to prepare for the forthcoming meeting and then walked to the Jobcentre.

He introduced himself at the desk, and a few minutes later, a red-haired woman with Harry Potter-style glasses and larger-than-life lips coated in orange, glossy lipstick called his name.

Where was Josh?

James felt pretty intimidated by her, but on his way over, he pictured her as a goldfish and fought hard to hide his smile. But the smile didn't last long.

She introduced herself as Niamh Wanless and explained that she was filling in for Josh while he was on holiday.

The only job search evidence James could offer her for the last fortnight was pointing at a few adverts in the newspaper, which he said he'd phoned about. *Was that even evidence?*

Niamh didn't think so. By the end of the meeting, James felt like he'd been through an inquisition and felt absolutely shite about himself—it was like he'd been found guilty of a crime without ever standing trial.

He'd lost his job. He was unemployed. On the dole. Redundant. He didn't have a job. He needed a job. So, he'd have to find one.

What was the big deal?

'Why don't you have a look at the jobs we have on offer here?' asked Niamh. 'We have a much better selection than the local papers.'

She led the way to the search area and left him to browse

through the multitude of vacancies. James began looking for a job that might suit him, but a niggling feeling in the back of his mind told him he'd forgotten something. Something important. He suddenly remembered what it was—Dan Howard had an appointment at the hairdresser's later that day, so his property would be empty. Could he miss an opportunity like that?

He left the Jobcentre and headed towards Jesmond. On the way, he saw a place selling bulk animal feed, and a pallet of wild bird food stood outside the door. This brought to mind a story he'd heard about a woman who unwittingly grew cannabis in her garden. It turned out the cannabis seed had been in a pack of mixed bird seed she'd bought to fill a bird feeder in her garden, and she was innocent of any crime.

It was September now. Seeds were sown in spring, weren't they? Would seeds grow at this time of the year, he wondered, and would all bags of birdseed contain cannabis seeds, or just the odd one? James wished he knew more about growing stuff, but he'd never had the opportunity. And he didn't have money to waste. He'd already spent quite a lot on Dan Howard, but it had been worth it. He couldn't chance buying seeds, though, because he thought the chances of them producing cannabis plants, especially at that time of year, would be slim.

Matt!

James remembered Matt had said he'd bought some cannabis seeds online. But that still didn't change the fact that it was the wrong time of year to plant them. They might not grow. Matt had planted some in the summer for his own use, for valid medical reasons. Might he have a plant he could spare?

James decided he would visit Matt and Amanda at the fancy

dress shop. Walking the familiar route to the city centre, he approached the shop. His heart beat faster, and his hands felt clammy, and he wiped them on his jeans. Why was he nervous? These people had been his best friends until a couple of months ago. They didn't fire him by choice; they didn't have the money coming in to pay him. *Would seeing them again be so difficult?*

The door hit the bell as he opened it, announcing his arrival in the shop.

Matt sat at the counter where he usually did and looked up.

'Hey, James. How are you?'

'Not bad,' said James. 'Yourself?'

James saw Matt flinch. Or had he imagined it?

'We're good, thanks.'

'James!' said Amanda, pushing the curtain to one side and entering the shop from the back room where he used to work. 'I thought I heard your voice. It's so good to see you!'

She hugged him, and it felt wonderful to be embraced by someone, even for a few seconds.

'What brings you here?' she asked.

'It's Matt I came to see, really,' said James. 'You said you'd planted some cannabis seeds. I just wondered if you had a plant you could spare.'

'I didn't know you were into weed,' said Matt, raising his eyebrows.

James didn't reply because he wasn't. As far as he was concerned, it was foul-smelling stuff, and others were welcome to it.

'I'm sure I could spare one since it's you asking—it's the least I can do—but don't let on to anyone where you got it from.'

'Your secret's safe with me.'

'It's dead in here today, Amanda. Why don't we finish early so James can come to ours and pick up a plant? What do you think?'

'Why not? I don't have any appointments booked in for this afternoon.'

They closed the shop and went to the John Dobson car park, taking the lift to the tenth floor, where Amanda had parked her car. James wasn't surprised she drove a flash car. The red Range Rover Sport was a practical vehicle with ample space in the back for Matt's wheelchair, but it also matched her personality.

'Nice car,' said James, as they climbed inside.

'Yes, I love it,' said Amanda, starting the engine. 'Unfortunately, it's going back to the garage next week.'

'Is there something wrong with it?'

'We can't afford the payments on it,' said Matt, looking straight ahead in the passenger seat.

James felt sorry for them and wondered how Matt would cope if they had to rely on public transport. It wouldn't be easy for him to use the metro or buses with a wheelchair, especially when travelling alone.

When they pulled up outside the terraced house in South Gosforth, Amanda helped Matt into the wheelchair she'd taken from the boot and opened the front door.

'Come in,' said Matt. 'Would you like a coffee?'

'No, thanks. I'm fine.'

Amanda went up the stairs, which had a stairlift for Matt, and returned a few seconds later, carrying a potted plant about thirty centimetres tall, which she handed to James.

'Wow!' said James. 'I wasn't expecting it to be that big. It doesn't seem long since you got the seeds.'

'They grow fast,' said Matt. 'Or maybe I have green fingers!'

James thanked him for the plant and took his wallet from his pocket.

'Can I give you something for it?'

'No!' Matt and Amanda replied in unison.

'Thanks again. I'd better be off then.'

'You can't walk back to Heaton carrying that in broad daylight,' said Amanda. 'I'll drive you home.'

'Good idea,' said Matt. 'Hope to see you again soon, mate.'

Before leaving the house, James took off his hoodie and wrapped it around the plant. He didn't want to get caught with it. Amanda unlocked the car, and James climbed into the passenger seat.

'What's your address?' asked Amanda, poised to key the postcode into the Sat Nav.

'If you could drop me off in Jesmond, that would be great.'

'Okay. That's closer than Heaton, and I know the way there,' said Amanda. 'Me and Matt go to Jesmond Dene sometimes. It's lovely there. I like the pets' corner, and he likes the tracks through the trees. It feels like you're out in the countryside when you're at Jesmond Dene.'

Amanda parked the car on a side street near the main road, just a few streets away from Somerset Road.

'Is here OK for you?'

'Yes, thanks for the ride.'

James got out of the car and stood on the pavement until the car pulled away. Amanda waved, and only when she was out of sight did James move towards Somerset Road, the plant still hidden by his hoodie.

James looked at his phone. It was almost three thirty. Dan should be at the hairdresser's in the city centre now. His car was not parked on the street, so James presumed he must have gone there as planned. Pulling down his baseball cap, he walked to the back of the house.

All was quiet on the back street. James looked around to see if anyone was watching, and confident that nobody could see him, he lifted the plant over the low wall into Dan's garden.

He looked for a gap among the taller plants that edged the garden and found a space large enough for the cannabis plant to grow. But he didn't have any tools with which to dig a hole. Why hadn't he thought of that? He tried to move the soil with his hands, but it was rock hard. Using his penknife, he pushed it into the soil to loosen it, and then used his hands to push it aside. When the hole was about fifteen centimetres deep, he removed the plant from the pot and placed it in the hole. Then he covered the roots with the soil he'd removed, pushing it down until it was flush with the rest of the garden. When he'd finished, it looked like the plant had been growing there for months.

As he admired his handiwork, he felt as though he was being watched, and a shiver ran down his spine. If somebody caught him in Dan's garden, how could he explain being there?

Cautiously, he looked around. A man stood at the kitchen window of the house next door. With his cap low, James waved to avert suspicion, and the man waved back.

James moved across to the decking area, out of sight from next door, and a short while later, he checked to see if the man had gone. The kitchen window was clear. He climbed over the wall into the back street, put the empty plant pot in a wheelie bin halfway down the back street, and walked away. He was tempted to run, as his heart was pounding, but he didn't want to draw attention to himself.

He went home to Heaton, and as he turned onto his road, he heard laughter and saw a couple of boys larking about. When he got closer, he saw them chasing the black and white kitten that had befriended him.

James ran over and shouted, 'Leave that cat alone!'

'What's it to you, mister?'

'It's mine!'

James picked up the frightened kitten and gave the boys a hard stare.

'Sorry, mate, we thought it was a stray.'

'That's no way to treat any animal,' said James. 'It doesn't matter if it's a stray or not. Don't let me catch you doing anything like that again. Do you hear me?'

The boys, glancing back at James several times, wandered off, muttering to themselves.

James carried the kitten to his flat.

'It looks like you've found yourself a new home. If you're going to stay with me, you're going to need a name. What should we call you?'

Looking at its prominent white whiskers against its black face, he said, 'Whiskers! That's perfect!'

26

The Electric Company

Dan had a lazy morning surfing the net, and after lunch, he went to Saks in the city centre. He wanted to look great for his upcoming holiday, and the stylists there were fab.

When he returned from the hairdresser's, he parked his car outside the house and saw his next-door neighbour pruning the roses in his front garden. Dan wondered if he should drive away again and go somewhere else for a while until Mr Backworth finished because his neighbour always stopped him and talked for ages.

He had already shopped at Asda; he'd called there after getting his hair cut, and the groceries were in the back of the car. He needed to get the fresh stuff into the fridge and make a start on dinner—one couldn't rush *coq au vin*.

Climbing out of the car, he retrieved his shopping bags from the boot and walked to his front door, hoping his neighbour wouldn't notice him, but he did.

'Good afternoon, Mr Howard,' said Mr Backworth, waving a green-gloved hand. 'It's a nice day for the time of year, isn't it?'

Dan looked up at the blue, cloudless sky and nodded.

'It was seeing your gardener earlier that spurred me on to prune my roses. They flower much better after being cut back, I find.'

Again, Dan nodded, thinking this neighbour must have lost his mind. *His gardener?* He'd never employed a gardener in his life. Dan didn't reply, though. He didn't want to add to the conversation in case he extended it. He wasn't keen on his neighbour, but he didn't want to offend him either.

'I see you've been shopping,' said Mr Backworth. 'What have you got for your tea tonight?'

How could he ignore that one?

'Just some chicken. I'd better get it in the oven.'

'Righto. Nice to see you.'

His neighbour resumed his attack on the thorny stems.

Dan nodded and went indoors with an enormous sigh of relief. That was the shortest conversation he'd ever had with Mr Backworth, and he silently congratulated himself.

He thought it strange that Chris had seen a mouse in the house and Mr Backworth had seen a gardener in his garden. *Were they hallucinating? What were they on?* Mr Backworth was quite old, he supposed. Maybe he had dementia?

Thank God there had been no more sightings of the mouse or rat that Chris had seen the other evening. The thought of dirty animals contaminating his home made him want to scrub everything, including himself.

Dan washed his hands at the kitchen sink and prepared the evening meal. While he was chopping an onion, the doorbell rang, and he opened it wearing an apron and wielding a paring knife.

A man wearing overalls and a cap stood on the doorstep and

said, 'Meter reader.' He looked up from his clipboard, his eyes widening when he saw the knife in Dan's hand.

'The meter has already been read. One of your lot was here last week or the week before.'

He was about to close the door when he heard the man say, 'It'll only take a minute, Mr Howard.'

'Alright, check the meter if you have to, but I am busy. This is a major inconvenience, and I'll be informing your head office about it!'

Sheepishly, the meter reader went to the under-stairs cupboard, noted the reading, and returned to the door.

'Don't forget to shut the door!' Dan shouted from the kitchen, thinking how incompetent the company was for sending two different meter readers to his house in two consecutive weeks. No wonder his electricity bills were so high!

When Chris returned home about an hour later, he looked tired. Before he went for a shower, he asked, 'Did you remember to remove your profile from the dating website?'

Earlier that day, Dan had trawled through all the dating sites he'd ever used, and none of his profiles were on any of them. He didn't understand how Rick and Dave had found his number, but he didn't dare tell Chris that.

'Of course I did.'

Dan turned away to set the table and missed the suspicious look in Chris's eyes.

After eating the coq au vin, they sat down to watch EastEnders with a glass of Chardonnay, and before long, Chris was snoring in his armchair.

When the soap finished, Dan channel-hopped for a while but couldn't find anything to watch, so he selected Netflix, chose a romantic film he loved and sat back to enjoy it.

Towards the climax of the movie, the part he'd been waiting for, his phone beeped.

Chris opened his eyes.

Dan checked the message on his phone, which read: *If you're still up for some fun, I'm free all weekend. Call me. Mark R.*

'Who's the text from?' Chris got up from his chair and took the phone from Dan's hand. 'Another one! I don't believe this. You said you'd taken your profile down, but you mustn't have. You lied to me, Dan. How can I believe a word you say?'

Chris stormed out of the room.

Dan heard him run upstairs and lock the bathroom door, which was something he never did. He must be upset, thought Dan. He looked at the message again, wondering if he should call Mark R and ask him where he'd found his phone number. Thinking better of it, he rewound the film on Netflix and watched the ending with a wistful smile and tears in his eyes.

When it finished, he switched off the television and opened his laptop. He hadn't written to the electricity company yet, and he needed to do that while the incident was still fresh in his mind.

Dear Sirs, Your company is incompetent. This week, you have sent two different meter readers to my house. It's inconvenient enough having one of them call, but sending two is just ridiculous. It's no wonder I've seen an increase in my bills when you're paying two people to do the same job. Your training program is completely inadequate. One of the meter readers left my door wide open. Anyone could have walked in off the street and robbed my house. I trust that you will see fit to reduce my next bill due to the inconvenience caused and for the potential crime that could have been committed while my house was left unsecured. Yours faithfully, Dan J. Howard.

When Dan went to bed later that night, he was glad that Chris was sound asleep. He lay in bed thinking about what he should pack for his holiday. His flight was just after lunch, and by this time tomorrow, he would be in Tenerife at an all-inclusive, four-star hotel right by the beach. He loved escaping to hot and sunny tropical islands.

Everything that could go wrong had gone wrong recently, and he couldn't wait to get away for a week and relax.

Dan was disappointed that Chris couldn't go with him, but he was sure he'd have a wonderful time in Tenerife on his own. Glorious sunshine, delicious food and cocktails served by handsome Spanish waiters, and no Chris to complain about everything he did. *It would be heaven!*

27

Empty Cupboards

The postman delivered a handful of letters addressed to James, and he took them upstairs to open. The first was a reply to a job application, which he read.

Dear Mr Webster, Thank you for your interest in working at the Freeman Hospital. Unfortunately, your application has not been successful on this occasion. Yours faithfully, Mrs K Knight.

He dropped the letter in the bin and fished it back out again when he realised he might need to take it to the Jobcentre as evidence of his job search.

The second letter was from his landlord, reminding him that his rent was overdue. That went in the bin and stayed there.

The third was a bank statement, and he saw that his bank balance was rapidly decreasing; he fancied a drink. He opened the fridge, but it was empty. *Bugger!* He poured a glass of water, sat on the sofa, and switched on the telly. Whiskers jumped onto his knee and lay down beside him.

Game shows and antique auctions were on all the channels, or so it seemed. He missed having Sky Sports. On Freeview, he found a wildlife documentary he'd already seen and sat back to watch it again, but his mind was on the letters he'd received.

If he didn't find a job soon, he would be unable to pay his bills, and he dreaded to think about what would happen then. He should look for a job more seriously, and he decided to visit the Jobcentre again.

Half an hour later, he walked into the building that he had come to despise. There was nothing wrong with the building itself, but the demoralising atmosphere inside was depressing.

'It's good to see you here when it's not your signing-on day,' said Josh. 'Can I help you at all?'

'I hope so, mate. I need to find a job.'

'That's what we specialise in.'

After an extensive search, James left with a couple of printouts, one for a job as a fishmonger's assistant at a supermarket and the other for a school crossing patrol officer, or lollipop man, as he thought of it, but that was only part-time, and the income would not be sufficient for his needs.

Realising he was hungry, he went to the kitchen and searched the cupboards for anything edible. They were almost empty. He had a packet of Walkers Worcester Sauce crisps, which he hadn't eaten before because he wasn't keen on the flavour, and six soft Rich Tea biscuits from a packet he'd opened weeks ago. He soaked one of them in milk and gave it to Whiskers.

'I'm sorry I don't have any fish or meat for you today, but I'll get some soon. I promise.'

James stroked Whiskers, and she purred loudly. Thinking about his financial situation, he needed to go shopping but didn't want to spend any money. The rent was due at the end of the week, and the pile of bills to pay was growing daily. He needed to find a job—and fast.

His anxiety levels were rising, so he went for a walk in the park to calm himself.

28

Little Pests

Dan had just returned home after a wonderful holiday in the Canary Islands, if he overlooked the cockroaches on his terrace, the over-priced food and drinks on the plane, and his bathroom scales that morning. He had gained seven pounds in weight, one for each day he was away. It was disappointing that the hotel didn't hold a special event to celebrate the eightieth anniversary of Batman, which he thought they should have. Still, overall, he felt pleasantly happy and relaxed while he ate his breakfast.

Chris, who had been disturbed by Dan returning from the airport in the middle of the night, had overslept. He rushed around getting ready for work.

'Do you know where my badminton racket is?'

'I think it's under the stairs. I'll have a look for you.'

Dan opened the cupboard door. Seeing the clutter inside, he thought he should sort out the mess. He pulled out the vacuum cleaner, lifted out two pairs of walking boots, a pair of Chris's football boots, and the bag for life that he used to store plastic carrier bags, just in case he ever needed one, although some looked as though they had biodegraded into tiny pieces. Then, the peg bag he used on the few occasions each year that he dried clothes on the washing line in the garden, half a tin of kitchen paint and an old coat that he hadn't worn for years.

He stood up and sighed when he saw the massive pile in the hall. He wasn't even halfway into the cupboard yet. *How had all that stuff come out of such a small space?*

Returning to the closet, he saw the handle of a racket near the back. He reached over, grabbed it, and pulled it out. *Hurray!* Chris's badminton racket. Dan held it up proudly.

'I've found it!'

'Thank you!'

Chris ran downstairs, walked past the pile of junk, took the racket from Dan, and headed to the door.

'Sorry, I'm running late, but I'm glad you're back. And that tan suits you!'

Dan smiled goofily at the compliment until a tiny mouse ran over his foot, and he screamed.

Chris stopped in the doorway and turned towards Dan.

'What's wrong?'

'A mouse!' Dan shrieked, pointing to the baby mouse running alongside the skirting board.

'Oh no! That's a young one, so there are probably loads of them,' said Chris. 'I really have to go. Call the pest control officer at the council and get someone to come out. If only you'd bought a mousetrap when I saw the first one, we wouldn't be in this mess. There could be hundreds of them by now.' He looked at his smartwatch. 'God! I'm so late. I'll have to sprint. See you later!'

Chris rushed out, leaving Dan alone in the house with the mice. He could hear scratching noises coming from inside the cupboard, and the little mouse in the hall was running back towards his feet.

Dan ran into the kitchen and sat on the tabletop with his feet on a chair. He picked up his phone, found the number for the city council's pest control department and waited in the queue to be connected to a human.

When a woman answered, Dan explained the situation and asked, 'When can you send somebody out?'

'Thursday morning is the first appointment. Would that be convenient for you?'

'Thursday morning!' screeched Dan. 'But that's three days away. What am I supposed to do in the meantime? They're all over the place.'

'A family of mice can't do too much harm in that time frame,' she said calmly. 'What you can do to help is clean the place up and make sure there's no food lying around.'

'I can assure you that my house is spotless. There's never any food lying around.'

'Okay, if you say so.' The woman sounded sceptical. 'One of our team will see you on Thursday morning.'

The line went dead.

Dan didn't know what to do. He hated vermin. He'd been terrified of them since he read James Herbert's book, The Rats, as a teenager. Closing the cupboard door would make him feel safer, but that meant getting down from the table and going near them. That might not help, because the mouse Chris saw went underneath the door. *What if one of them touched him again?* He looked at his foot in disgust, wishing he dared to leave the table so he could wash his shoes and take another shower.

Instead, Dan sat on the tabletop all day, playing on his phone, and was relieved when Chris eventually returned from work because, by then, his phone battery was dangerously low, and he desperately needed to pee.

'Why are you sitting on the table?' asked Chris, putting the badminton racket in the cupboard and closing the door. 'And why is all this junk still in the hall?'

Dan mumbled a reply, so Chris couldn't hear what he said, too embarrassed to admit he was afraid of mice and had been sitting there all day.

'Did you contact the pest control people?' asked Chris.

'Yes, they're coming on Thursday morning.'

'Good. Now come down off the table.'

With Chris at home and the cupboard door closed, Dan thought it should be safe. He stepped down, hurriedly plugged his phone into the charger on the kitchen worktop and ran to the bathroom. When he returned to the kitchen, he realised he was thirsty. He hadn't had a drink since breakfast, so he filled a pint glass with water and drank it all.

'It's good to see you drinking water,' said Chris. 'It's so much better for your body than the coffee and soft drinks you usually have. What's for dinner tonight?'

'I thought we could go out for something,' said Dan, who had bought nothing for dinner because he'd been unable to leave the house because of the mice. 'But I could get something out of the freezer.'

'It would be nice to go out for dinner for a change,' said Chris, smiling at him. 'I missed you when you were away.'

Their taxi arrived about an hour later. As they stepped out of the house, Dan's phone beeped, and sheepishly, he hid it in his pocket. He was still receiving messages from random, unknown men who wanted to hook up, and he didn't want

Chris to know.

They went to a Japanese restaurant in town. While browsing the menu, the waitress brought a complimentary sake shot to each of the men, which they drank. Dan ordered more sake to have with his meal, while Chris drank sparkling water.

The sake was stronger than Dan expected, and he felt tipsy when they left the restaurant. He suggested going to a club, but Chris talked him out of it because he had work the following morning, so they got a taxi home instead.

After Chris went to bed that evening, Dan checked the message he'd received earlier. He had been right. It was from another man—a guy called Jon, who wanted to do all sorts of things to him.

Feeling brave and a little intoxicated, Dan dialled Jon's number, and he answered on the second ring.

'Hi! I hoped I'd hear from you tonight. I'm only in town until tomorrow.'

'Hi Jon,' said Dan. 'Sorry! I'm not calling for the reason you think. I'm in a serious relationship at the moment and I'm not looking for anything else right now.'

'That's a shame, Dan. We could have had so much fun together.'

The line went dead. Jon had hung up on him. Dan sat there, open-mouthed—he hadn't had time to ask Jon the question he desperately wanted to know the answer to. *Where did you get my number?*

Dan wondered about calling Jon back, but after turning down his offer of unspeakable deeds, Dan didn't want to disturb him again. But he still needed to find out where these men were getting his details from, so he scrolled down to the message from Mark R and dialled his number.

'Hi Mark, it's Dan here. You messaged me a while back.'

'Oh! You must be the guy in Jesmond. When I didn't hear from you, I thought you weren't interested. I'm sorry, but my circumstances have changed since then. I'm seeing somebody now, and he's a great guy!'

'That's fine, Mark. I'm in a relationship as well,' said Dan. 'I just wondered if you'd mind telling me who gave you my number.'

'Nobody gave it to me,' said Mark. 'I found it in a little pub on Campbell Street near the city centre. It was written on a card by the payphone. Didn't you put it there?'

'No, I didn't,' said Dan. 'I think somebody's messing with me.'

'I'm sorry to hear that, Dan,' said Mark. 'I'm out of town this week, or I'd take the card down myself. I live just around the corner from there.'

'It's okay. I'll go tomorrow. Thanks for your help, Mark, and take care.'

'You too, Dan.'

Dan put down his phone, thinking that Mark sounded like a nice guy. He was glad he'd made the call. Now that he knew the source of his mobile number, he could put a stop to the booty calls once and for all, and he wouldn't have to hide his phone from Chris any more.

But who had put the card in the pub?

29

Impersonating a Neighbour

James's hand shook as he opened his bank statement, and immediately his eyes were drawn to the balance at the bottom of the sheet. He groaned as he looked through the list of transactions. After he'd bought some groceries from Lidl, he'd had a few quid left in his account. Then, it appeared that the bank had stopped a standing order payment to his landlord because he had insufficient funds in the account to cover the rent and charged him £20 for bouncing the payment, which made his account overdrawn.

There was no money in the bank, and his rent was unpaid. He shook his head. Checking his wallet, he found a five-pound note and counted the loose change on the kitchen top, which amounted to just over £3. He had eight quid in cash and an overdraft of £14. When was his dole money due to be paid?

Signing-on day had come around again, and the gap between visits seemed to be getting shorter each time.

James couldn't face the Jobcentre just yet. He took a deep breath to calm himself and went for a brisk walk to clear his head. He put on his hoodie and cap and headed outside. It was a cool, overcast day, but at least it was dry. He walked to the city centre and wandered through the streets until he found a public telephone and dialled 101, the number for non-urgent police enquiries.

A male operator answered the call immediately and asked how he could help.

'I think my neighbour is growing cannabis in his garden. That's illegal, isn't it?' said James.

'Yes, sir. It is illegal to grow cannabis. May I take your name, please?'

'Mr John Backworth,' said James.

'What's the address of the property where you suspect cannabis is being grown?'

'The address is Sixty-Six Somerset Road in Jesmond. I live at number sixty-four next door.'

'Thank you, Mr Backworth. We'll send an officer to the address to investigate this further.'

James thanked him and hung up the phone.

He was hungry, so he went to Greggs for something to eat. As he joined the queue, he couldn't believe his eyes—standing in front of him was Amanda Armstrong.

'Amanda!' he said. 'How are you?'

'James!' said Amanda, turning around to face him. 'I'm fine, thanks. How are you?'

James could see that Amanda was not fine. She was thinner than when he'd last seen her, and she had dark circles under her eyes. Her sparkle had gone; she was not the bubbly Amanda he had known.

'I'm alright,' he replied, knowing it was a lie.

'Have you found a job yet?'

'No, I'm still looking.'

'If I hear of anything, I'll let you know.'

'Thanks. How's it going at Glad Rags?' he asked. 'Have things picked up yet?'

'Oh, James. It's been awful,' said Amanda. 'The orders have practically stopped. I don't know what we're going to do.'

Tears in her eyes threatened to spill.

'I'm sorry. You didn't deserve any of this.'

'Thank you.'

Amanda hugged him and then turned to the counter to pay for her order.

'See you soon,' she said as she left the shop. 'Take care of yourself and stay in touch!'

James bought a tuna baguette and a bottle of Coca-Cola. Outside, he found an empty bench and ate his lunch, watching the pigeons gathering around him, waiting for scraps.

After finishing his meal, he put his rubbish in a bin and headed for Jesmond. He didn't know how long it would be before the police arrived at Dan Howard's place, but he hoped to be there in time.

As he approached Dan's house, he saw a police car parked out front. With his hood up, he wandered to the back street, his phone in his hand, pretending to text as he walked past Dan's garden.

30

Park and Smash

That same day, after breakfast, Dan checked his emails, and his eyes lit up when he saw a reply from the electricity company. It had been ages since he'd written to them, and with his holiday and everything, he'd forgotten all about the complaint he had made. He opened the message.

Dear Mr Howard, We have investigated your complaint, and we can assure you that only one meter reader was sent to your property by our company to read your electricity meter. We don't know who the other person you allege came to your house to read the meter is, but they were not a member of our team. Our staff training emphasises the importance of property security, and our staff are instructed to never leave an external door ajar when exiting a property. I hope this concludes this matter satisfactorily. Yours sincerely, Peter Spurgeon, Regional Manager.

Dan slammed his fist down on the table. Peter Spurgeon was lying through his rotten teeth. Two people had definitely been to his house to read the meter. He was damned sure of that.

He wouldn't leave the matter there. He would have to go higher than the regional manager and wondered if perhaps he should try the CEO and copy Ofgem or his MP into the following reply. That might do the trick.

Dan wrote a long-winded reply detailing precisely when the two men had visited the house and copied in Ofgem. Surely, he must be entitled to a discount on his electricity bill for the inconvenience of being disturbed twice, and then being fobbed off by the regional manager.

After eating a light lunch, because he had taken to heart what Chris had said about his weight, Dan drove to Campbell Street, a side road near the city centre, and crawled along the kerb. There was only one pub he could see, so he parked opposite it, on double yellow lines, and went inside.

Dan's skin crawled as he looked around the dismal room. Repulsed by the filth and grime, he was loath to go further, but he needed to remove the card advertising his number. He saw the alcove at the back and made a beeline for it, grimacing with every step as his shoes stuck to the disgusting, patterned carpet.

Shocked by the number of cards pinned to the wall beside the payphone, Dan was surprised that any of the guys had found the one bearing his number. When he spotted it several minutes later, he pulled out the drawing pin, removed the card, and pushed the pin back into the wall. Then, he tore the card in half, put the pieces in his pocket and smiled.

Success!

Now, no more strangers could text him, and hopefully, that would be the end of Chris's jealous behaviour.

But who could have put the card there? Taking the pieces of card from his pocket, he examined the handwriting. It might be the same writing as that on the box he received in the post, but he couldn't be sure. He wished he'd kept the box so he could compare them. He wondered if a disgruntled ex could be messing with him. *Who else would do something like that?*

As he left the pub, a lorry was travelling past the pub at a snail's pace, so he stood in the doorway and waited. As he grew increasingly frustrated, he heard a noise that sounded like breaking glass and wondered what it could be.

When the lorry finally passed, it sped up. Dan saw his car, which was parked on the opposite side of the road, and stared open-mouthed at the driver's side wing mirror, dangling from colourful wires. A pile of mirrored glass lay on the tarmac beneath. He ran down the road after the lorry, shouting obscenities, his hands fisted in the air, but it turned a corner and disappeared from view.

He never considered the fact that his car had obstructed the heavy goods vehicle, which was why he'd had to wait to cross the road and why his car had been hit.

Dan returned to the car and saw a parking ticket on the windscreen. He looked up and down the road, but couldn't see a traffic warden. Yes, he had knowingly parked on double yellow lines because he only intended to be in the pub for a few minutes at most. How had he been given a parking ticket in such a short time?

He removed the notice from under the wiper, threw it onto the passenger seat and drove home, with the wing mirror banging against the paintwork with every bump in the road.

When he turned onto Somerset Road, he saw a police car parked outside his house. His first thought was that something had happened to Chris. Pulling up in front of the patrol car, he rushed over to the open window and asked, 'What's wrong?'

Dan recognised the policeman inside the car as Police Constable Rob Marshall and sighed. 'You nearly gave me a heart attack. I thought something awful had happened to my partner. I hope this isn't about the fish shop again.'

'Mr Daniel John Howard?' asked the policeman.

'Yes, you know who I am,' said Dan.

'May I look in your garden?'

'My garden?' asked Dan, his brow furrowed. 'Why do you want to see my garden?'

'Just lead the way, Mr Howard.'

Dan unlocked the front door and led the constable through the house and conservatory into the back garden. He looked around, thinking the lawn needed cutting and treating for weeds and moss, and the flower beds could also do with weeding.

Maybe I should employ a gardener.

The policeman glanced around the garden, went directly to the shrubs at the edge and spoke into his radio.

Dan heard him say the word SOCO. He knew what that meant. His garden was the scene of a crime. At any time, a group of people clothed in white suits and facemasks could descend on his garden. But he'd only been gone for an hour.

What could possibly have happened in just an hour?

The police constable faced Dan and said, 'Daniel John Howard. I'm arresting you on suspicion of growing cannabis on this property.'

'What? No!'

'Please let me finish.' The constable read him his rights. 'You need to come with me now.'

'Are you going to handcuff me and embarrass me in front of my neighbours?' asked Dan.

'I will if I have to,' said the constable, with a severe look. 'Are you going to come with me quietly or not?'

Dan followed him back through the house, locking the doors behind them. The policeman opened the back door of the police car, and Dan climbed into the back seat.

'Your wing mirror is damaged,' said the policeman. 'I could give you a fixed penalty for driving it when it's hanging off like that, but you're in enough bother already. Get it fixed before you drive that car again. It's not roadworthy like that. Do you understand?'

Dan nodded, thinking, could this day get any worse?

He was driven to the police station and walked into the building with the policeman. He had never been arrested before and didn't know what to expect, but he was glad the policeman hadn't handcuffed him. How embarrassing that would have been?

Police Constable Marshall talked to a stout man at a desk. The custody officer then took charge and explained to Dan what would happen. Dan's hands shook as he emptied his pockets, removed his belt and shoelaces, and put the items in a plastic tray. The policeman put the two pieces of card Dan had removed from his pocket together, raised his eyebrows, and looked at him disapprovingly.

The policeman accompanied Dan to a cell and locked the door behind him.

Never in his life had he felt so humiliated. He knew nothing about any cannabis growing in his garden. He wasn't even sure what cannabis plants looked like. Were they the leaves he'd seen in images of Bob Marley? They could have been growing in his garden for years, and he wouldn't have known.

Could Chris have planted them?

Dan didn't think so. He'd never seen Chris use drugs. He was so careful with everything he ate and drank, so he didn't think he'd poison his body with drugs. As far as Dan was aware, Chris's only sin was a glass of wine in the evening.

But if not Chris, then who?

His mother had been the gardener in the family, and she had been in a lot of pain towards the end of her life when the cancer had spread through her body, but he couldn't remember her smoking weed, and he was sure he would have if she had.

Maybe the police officer had been mistaken, and it wasn't cannabis. He hoped this was all a big misunderstanding because growing cannabis was a serious offence. Would he go to prison?

No! He couldn't go to prison. He'd seen lots of prisons in films and television shows and knew that he'd hate to be incarcerated in one; it would be worse than working for a living. He liked the comfortable life he had.

Another police officer opened the door.

'Hello, Mr Howard,' she said. 'May I call you Daniel?'

'I prefer Dan, if you don't mind.'

'Okay, Dan,' she said. 'I'm Sergeant Ali Hanlon. Come with me.'

Dan followed her along a passage and into a small room. Looking around it, he saw a board against the wall with height marks and a long table.

'Steve will be along any second to take your photo,' said Sergeant Hanlon. 'Please stand with your back against the wall.'

Dan moved to where she pointed, and the top of his head almost reached the five-foot-nine line.

A balding man entered the room, carrying a camera. He took photos of Dan from various angles, looking straight ahead, then to the left and right.

'Now, he'll take your fingerprints,' said Sergeant Hanlon, as though it were an everyday occurrence. He supposed it was for her, but not for him.

'Put your hand flat on the glass,' said Steve, demonstrating how to use the Livescan laser. 'It'll take a copy of your fingerprints, which we'll load into the national database. We'll soon see if you've been in trouble anywhere else.'

He laughed loudly, which Dan thought was highly inappropriate, considering the seriousness of his predicament. He followed the instructions and saw the finger and thumb prints appear on a large screen. Then Steve sat down in front of a computer to enter some data.

'We need to take a DNA sample now,' said the sergeant, holding what looked like a large cotton bud. 'Open your mouth wide.'

Dan opened his mouth, and he felt the swab rub against the inside of his cheek. She put the swab into a container and sealed it.

'And finally, we need to swab your hands and arms.'

'Why?'

'To check for any drug residue.'

Dan shook his head despondently and held out his arms for her to test with another swab.

'We're done in here,' she said. 'I'm going to take you to the interview room now and ask you a few questions. Come this way.'

Dan followed her along a corridor, and they entered a sparse room with grey-painted walls. They sat on hard chairs on opposite sides of a cheap melamine table. A young man wearing a uniform, who didn't look old enough to be a policeman, followed them into the room and sat beside

Sergeant Hanlon at the table.

Sergeant Hanlon explained that she would record the conversation and reminded Dan that anything he said could be used as evidence against him if he were to be charged with an offence and his case went to trial.

Dan knew he was in serious trouble. He'd seen these interviews played out on television many times. The police officers were usually mean and kept hammering the prisoner with questions until they broke down and confessed. Sometimes, they were overly sympathetic, and the prisoner would feel safe enough to tell them everything, believing that the interviewer genuinely cared about them. Then, sometimes, they would use the good cop and bad cop routine to confuse the prisoner into confessing to his crime.

His mind was working overtime, and he knew he needed to calm down. He took a deep breath and exhaled slowly, as Chris had taught him to do when he was anxious or stressed.

'We received a tip-off that you are growing cannabis in your garden, and when PC Marshall went to your garden this afternoon, he saw a cannabis plant growing in your garden,' she said, pointing to a photograph of his shrubbery. 'Since then, a specially trained officer has been to your property to confirm that the plant growing in your garden is a cannabis plant. He has photographed it for evidence, removed it, and it will be disposed of safely. Now what have you got to say for yourself?'

'I don't know anything about it,' said Dan, shaking his head. 'I don't know how it got there.'

'Does anyone else live in your house with you?'

'Yes, my partner, Chris Smith,' said Dan. 'But he's super fit and careful about what he eats and drinks. I'm sure he wouldn't use drugs.'

'Do you use drugs?'

Dan's cheeks flushed.

'I'm waiting for an answer,' she said.

'I did when I was a teenager, but I haven't for years.'

'Where did you buy the seed?'

'What seed?' he asked blankly.

'The seed you used to grow the cannabis plant.'

'I've never bought seeds in my life,' he said. 'I have what my mother called an easy-care garden. There are mature shrubs in the borders and perennial flowers in the flower beds—the ones that grow back every year. My mother planted them for me before she died. She was so thoughtful. She didn't want me to have too much gardening to do after she passed. All I need to do is cut the grass in the summer and some weeding. So, I've never needed to buy any seeds.'

'Wait here, Dan. I'll be back soon. PC Williams, we'll take a quick break. Stand outside the door, please.'

Sergeant Hanlon and the constable left the room, locking the door behind them, leaving Dan alone with his downward-spiralling thoughts.

31

Another Chance

James had enjoyed watching the policeman searching for the cannabis plant in Dan's garden. It hadn't taken him long to find it. The look on Dan's face had been brilliant!

Neither noticed him walking past, then turning around further up the road, and passing the property again, when he heard the policeman reading Dan his rights. He then walked around to the bus stop near the front of the house and stood there, pretending to wait for a bus. He watched the policeman take Dan away in the patrol car. His plan worked. The police had arrested Dan for growing cannabis. *Another successful mission!*

James was chuffed with his achievement as he walked home, but the satisfaction soon evaporated when he entered his empty flat.

He had never been so lonely in his life. There wasn't any beer left in the fridge, so he couldn't even drown his sorrows. He switched on the telly and watched a game show with Whiskers lying on his lap, purring happily. Thank God for the cat. At least he had some company.

He still needed to go to the Jobcentre, but he couldn't face that yet.

James sat in front of the telly for over an hour, thinking about how he used to enjoy watching football and films with Lisa. He missed her so much. Everything had been more fun when Lisa was around. He lowered Whiskers to the floor, leapt up from his seat, and went round to Lisa's flat. He knocked at the door, stepped back, and waited. Standing by the doorstep, he tapped his foot, thinking she should be back from work by now.

Eventually, Lisa came to the door wearing a dressing gown and with a towel wrapped around her head.

'James! What are you doing here?'

'Can I come in?'

'I'm going out soon, but I suppose so.'

She opened the door for him to enter, and he followed her into the downstairs flat, where he'd spent some fantastic nights. Memories of their time together flooded his mind, and he swallowed hard.

'What is it?' she asked, looking concerned. 'Has something happened?'

He shuffled on the spot, trying to find the right words, wondering why he hadn't thought to rehearse what he wanted to say before marching over to her place to confront her.

'I was wondering—well, it's just that I miss you a lot, Lisa. Is there any chance that we could try again?'

Now it was Lisa's turn to be stuck for words.

'Aww, James,' she said after a brief pause. 'I thought a lot about you, I really did, and I waited so long for you to make a commitment. But you didn't. As you know, I'm seeing someone else now, and he's serious about me. He's already asked me to live with him, and I'm moving into his place in Gosforth at the end of the month. I'm so sorry, James. I hope things work out for you. I really do.'

James was so choked up that he couldn't speak. So, that was that. There was no hope of reconciliation between them. He had lost her for good. Tears threatened to fall, and his throat felt constricted. He didn't know if any words would come out, so he nodded in her direction, letting her know he understood, before making his escape.

It was definitely over between them. Lisa wasn't just having a fling to make him jealous and spur him into making a commitment. Her new relationship was serious. She was moving to another part of the city, a posh area as well. Her new bloke must have money, like Dan Howard, he thought bitterly, remembering the shopping bags he'd seen Lisa carry from his car.

By the time James returned home, he was fixated on Dan Howard. What else did he have to take his mind off his fucked up, useless life?

James picked up his laptop, searched for Google Play, and entered the website using Dan's username and password. Let's have some fun, he thought, searching through the apps. He bought an auto-expand app using the saved card details on the account and downloaded it to Dan's phone. He then logged onto the app, which was designed to auto-expand text. It could be set to expand any word to make a phrase. The examples given were that 'Merry' could be expanded to 'Merry Christmas,' and 'Kind' could be expanded to 'Kind regards, John Smith'.

Wondering which words Dan would use regularly while texting, James decided to auto-expand the words 'hi,' 'thanks,' and 'Dan.'

Playing on the app and setting it up had provided a great distraction, and his requirement to sign on at the Jobcentre that day had been forgotten.

32

In Trouble

Sergeant Ali Hanlon found her colleague, Police Constable Rob Marshall, eating a late lunch in the police canteen. She walked over to his table.

'Can I have a chat with you about the bloke you just brought in, Rob?' she asked.

'Aye, grab a cuppa and take a seat.'

She returned a few minutes later with a latte and a large chocolate cookie.

'I didn't have time for breakfast this morning,' she said. 'By the time I got the kids ready for school, we had to leave.' She took a large bite of the biscuit.

'Are you still on your own, then?'

'Yes,' said Ali. A look of sadness crossed her face. 'My errant husband hasn't been home in weeks. It looks like he's made his choice—and he's chosen her.'

'The stupid prick,' said Rob. 'He didn't know how lucky he was to have you and the bairns.'

'Tell me what you know about Dan Howard,' she said, changing the subject because her husband's abandonment of her and their children to live with that bitch he worked with was still too raw to talk about.

'I met him for the first time a few weeks ago,' said Rob. 'We received a report of a car obstructing a parked car outside Mike's Fish Bar, and I went to sort it out. Howard was double-parked, feeding his face, knowing full well that he was preventing a young mother from leaving.'

'What a jerk! What did you do?'

'I gave him a fixed penalty.'

'And what about today?' she asked. 'It's just he doesn't seem the sort to grow cannabis.'

'It was his neighbour who tipped us off,' he said. 'I went to Howard's place. A nice place it is, too! And I found a cannabis plant growing in the garden—in full view. He hadn't tried to hide it.'

Ali sipped her hot drink and took another large bite of the cookie, wondering what action she should take. Howard was hardly a criminal mastermind growing cannabis to supply a town. He said he knew nothing about the plants, and there was no evidence to suggest otherwise. She would never get a conviction on one plant found in full view in a back garden; the case would be laughed out of the court.

'How are you going to play this one?' asked Rob.

'I'll have to let him off—with a caution.'

'Yeah, that's what I thought,' he said, finishing his sandwich. 'As it was his neighbour who reported it, I suspect he might be behind this. It makes you wonder what Howard's done to upset him.'

'After the stunt he pulled outside the fish shop, I can't see him winning any best neighbour awards,' she said. 'Thanks for your help, Rob.'

'Anytime. You take care of yourself.'

Rob stood up and left the table.

Ali finished her biscuit, drank the rest of her coffee, and placed the empty cup on the table. When she returned to the interview room a few moments later, Dan's face was ashen.

'Are you alright, Dan?' she asked.

'Yes, I'm fine,' he said, sitting upright and taking several deep breaths.

'We found a cannabis plant in your garden, and you haven't been able to account for how it came to be there.' She gave Dan a stern look. 'As there were fewer than nine plants growing on your premises, if you admit to the offence of cultivation of cannabis on a small scale, I can let you off with a caution today. That doesn't mean you get off scot-free, mind you. If you re-offend in the future, this incident will be taken into account. Do you understand?'

'Yes, thank you,' said Dan, exhaling loudly. 'You mentioned you had a tip-off about the cannabis plant. Who was it from?'

'I'm afraid I can't tell you that.'

Dan sat back in his chair and looked deep in thought.

Sergeant Hanlon prepared the paperwork while Dan waited. Afterwards, the custody officer at the front desk returned his belongings, and then Dan walked out of the building, a free man with a police caution on his record.

33

Sympathy and Wine

When Chris came home from work, Dan was sitting in his armchair, reflecting on the day's horrendous events.

'Hiya,' said Dan, but his voice lacked the joy and enthusiasm it usually had when he greeted his partner.

'What's up?' asked Chris, sitting on the chair arm.

Dan shook his head.

'Tell me about it,' said Chris. 'A problem shared is a problem halved, you know.'

Dan looked up at him with a regretful smile.

'I don't think you'd believe me if I told you.'

'Go on, try me.'

'Okay,' said Dan. 'I went out this morning, and when I got back, there was a police car parked outside our house.'

Chris stood up and stepped back, leaning against the door frame, from where he could see Dan's face.

'The policeman asked to see our garden,' said Dan.

'Don't tell me you've buried a body out there,' said Chris, only half joking.

'No, Chris, just listen, will you?' said Dan. 'He found a

cannabis plant growing out there.'

'You told me you hadn't taken drugs since you were at college.'

'I haven't,' said Dan. 'Honest, Chris. I don't know how it got there. The police said they'd had a tip-off from somebody to search my garden. Someone must have planted it there and then informed the police.'

'Come off it, Dan,' said Chris. 'Who would do something like that?'

'I don't know, but I intend to find out. I'm going to fill out a freedom of information request to find out who contacted them. I won't let this lie.'

'You have a wild imagination, Dan, and you're always looking for problems. Please don't bother the police any more. They won't tell you who their informant was, freedom of information request or not. I don't know what planet you're on sometimes.'

'It did cross my mind that you might have sown the seed,' said Dan maliciously, in retaliation for Chris's harsh words.

'What!' said Chris. 'Why would I do that? I never touch the stuff.'

'Yeah, I know that, but I can't think of any other explanation. Can you?'

'A cannabis seed could have blown in on the wind or been pooped out by a bird.'

Dan snorted loudly.

'A stoned bird—that's something I'd like to see. But seriously, Chris. I'm getting worried about all this. I can't help thinking about what could happen next.'

'Maybe it's karma catching up with you,' laughed Chris.

'Karma,' said Dan, puzzling over the word. 'But why would

I have bad karma?'

Chris rolled his eyes.

'Have you made any food tonight? I'm absolutely ravenous.'

'I was at the police station all afternoon,' said Dan. 'I've just got in, and I feel completely drained.'

'The police station!' Chris's eyes widened. 'They didn't charge you, did they? You can do serious time for growing cannabis.'

'They let me off with a caution.'

'Thank God for that. I thought for a minute there that I might be visiting you in Durham—at the high-security prison.'

'Don't even go there, please,' said Dan. 'I was so scared.'

Chris hugged Dan and said, 'It's alright. You're safe now. Come on, let's get ready. We'll go out for dinner tonight. It looks like you could do with cheering up.'

'Do you fancy trying that new Thai restaurant that's just opened in Gosforth?' asked Dan, immediately perking up at the thought of food.

'If that's where you want to go, that's fine by me.'

'Great! I'll text them and reserve a table,' said Dan. 'I've heard it gets busy, even mid-week.'

Dan picked up his phone and sent a message: *Hi, please reserve a table for two for Dan Howard at 8:00 p.m. Thanks.*

He didn't notice the auto-extend changing his words into phrases, and the message he sent to the restaurant staff read: *Hi, I'm the biggest tosser in the toon. Please reserve a table for two for Dan The Man Howard at 8:00 p.m. Thanks. I'll forever be in your debt.*

When they arrived, the restaurant was busy. A waiter showed the men to a table by the window, and they ordered their meals. Dan couldn't understand why the staff kept looking at him curiously while he and Chris ate their food and polished off two bottles of wine. Perhaps they had mistaken him for a celebrity, and he wondered who he might have been mistaken for.

Dan thought he looked a little like Declan Donnelly from the television duo Ant and Dec, but he was much taller than Dec and much younger, too, so they were unlikely to confuse him with Dec. Sam Fender was a local lad, and they had similar colouring, but Sam was a little slimmer. What about James Arthur, the X-Factor singer? Now, that was more like it. They had a similar build and colouring, and he was from the northeast. Yes, he believed he could be mistaken for James Arthur.

When Dan emptied the second bottle of wine, Chris said, 'Come on, it's time to go home.'

Dan finished the glass and followed him outside, took his car keys from his trouser pocket and headed for his car.

'What do you think you're doing?' asked Chris. 'You're in no state to drive. You've had one and a half bottles of wine.'

'I'm okay,' said Dan, staggering towards the Mercedes. 'We don't have far to go.'

'No, you're not.' Chris grabbed his arm and said, 'We'll walk back.'

'Can't we get a taxi?'

'What! To take us one mile down the road. No!'

The walk home didn't sober Dan up much, but it wore him out. By the time they turned onto the path to the house, he was out of breath and leaning on Chris for support.

Chris helped him to the front door, unlocked it, and they went inside. Chris grabbed Dan to stop him from falling over in the hall.

'I'm taking you up to bed,' said Chris, putting his arm around

Dan to support him.

Dan flopped onto the bed, fully clothed, and within a minute, he was snoring softly.

Chris looked down at him and shook his head. From what Dan had said about his experience at the police station, he'd had a tough day. Chris removed Dan's shoes, placed them together by the wall, and removed his jacket. As he pulled the jacket free, a piece of white card fell to the floor.

He picked it up. It was half of a business card for a Newcastle taxi firm. He wondered why Dan had torn it. Then he turned it over and saw part of a handwritten message, and his stomach flipped. It contained the first half of Dan's phone number. He fished in Dan's jacket pockets and found the other half of the card. Putting them together, he read the message above the phone number: *Good-looking gay guy wanting a good time, Jesmond.*

34

Cowboys

October 2019

James spent the next few days lying in bed or moping around his flat. He had little interest in anything, apart from looking after Whiskers, who had become his constant companion.

On Thursday morning, he charged his phone and saw that he had received a message two days earlier. Wondering who it was from, he played the message: *Hello, this is a message for James Webster. This is Josh McIntosh from the Jobcentre. We were expecting to see you yesterday at ten o'clock for your appointment. If you've got a job, that's great. Let us know. If you missed signing on for any other reason, please contact us immediately, and we'll reschedule the appointment. This is important, Mr Webster. If we don't hear from you, your benefits will be stopped.*

Shit! He had forgotten all about the appointment. They couldn't stop his payments. He desperately needed the money.

James returned the call, apologised for missing the appointment, and asked if he could come in that afternoon. They agreed he could attend at three o'clock that day.

The skies were grey and gloomy as James walked to the

Jobcentre in Byker. On the way there, he became more and more depressed, thinking about his futile job search. He had attended the Jobcentre every two weeks to sign on, and after the initial period when he had been preoccupied with Dan Howard, he had applied for two jobs without fail. But with every turndown he received, he became more certain that he wouldn't get another job in time to pay his outstanding bills.

The reminders he was receiving now were more demanding than before, threatening him with debt collection agencies, bailiffs and court action if he didn't pay them.

He couldn't pay. His dole money was just £73.10 per week, enough to feed him and Whiskers, but it wouldn't stretch to pay his rent, electricity, gas, council tax, phone contract and internet connection.

At the Jobcentre, he saw Josh Macintosh, showed him the letter from the Freeman Hospital that he had retrieved from the bin, and signed the claim form.

'Do you need a hand with your job search today?'

'To tell you the truth,' said James, 'I need a hand with a lot more than my job search.'

'I'm sorry, Mr Webster, we can't help with personal problems,' said Josh, 'but there are some new jobs that have just come in that might be suitable for you. Let's have a look, shall we?'

After trawling through lots of vacancies, Josh looked apologetic. He hadn't found as many for James as he'd hoped.

'There's a part-time job here at a car wash in Washington,' he said. 'Mornings only, from eight until twelve.'

'I don't drive,' said James. 'How would I get to Washington?'

'By bus?' suggested Josh. 'I think there's one every hour from Eldon Square.'

'What's the pay like?' asked James.

'Minimum wage.'

'Nah,' said James. 'That'll be three hours of travelling each day for four hours of work, and by the time I pay the bus fare, there won't be enough left over to pay my bills.'

'I'm struggling here, Mr Webster,' said Josh. 'I'm afraid there aren't many jobs for unskilled workers. Why not give it a try?'

'Okay,' said Josh, knowing that by applying, he would waste his time and the company's time, but he had to do it to continue receiving his Job Seeker's Allowance payments.

'Let's see what else there is,' said Josh, resuming his search. 'Ah! This might be better. A ground maintenance assistant for the city council. It looks like it involves cutting grass in the parks and schools, some planting of flower beds, a bit of litter picking, emptying bins and that sort of thing. It says a driving licence is preferred but not essential.'

'Yeah, I'll give that a go,' said James, thinking he might enjoy doing that. 'Thank you.'

Armed with the print-outs, James went home and applied for the jobs online, with little hope of getting them, but at least he'd done what was necessary to get his dole money.

Feeling low, he went out for a walk and ended up in Jesmond. He saw a beat-up red transit van on a street near Somerset Road. Two workmen carried rubbish bags, put them in the back of the van and then poured themselves a drink from tartan thermos flasks. *Did they still make those?*

'There's a couple more bags of rubbish to bring out,' said a man in blue overalls. 'What are you going to do with it?'

'I need the van first thing in the morning to pick up some plasterboard, so I'll get rid of it tonight,' said the other man, wearing a lumberjack shirt and scruffy jeans. 'Don't you worry yourself about it.'

James was certain the guys were cowboy builders because their van wasn't sign-written and because legitimate builders hired skips to dispose of the waste.

He had an idea. He went to Somerset Road and found Dan's rubbish bin on the back street. With his sleeves covering his hands, he lifted a pile of papers that looked like envelopes and letters, checked that there was a name and address on one of them, and took them to the street where he'd seen the van. He waited for the men to enter the house they were working in, and then he approached the rear of the van. It was almost full of strong black rubbish bags. He had his eye on one that was gaping open and reached over to deposit the letters in it when he heard a voice behind him.

'Get out of my van, you thieving bastard!'

James dropped the letters and sprinted away from the van.

'If I see you again, you're a dead man.'

The builder ran after him but couldn't keep up.

James didn't stop running until he entered Heaton Park, then doubled over to catch his breath. He looked back to make sure the men weren't following him, and then he walked home, thinking that if his instincts were correct, the guy would illegally dump those bags somewhere later that night.

35

Closing Shop

'This was the first outfit I bought for the shop,' said Amanda, holding up a sexy nun outfit.

'I remember it well,' said Matt. 'You wore it at that vicars and tarts party, and you looked amazing in it. What a fantastic night that was!'

Amanda smiled wistfully as she folded the costume and packed it in a large cardboard box.

'I don't think this one has been worn,' said Matt, folding a child-size pirate outfit and placing it in the box.

'It hasn't. It was from that last batch that arrived late, after everything went wrong for us. Hardly any of those costumes were hired out.'

When Amanda and Matt packed the last of the clothes and taped the boxes, a massive pile of boxes stood by the door. She removed her mobile phone from her bag and booked a parcel collection.

'A van will be here for them at about three o'clock,' she said, putting her phone back in her bag. 'And the estate agent said she'd be here between four and five.'

'It's two o'clock now, so we have an hour to spare before the collection. I know you didn't have breakfast this morning, so you must be starving. Do you fancy a late lunch?'

'I couldn't. The last thing I feel like doing is eating. My stomach's all churned up. It feels like there's a huge knot inside.'

Holding her stomach, she rushed to the toilet, and Matt heard her retching.

When she returned to the shop, her face was blotchy and her eyes red.

'I'm so sorry, love,' said Matt, taking her hand, pulling her into his lap and holding her close. 'It'll all be over after today, and then we can put this behind us.'

Amanda looked around the empty shop. The velvet curtain, the rails and the clothes from the back room were gone, and the shelves behind the counter were empty. Her desk, the computers and printers had already been sold and collected. She had removed the window display a few days earlier and smeared the glass in Windolene cream so they could hide their shame from passers-by while they cleared the shop. Her bottom lip quivered, and tears sprang to her eyes.

'I put everything I had into this shop,' she said, shaking her head sadly. 'And I feel awful because I persuaded you to do the same. We've lost it all, Matt. Everything.'

'I would never do something I didn't want to, Amanda, so don't beat yourself up about that. And no matter what happens, don't forget that we still have each other.'

'Everything was going so well,' she said, her voice wavering. 'What did I do wrong?'

A tear overflowed and ran down her cheek, and Matt wiped it away.

'You did nothing wrong, love. Get that idea out of your head right now.'

'But I must have. My business is in receivership,' she said. 'We've had to sell everything off at a fraction of its value. Once we pay our debts off, we'll have nothing left to show for five years of blood, sweat, and tears. Nobody appreciates how hard it is to run a small business unless they've done it themselves. I tried my best, Matt, but I failed!'

Amanda sobbed loudly and rested her head on Matt's shoulder.

'We'll be okay,' he said. 'We can get through this. I know how strong you are. You did very well to avoid bankruptcy. That means you can start up another business when we're back on our feet, if you want to have another go.'

A little while later, Amanda stood up and reached for a tissue from her bag. She wiped her face and blew her nose.

'You go and get something to eat if you're hungry. I don't mind waiting here for the courier to collect the boxes.'

'It's okay. I'm not hungry,' said Matt, although his rumbling stomach betrayed his lie. 'I'm going to stay here with you until the shop's empty and we've handed the keys over to the estate agent. Then, we'll go home, love.'

36

Planting Potatoes

At the Jobcentre, James saw Niamh again, because Josh was on personal leave.

'It says here that you've applied for six jobs since you started your claim,' she said. 'Have you had replies from them?'

'I didn't get the one at the Freeman Hospital,' said James, showing her the letter that was folded in his booklet. 'I haven't heard from any of the others yet.'

'Have you applied for more jobs?'

'No, I haven't seen any that I'm likely to get.'

'I shouldn't have to remind you that you need to apply for at least two jobs every week, regardless of whether you think you'll get them or not. And, if you apply for more, you'll improve your chances of getting one, won't you? Now, let's see if we have anything for you today.'

She searched the current vacancies and found two jobs that she thought James would be a suitable candidate for—a cleaner at a warehouse in Byker and a bakery assistant in the city centre.

Not a chance, thought James. He couldn't clean, and he

couldn't cook, but he took the slips, rushed for the door, and was glad to be outside again. The more time he spent at the Jobcentre, the more worthless he felt.

On his way home, he called at Lidl to buy some groceries. As he walked through the vegetable aisle, he saw a pile of potatoes and smiled as an idea popped into his head.

At the checkout, he paid for three pot noodles, a box of breakfast cereal, a loaf of bread, a tin of baked beans, a box of dry cat food, two pints of milk and one potato. He took the shopping home to his flat and dumped it on the kitchen worktop. Then he fed Whiskers. The kitten hovered over the food for a while, letting him know she preferred tuna to the dry cat biscuits he'd bought, but eventually, she ate it.

James put the round potato into his pocket and left the flat. When he reached Somerset Road in Jesmond, he looked around to ensure nobody was watching him and then approached the rear of Dan's car, kneeling on the ground between it and a Skoda parked close behind it.

He took the potato from his pocket and pushed it into the exhaust pipe. When he felt some resistance, he forced it further in until it was firmly jammed in place.

James smiled all the way home, wondering how Dan would react when his car wouldn't start. *Maybe he would blow a gasket!*

37

Hot Potato

Dan rushed around the house with a duster and spray. He wanted to get the cleaning done as quickly as possible because he needed to go into town for some shopping. It had been weeks since he'd bought any new clothes.

When he finished, he changed into some clean clothes, put on his jacket, and grabbed his car keys. He sat in the leather driver's seat, pressed the start button, and the engine purred quietly. Just as he was about to pull away from the kerb, it stopped. He pressed the ignition button again. This time, the engine spluttered and stopped.

Dan returned to the house, swearing under his breath. He called the local garage and explained what had happened.

'Is this the Dan Howard who lives at Sixty-Six Somerset Road?' asked the man on the other end of the phone.

'Yes, that's me,' said Dan. 'Can you send someone around to fix it, please?'

'Well, I don't know about that,' said the man. 'The last time I sent one of my mechanics to help you out, we got a load of grief.'

'I don't know what you mean.'

'You left a bad review of my company!'

'Oh! I'd forgotten about that.'

'Yes, I suspected you must have when you phoned us to ask for help,' said the garage owner. 'As things stand, I am not willing to send anyone there to fix your car, but if you take that review off Google, I might reconsider.'

'But that's blackmail! That review was an honest account of how I felt about your company when I wrote it.'

'Are you going to remove it or not?'

'Alright, I will,' conceded Dan, reaching for his laptop and logging into his Google account. 'I'm taking it off now. When can you come and fix my car?'

The man on the phone waited until he saw the review disappear from his Google business page, and then said he'd send somebody out to look at it that afternoon.

Dan waited and waited, hoping it wouldn't be too long before a mechanic would arrive. He still wanted to go shopping, but the day dragged on. The doorbell rang precisely at three o'clock.

When Dan opened the door, he was surprised to see the same man who had come to fix his tyre. He wouldn't have remembered the guy, but he would recognise that hand-knitted hat anywhere. It was vile.

'What's the trouble with it this time?' asked the mechanic.

'It won't start,' said Dan. 'When I tried, the engine started, but stopped a few seconds later.'

'Can I take the key and have a look?'

Dan handed the mechanic his key and watched him walk down the path to his car, which he'd parked right in front of the house as usual. He closed the door and went to the lounge window for a better view of what was going on.

The man climbed into the car. The engine spluttered and then stopped, as it had when Dan tried it. He started the car again, revving the engine very hard, and Dan heard a sound like a gun firing, and then a metallic-sounding bang.

The mechanic got out, walked down the road, picked something up from the ground and then returned to the house. Dan met him at the door.

'Do you know what's wrong with it?' asked Dan. 'Can you fix it?'

'Aye, I know what the problem is,' said the man with a smile, holding up a potato covered in soot.

'A potato?' said Dan, looking puzzled.

'Aye. It's an old prank the bairns pull,' said the mechanic. 'If you stick a potato up an exhaust pipe, the car will do one of two things. It'll either stall, like it did for you, or shoot the potato out of the exhaust pipe, like it did for me. Do you know who that red Skoda belongs to?'

'Yes, it's Mr Backworth's from next door. Why?'

'I'm afraid you're going to have to apologise to him. The potato smashed his car's grille.'

'But my car is okay now, isn't it?' asked Dan.

'Yes, it starts well, and it's safe to drive,' said the mechanic, handing back Dan's keys. 'That'll be £75 please.'

Dan gave the man the money and closed the door, wondering who might have put a potato in the Merc's exhaust pipe. Was it the same person who had planted the cannabis plant in his garden and sent him the box full of glitter, which he still hadn't got out of the carpet?

Hmph! Perhaps the guy from the garage had planted the potato, as he had the most to gain from it—another £75 in his pocket and a negative review removed from his business page.

Dan picked up his phone and dialled 101 to report the incident to the police. He wanted them to know that he was being victimised in his own home. The operator didn't seem interested in his story, so Dan exaggerated the situation and said that his car had been vandalised, to which he got the standard reply that someone would call around later to take the details.

Realising the time, Dan rushed out to his car.

Mr Backworth was standing in front of his Skoda, running his finger over the crack in the car grille.

'Hello, Mr Howard. I don't suppose you saw who did this to my car, did you?' he asked, pointing to the damage.

'No.'

'This used to be such a pleasant neighbourhood,' said his neighbour. 'This would never have happened when we moved here in the sixties. I'll take it to the garage and see how much it'll cost to repair. I hope it won't be an insurance claim. God only knows what the premium will go up to. It's high enough already.'

'I'm sorry, I have to go,' said Dan, getting into the Merc without giving the man a chance to say anything else.

He wondered why he hadn't confessed to Mr Backworth that the damage to his Skoda was from a potato being shot from his car's exhaust pipe. He didn't want to pay for the repair; it was as simple as that. Did he feel guilty? No, because it wasn't his fault. He wasn't the one who had put the potato in the exhaust pipe.

At Asda, he picked up some chicken breasts and vegetables for a stir-fry. Chris would be home soon, and he didn't have time to cook anything more elaborate for dinner.

HOT POTATO

When Dan parked outside his house after his shopping trip, Chris was unlocking the front door. Dan grabbed the bags from the car boot and jogged up the path to meet him.

'Chris, what a day I've had,' said Dan. 'I'll tell you about it over dinner. I'm going to make a stir-fry.'

Chris took a shower while Dan prepared and cooked the food. It was ready when Chris came downstairs. Dan knew Merlot wasn't the right wine to drink with chicken stir-fry, but he opened a bottle anyway because he felt he needed a drink, and he filled two large glasses to the brim.

'Steady on, Dan,' said Chris. 'A small glass of red wine is good for you, but that much isn't.'

'Oh, Chris!' said Dan. 'If you'd had the day I've had today, you'd want a large glass, too.'

'What's happened this time?' asked Chris.

Dan took a sip of wine.

'You won't believe this. My car wouldn't start this morning, so I called the garage. The guy came out, the same one who fixed the tyre, and he worked out what the problem was pretty quickly.'

Dan gulped his wine.

'What was it?' asked Chris, digging into his food.

'Somebody had stuck a potato in the exhaust pipe! Can you believe that?'

Dan finished the glass and poured himself another.

'A potato!'

Chris roared with laughter.

'Yes, a potato,' said Dan, 'and it's not funny!'

'My brother did that to my dad's car when he was little. He got his backside skelped for it, and he never dared to do it again.'

'I reported it to the police,' said Dan.

'You didn't? It's just a kid's trick, Dan. There's really no need to involve the police.'

'It's too late now. I've already called them.'

'I didn't realise until recently what a drama queen you are,' said Chris. 'Everything is either a drama or a crisis with you.'

Chris finished the stir-fry on his plate and sipped his wine.

Dan hadn't touched his food but had almost emptied his second large glass of Merlot.

'If you're not going to eat that, can I have it?' asked Chris. 'It's delicious.'

Dan handed his plate to Chris and opened another bottle of wine.

'Somebody is out to get me,' said Dan. 'I know it. How else can you explain everything? The empty box on my birthday, the cannabis plant, and now this?'

He didn't mention the card in the pub, inviting men to call him, because Chris had been so jealous when he'd received texts from other men.

Chris pushed his plate to one side and replaced it with Dan's. Between mouthfuls of food, he said, 'You have too much time on your hands if you're worrying about trivial stuff like that. You need something to keep your mind occupied. Have you thought about getting a part-time job or doing some charity work? It would do you good to get out more and mix with other people.'

'Mix with other people—no, thank you!' said Dan, pulling a face.

Dan was halfway through his third large glass of wine when the doorbell rang, and he rushed to the door with his glass in his hand.

'Mr Howard,' said Police Constable Rob Marshall. 'We meet again. Can I come in?'

Dan stepped aside, and the policeman entered the house, following Dan into the lounge and sitting on the sofa.

'Tell me what happened today,' he said.

Dan sat in his armchair and told the story again, and Chris wandered into the room just as he finished.

'May I ask who you are?' asked the constable.

'Hi, I'm Chris Smith. Dan's partner. I told him this wasn't a matter for the police, but he'd already called you before I got in from work.'

'It's hardly vandalism as you reported, Mr Howard,' said the policeman, returning his attention to Dan. 'There's no damage to the vehicle, and there's nothing we can do about the potato incident.'

'Surely you can find out who put it there,' said Dan. 'Can't you use fingerprints or CCTV or something?'

'We'll not get fingerprints off a potato,' he replied, trying to keep a straight face. 'Do you have a camera on the front of your house?'

'No,' said Dan, taking a gulp of wine.

'Well, that means there's no CCTV either. We'll put this incident on record. If anything else happens, let us know.'

The policeman stood up, and Chris saw him out, apologising on Dan's behalf for wasting his time.

When Chris returned to the lounge, he sat in his armchair and looked at Dan.

'I'm worried about you. You're getting paranoid, thinking that somebody's out to get you. Stuff like this happens to everyone all the time, and they shrug it off. You really need to relax more.'

'Thanks for your support!' said Dan sarcastically as he stumbled to the kitchen to refill his empty glass. When he returned, he said, 'We should get some CCTV cameras fitted to the house, and then you'll see that I'm right.'

'Talking about support, I guess you must have forgotten about my birthday,' said Chris.

Dan's eyebrows furrowed as he tried to recall the date of Chris's birthday.

'It's today!' said Chris. 'No card, no present, no nothing. You never think about anyone but yourself.'

He went to the lounge and picked up a magazine to read.

38

Down at the Station

The following afternoon, Police Constable Rob Marshall entered the police station and saw Sergeant Ali Hanlon sitting at her desk doing paperwork. He made a beeline for her.

'You'll never guess who I saw last night,' he said, raising his eyebrows.

'No idea,' she said. 'Tell me.'

'Daniel Howard. The guy from Jesmond who had the cannabis plant growing in his garden,' said Rob. 'He phoned an incident in earlier. Under normal circumstances, it wouldn't have warranted a visit, but because he's been involved in several incidents recently, I wanted to see what was going on.'

'And—'

'Apparently, somebody stuck a potato up his exhaust pipe.'

'That's not a euphemism, is it?' she asked, pulling a face. 'I hope you're talking about his car.'

'Yes, the exhaust pipe on his car,' said Rob, rolling his eyes. 'I got there about six o'clock in the evening, and Howard had already had quite a bit to drink. He was slurring his words and was unsteady on his feet. He could have a drink or drug problem.'

'Maybe,' said Ali. 'Do you know who pulled the potato prank on him?'

'There's no way we'll find out who did that,' he said, 'but my money's on his next-door neighbour. The one who reported him for growing cannabis in his garden.'

'Yes, he's a strong contender,' she agreed. 'Howard's name has cropped up in another case. I had a constable from Gateshead on the phone earlier, asking about him in relation to a fly-tipping complaint. As you seem to have a handle on him, I'll let you talk to him about it.'

'I'm off for a few days now,' said Rob, 'but I'll pop round to see him next week, if that's okay?'

'Yeah, it's not urgent. Have you got any plans?'

'I have a date on Friday night,' he said, raising his eyebrows.

'That's great! And about time, I might add. It must be five years since you got divorced.'

'Four and a half years, and I have no regrets,' said Rob. 'That woman was a psycho—I'm well rid of her.'

'You must remember, not all women are like that. There are plenty of decent ones around.'

'Once bitten, twice shy.'

Rob winked at her. If things didn't go well with his date at the weekend, and Ali's husband didn't come crawling back to her, begging for forgiveness, he would ask Ali out. She was a decent woman, attractive as well, and he could see them having a future together.

39

Abject Failure

'Amanda, are you getting up? It's ten o'clock,' said Matt. 'I've made bacon and eggs for breakfast.'

Amanda lay in bed, covered by the duvet, the curtains drawn. She sought comfort by cuddling Matt's pillow, needing to feel safe, but the damage had already been done. Her business had failed; she had failed; and nothing mattered any more.

She heard Matt speaking and was aware he was standing at the bottom of the bed, but she didn't turn to look at him or answer his question. His voice sounded distant and hollow, and her mind couldn't make sense of the words, so she ignored them.

He came closer and held her hand.

'Amanda. You have to eat something. Do you want me to bring your breakfast in here?'

Breakfast.

She used to enjoy food, but she had lost her appetite. She laughed silently, thinking what a strange saying. Where had she lost her appetite, and could she find it again if she tried? She couldn't care less about eating, because eating made her vomit, and she hated throwing up.

Matt climbed out of his wheelchair, lay on the bed beside her, and held her in his arms. That felt nice. Amanda felt warm and protected, and for a few minutes, she almost forgot about her fancy dress business and the shame, embarrassment and humiliation of its closure, its failure, and all the grief she'd dealt with in the process.

But had she dealt with it?

She was haunted by Spider-Man and the Lone Ranger. They came to her in her sleep and taunted her about the comments and reviews that the guy posted on the internet. They were written in black and white and would be in the public domain forever, for everyone to see.

No, she hadn't dealt with it. How could she?

Powerless to clear her name and repair Glad Rag's reputation, she had shed tears, many tears, and become angry, taking it out on those she loved, namely Matt, which had made her feel wretched and achieved nothing. Matt didn't deserve her rage, but she had nowhere else to direct it.

Spider-Man and the Lone Ranger both fought for justice. *What a joke!* There was no such thing as justice. If there were, she and Matt would be in their shop right now, sending outfits to people throughout the country and fitting customers' costumes in the store, but instead, she was lying in his arms in their bed, feeling as though there was nothing left to live for. After everything that had happened, how could she show her face to the outside world?

40

Seafood Paella and Prison

Dan weighed the pros and cons of installing CCTV at his house for several days before deciding to go ahead. Online, he found a company based in Newcastle that appeared to be reputable and called them.

He explained he wanted two cameras fitted: one at the front to show his door and path, as well as his car in the street, and another at the back to cover the rear garden and the back lane.

'If the camera captures a view of the street, you'll have to comply with the new GDPR laws because you're filming a public place.'

Dan didn't know what GDPR laws were and didn't care. He just wanted the cameras up to protect himself and his property from harassment and damage.

After receiving an acceptable quote for the work, Dan confirmed he would like to proceed.

'When can you fit them?' he asked.

'Let me see. We're looking at November now. How does Monday, the fourth, sound?'

'I was hoping you could fit them much sooner, to be honest,

but okay. If you have a cancellation before then, please let me know.'

'Yes, of course. Now, if I could just take some details and a deposit.'

Dan gave her the requested information and paid the deposit by card. He ended the call, feeling happier that he would soon have security cameras in place. If anything else happened, he would have video footage to show the police.

Now, it was time to visit Asda. Dan wandered along the aisles pushing a shopping trolley, browsing the shelves and selecting the ingredients to make seafood paella. He started at the fish counter and chose cartons of king prawns, live mussels, and monkfish. At the vegetable section, he grabbed a large onion, a garlic bulb, and a pot of fresh parsley. He added a tin of chopped tomatoes from the tinned vegetable aisle and then headed for the spices, where he found saffron and star anise. While engrossed by the offer on a selection of herbs and spices, he didn't notice a dark-haired young man in a hoodie watching him.

Dan checked his shopping list. He'd forgotten to get the paella rice, so he doubled back to get some. On rechecking the list, he saw that the other items he needed for the recipe were foodstuffs he already had at home. *Great!* He had everything he needed. He wanted to impress Chris with dinner that evening; he needed to do something to make amends for forgetting his birthday!

He added a high-end bottle of Sauvignon Blanc, which cost a whopping £20, and went to the checkout, where he transferred his shopping from the basket to the conveyor belt. The till operator scanned the barcodes, and Dan packed the food into carrier bags, which he placed in the trolley. He then paid for the shopping with his card and pushed the trolley out of the supermarket.

On his way out of the store, he saw a stall selling fresh flowers. He loved fresh flowers and stopped to admire the bouquets.

While Dan was distracted, the young man in the black hoodie reached into one of the carrier bags in Dan's trolley and took a pack of mussels, without breaking stride. By the time Dan had chosen and paid for some yellow roses with white gypsophila, James Webster had left the car park.

Dan placed the shopping bags and flowers in the boot of his car and returned the trolley to the shop. Then, he drove home, where he placed the fish in the fridge.

King prawns, monkfish. There was something missing. *The mussels! Where were the mussels?* He definitely remembered putting them in his trolley when he chose the king prawns and monkfish. Were they there when he packed his bags? He wasn't sure, but he thought there was something suspicious about the shop assistant at the till. She kept giving him funny looks. She must have taken them.

Dan took the receipt for his shopping from his wallet and saw that he had paid for the mussels. They were £3.25—not exactly cheap. The woman must have scanned the pack and then kept it for herself, he thought.

He couldn't make seafood paella without mussels, and he didn't have time to return to the shop to make a complaint and get another pack, so what could he do?

Looking at the ingredients, he decided to make a fish stew instead of a seafood paella, as he didn't need mussels for that. He hoped Chris liked fish stew.

Dan was chopping vegetables for the dish when the doorbell

rang. He whipped off his apron in a bit of a flap but failed to put the knife down. He opened the door to see Police Constable Rob Marshall standing on the doorstep.

'Please put down the knife,' said the constable.

'What? This is just a kitchen knife. I was chopping onions for dinner. What can I do for you?'

'You can start by putting down the knife, Mr Howard,' repeated the officer.

'Alright,' said Dan, rolling his eyes. He returned to the kitchen and left the knife on the worktop. Then, he invited the policeman in, and they sat in the lounge.

'We have reason to believe that you are responsible for some fly-tipping that occurred last week.'

'No!' said Dan. 'I would never do something like that.'

'That's what you said about growing cannabis in your garden, but I found some there, didn't I?'

The policeman raised his eyebrows.

'I still don't know how that came to be there. All our rubbish goes in the bins outside. I have a green bin for normal waste, a blue bin for recycling, and a brown bin for garden waste. I'm very particular about what I put in them.'

'Where were you between 6:00 p.m. on Wednesday and 10:00 a.m. on Thursday?'

'I was here. I rarely go out at night during the week, or on weekends now, for that matter.'

'Can anyone corroborate your whereabouts during that time?'

'Yes, Chris was here.' Then Dan's brow furrowed. 'No, he wasn't on Wednesday night. He and his colleagues had a training meeting after work. They went out for a drink afterwards, and he didn't get home until almost one in the morning, which I remember because it was very late for him, especially when he had to be at work at eight o'clock the next morning.'

'So you don't have an alibi for Wednesday evening or a few hours on Thursday morning?'

The police constable made a note.

'We have evidence that some building waste that was dumped illegally originated from this address, and nobody can confirm that you were here when it was dumped. Dan Howard, I'm arresting you for fly-tipping.'

The constable then read Dan his rights for the second time.

'I suppose you'll want me to come to the station again?'

'Yes, I'm going to take you to the station for questioning.'

'Can I put the fish back in the fridge before we leave?' asked Dan. 'It'll go off if it's left on the kitchen worktop.'

'Aye, go on.'

The constable watched Dan to ensure he didn't pick up anything, such as a kitchen knife, or try to escape through the back door and then took him outside to the police car.

After waiting in a cell at the station for what Dan guessed was about an hour, but could have been anything from twenty minutes to two hours, as he had no way of knowing, Sergeant Ali Hanlon and Police Constable Rob Marshall accompanied him to the same grey interview room as before.

'Sit down, Dan,' she said, as they took a seat opposite him. 'Do you know why you're here?'

'PC Marshall said it was something to do with fly-tipping,' said Dan. 'I can assure you it's got nothing to do with me. I'm meticulous with my waste.'

'Hmm. Can you explain how some discarded letters with your name and address on them were found in the waste bags along with half a tonne of building waste, most of which was old plaster and tiles?'

'No,' said Dan. 'I can't.'

'Have you recently fitted a new bathroom or kitchen in your house?'

'Not recently,' said Dan. 'The kitchen is ancient. The cupboards could do with replacing, and it's been a while since the bathroom was done. It was just after my mother died.'

'Have any builders been to your house to do work in the last few weeks?'

'No.'

Ali looked at Dan and thought that if he was lying, he was very good at it. She believed him. But the evidence strongly suggested that the rubbish had come from his property.

'There were some builders on my street last week,' said Dan. 'I think they were doing some work at the house across the road. Number sixty-three. The letters could have blown out of the bin lorry, and the builders might have picked them up and put them in their rubbish bags.'

Dodgy builders picking up rubbish. That sounded like a story, she thought. Howard was grasping at straws. *Good!*

'Dan, you haven't been able to provide us with a satisfactory account of how rubbish from your house was found in the waste illegally dumped in Gateshead last Monday night,' said Sergeant Hanlon. 'Therefore, I am charging you with fly-tipping.'

'What! But I didn't do anything!' said Dan, getting to his feet.

'Sit down!' shouted the constable.

Dan sat down again, and his shoulders slumped.

'That's for a court to decide,' said the sergeant, handing

him a charge sheet. 'The case will be heard at the Magistrate's Court in Newcastle. There's a bit of a backlog at the moment, so I expect the hearing will be after the New Year. You'll get a notice through the post with the date and time of the hearing.'

'I think I need a solicitor.'

'I'm afraid it's too late for that, Dan. The interview is over, and you have already been charged with the crime.'

'Does that mean I can go home now?' asked Dan.

'Yes, you're free to go.'

Three hours after his arrest, Dan returned home.

'Where have you been?' asked Chris, rushing to the door when it opened. 'I've been worried sick.'

'At the police station.'

'Not again!' said Chris. 'What for this time?'

'They think I dumped some building waste near Gateshead. But I didn't.'

'Why do they think you did it?'

'Some letters addressed to me were in one of the rubbish bags,' said Dan. 'So, they've charged me with fly-tipping.'

'They charged you?' said Chris, shaking his head, not knowing what to think. 'Oh, my God!'

Dan slumped down in an armchair, feeling numb. Shouldn't he be angry about being falsely accused? What was wrong with him?

'I'll make dinner tonight.' Chris went into the kitchen and opened the fridge. 'I can grill some of this fish and steam some veg.'

'That'll be fine,' said Dan, following him into the kitchen and reaching for the expensive bottle of white wine in the fridge. He poured himself a large glass.

'So, what happens next?' asked Chris, brushing the fish

fillets with olive oil and seasoning them.

'Because I wouldn't admit to doing it, the police say I have to go to the magistrate's court to prove my innocence.' Dan took a huge gulp of wine. 'They said the hearing would probably be in the New Year.'

'Jesus! That's serious.'

'I know. I'm bricking it, to be honest.'

'What happens if they find you guilty?' asked Chris, putting the fillets on the grill pan and lighting the grill.

'I don't know.'

Dan reached for his laptop and asked Google.

'Dear God! If they don't believe me, Chris, I'll have to pay a fine of at least a thousand, but it could be as much as fifty thousand. And possibly a prison sentence of up to twelve months. Oh, my God!'

Chris put down the bowl and hugged Dan.

'It'll be okay. You didn't do it, so everything will be alright,' he said, wishing he had that much faith in the British justice system.

That evening, while the couple watched television, Dan stewed over his day, but despite his arrest and the forthcoming trial, the thing that bothered him most was the missing pack of mussels. When EastEnders finished, he opened his laptop and drafted an email to Asda customer services.

Dear Sir or Madam, I was absolutely appalled today when I shopped at my local store. I had a pack of mussels in my trolley, but they were missing when I got home. The only conclusion I can come to is that the till operator must have removed them maliciously, or maybe took them for herself. She should be questioned about the matter to find out how this happened. Not having the correct ingredients for my seafood paella after shopping at your store for them meant I had to find an alternative dish to cook, and that caused me a great deal of unnecessary stress. I hope you will resolve this matter to my satisfaction. Yours faithfully, Daniel J. Howard.

'You're hitting that keyboard pretty hard,' said Chris, looking up from the latest edition of his sporting magazine. 'What are you doing?'

'Complaining to Asda,' said Dan, hitting the send button. 'Before all the police stuff happened today, I intended to make seafood paella for dinner tonight, but by the time I got home, the mussels had disappeared from my shopping bags. That's why I was going to make fish stew instead. As it happens, I never got to make either.'

'I can't believe that you're worked up about something so trivial as a pack of mussels and what we had for dinner when the police have charged you with fly-tipping,' said Chris. 'I know you must be very upset about that, but you shouldn't take it out on anyone else. That's hardly fair.'

'I'm not taking it out on anyone else,' said Dan, shrugging his shoulders. 'Asda isn't a person. It's a company.'

Chris rolled his eyes and returned to browsing Netflix for something to watch.

41

Coffee with Matt

James sat with his phone in his hand, scrolling through his short list of contacts. Could he reach out to his friends again? He hadn't seen them since he got the cannabis plant from Matt, and he missed their daily chats so much.

He texted Matt, changing the words several times, and eventually, he sent the text, asking Matt if he'd like to meet for coffee, thinking it would be good to catch up.

Matt replied, asking to meet at a coffee shop in the city centre, near Glad Rags. That was no surprise, thought James, as it was the most convenient place for Matt to pop out from work.

That afternoon, James walked past the shop that Glad Rags leased and saw an estate agent's sign nailed to the door frame stating that the shop was available to let. He stepped back and looked at the shop. Somebody had removed the Glad Rags sign from above the door. He couldn't see inside the shop because the window had been smeared with Windolene, but he guessed the property was empty. Glad Rags had gone.

'James, I thought it was you,' said Matt, pulling up beside

him in his electric wheelchair. 'How are you doing, mate?'

James thought Matt looked like he'd aged several years in the month since he'd last seen him. The hair at his temples was speckled with grey, the lines on his face had deepened, and the dark circles under his eyes matched Amanda's.

'Not bad, Matt. What happened here?' James nodded towards the shop.

Matt sighed and shook his head. 'Let's get that coffee?'

The men crossed the road, entered the coffee shop, and placed their orders—a latte and an espresso. James carried the cups to a table with plenty of space around it, and Matt parked his wheelchair beside it.

James passed the espresso to Matt and sipped at the latte.

'You asked about the shop back there,' said Matt. 'I'm afraid we had to close the business.'

'When did that happen?'

'Last Friday. Bit ironic, really. The run-up to Christmas was usually our busiest time of the year.'

'I'm sorry.'

'When the orders stopped coming in, we hoped we could keep the business going by reducing the costs,' said Matt, warming his hands on his mug. 'We both felt awful about letting you go, but we thought it might make a difference with one less salary to pay. We worked without pay for the last month, so we could pay the rent and rates on the place, but none of it made any difference in the end. There were still no orders, the bills kept mounting up, and there comes a point when you just can't—'

'How's Amanda taking it?' asked James.

'Not well, to be honest,' said Matt, swallowing loudly. 'She thinks she's a complete failure. You know, the business meant everything to her. It was her life.'

'Yes, I know how much she loved it,' said James.

Matt rubbed his face with both hands and said, 'I can't get her to leave the house. She can't face seeing anyone. She doesn't bother getting up some days and when she does, she doesn't bother getting dressed—she sits in her dressing gown all day and hardly says a word, and she's not eating much either—she's had no appetite for weeks. I don't know how to help her.'

James felt awful about his friends going through this. How could Dan Howard have reduced the lively Amanda he'd worked with to a nervous wreck?

'I'm sorry. Let me know if there's anything I can do.'

'Thanks, James. I appreciate that.'

'Give her my love and tell her the business going bust had nothing to do with her. It was that bloody customer's fault.'

'I know that, and she knows that, but it doesn't make it any easier. She's beating herself up about how we handled the situation and what would have happened if we'd done something different.'

'I think you did the right thing,' said James. 'You can't give people money just because they demand it. It's not right.'

Finishing their beverages, the men promised to keep in touch, exited the coffee shop and went in opposite directions.

On his way home, James saw a woman on the opposite side of the road behaving oddly, and he stopped to watch. She was frantically looking for her car. She jogged up and down the street and slowed as she approached every silver vehicle to check if it was hers. Then, she requested help from some passersby to find it.

James stood on the opposite pavement as the scene unfolded.

The woman's panic escalated when she couldn't find the car, and when she finally accepted that it had gone, she assumed someone had stolen it. Her fraught voice carried across the street when she phoned the police to report the theft of her vehicle. Several minutes later, a look of relief flashed across her face, and then it changed to one of annoyance.

'Thanks, everyone!' she said to her helpers. 'My car has been towed. The parking ticket must have expired. Sorry to have troubled you all.'

She marched to a taxi rank further up the road and got into a car on a mission to retrieve her vehicle.

While she thought her car was missing, James had felt sympathy for the woman. His mind wandered to Dan Howard. Now, if what he'd witnessed had happened to Dan, he wouldn't have felt any sympathy whatsoever. The man deserved to suffer because of the suffering he had caused. It wasn't just his life that Dan had ruined; it was Matt and Amanda Armstrong's as well.

When James entered his flat, he powered up his laptop, opened YouTube and watched a couple of videos on how to use relay technology to unlock and start keyless cars.

Half an hour later, he scoured the shops on Chilton Road for all the bits and pieces he needed to construct a device. When he returned to his flat, he laid out his spoils and replayed the video that was the easiest to understand, because he had never done anything like this before.

Later that day, James stood back and admired his handiwork. The device looked right. He just hoped it would work and wished there was some way to check before he used it.

James waited until it was dark outside, and then he walked through the rain to Dan's road and hung around the bus stop for a few minutes to check if anything was happening on the street. He saw no movement apart from a ginger cat that ran past, jumped onto a low wall in front of a house and lay down, waiting for its owners to return home, James presumed, as there wasn't a cat flap in the front door.

All was peaceful, so James crossed the road and walked towards Dan's house. Just as he was about to turn onto the path, the front door opened, and Chris Smith stepped out in his running gear, glanced in his direction, and said, 'Are you alright, mate?'

'I have a parcel delivery for number sixty-eight,' said James, holding up the bundle he carried. 'Do you know where number sixty-eight is? I can't find it.'

'There must be some mistake,' said Chris. 'Our house is sixty-six, and it's the last one on this street. It is Somerset Road you're after, isn't it?'

'Aye, it is,' said James. 'The number must be wrong. Cheers, mate.'

Chris nodded and jogged up the road.

Phew! That was close.

James hid around the side of the house until Chris was out of sight and his nerves had settled, and then he returned to the front and put the device, which would relay a signal from Dan's keys, which were hanging on a hook by the door, to his car and trick the vehicle into opening the doors and starting for him. He placed it at the corner of Dan's house, where nobody would see it, and then went to Dan's Mercedes, which was parked on the roadside.

The car door was unlocked when he reached it. James opened the door and climbed into the driver's seat, which was comfortable. He pressed the start button, and the sound of

Taylor Swift filled the car; he turned off the music. The engine purred under the bonnet as he drove the car, not knowing exactly how far it would travel using the relay. Manoeuvring the car around the tight bend and onto the narrow lane that led to the back street, he continued past Dan's house and brought it to a halt right outside his neighbour's back gate. He turned on the music and climbed out of the car. There wasn't much room as he'd parked close to the neighbour's gate, but he squeezed through the narrow gap.

James opened the boot door, removed Dan's missing carton of mussels from his jacket pocket, tore a hole in the plastic packaging and placed it under a neatly folded raincoat. *Perfect!*

Before he went home, he needed to retrieve the device, so he stood at the bus stop for a few seconds, checking that Chris wasn't running up the street and that nobody else was around. A man from a few houses down was getting into his car, and James watched him drive away before walking up the path, creeping past the window, and picking up the device.

James hurried home, wishing he could see Dan's face when his car was missing, and wondering how long it would take him to find it.

42

Where is my Car?

After clearing away the breakfast dishes and having a sneaky browse on the internet, Dan left the house, locked the door behind him and walked down the path to his car, but it wasn't there. He looked up and down the road repeatedly, shook his head, and shrugged.

Thinking back to the previous day, he remembered that he'd used his car to go to Asda, and he was sure that he'd parked it right outside his house on his return because he'd had bags of food to carry in.

Dan removed his phone from his pocket and texted Chris: *Hi Chris, do you know where my car is?* He held his phone, waiting for a reply, and got more and more impatient when nothing appeared on the screen. He sent another message: *Hi Chris. I left my car outside our house yesterday, and it's not here now. What should I do? Thanks. Dan x*

Dan's phone rang, and he sighed with relief when he saw it was Chris.

'Hello!' he said. 'So you got my message? Why did it take you so long to call me back?'

'What's going on, Dan? What's with the stupid messages?'

'They weren't stupid messages. I've lost my car!'

'Just listen for a minute. This is the last message you sent me. Tell me it isn't stupid,' said Chris. He read the text he'd received from Dan: *Hi, I'm the biggest tosser in the Toon Chris. I left my car outside our house yesterday, and it's not here now. What should I do? Thanks, I'll forever be in your debt. Dan the Man. Kiss.*

'That's not what I wrote,' said Dan. 'How did that happen?'

'I don't know. You tell me. Have you been drinking?'

'No, I haven't! I'm serious, Chris. My car isn't here!'

'Come to think of it, I don't remember seeing it this morning,' said Chris. 'Could it have been stolen?'

'Oh, God! I hope not. I love that car.'

'Phone the police,' said Chris. 'Tell them what you've just told me. I have to go now. My spin class is about to start.'

Chris ended the call.

Dan walked along the street to ensure he hadn't parked further away from the house, but his car was nowhere to be seen. He went back indoors and phoned the police.

'I would like to report a crime, please.'

He provided the police officer with his details and then informed him about the missing car, which he presumed had been stolen during the night.

The officer was sympathetic, suggested he contact his insurance company, and advised him that a police officer would visit him later that day or the following day to take more details.

Dan paced the floor for hours before the doorbell rang. When eventually it did, he rushed to open the door and saw Police Constable Rob Marshall standing there.

'Come in,' said Dan. 'Would you like a cup of coffee or tea?'

'Thank you, coffee would be nice,' said the constable. 'Milk and two sugars, please.'

'Take a seat in the lounge and I'll be right back,' said Dan, before darting into the kitchen.

Over coffee, Dan explained what had happened with his car, and the policeman took notes.

'It sounds like it has probably been stolen,' said the constable. 'Was there any glass on the road where the car was parked?'

'I didn't notice any. I think I would have seen it if there was.'

'Does anyone else have a set of keys to your car?'

'No, just me.'

'Is it one of those keyless cars?'

'Yes. The car doors open when you get close to the car, and it has a button to start it. How did you know?'

'I could have guessed it would be. We see more of them stolen than anything else. Do you remember the steering locks people used to have years ago? I'd recommend anyone who has a keyless car to get one of them, or ask the dealer to remove the keyless entry option.'

'What are the chances of getting the car back, do you think?'

The policeman shook his head and said, 'I wouldn't hold your breath, Mr Howard.'

Looking for a distraction after the constable left, Dan opened his laptop and scrolled through Facebook, checking out the business pages of some companies he'd dealt with in the past, hoping to find something to cheer him up.

He arrived at the Glad Rags page and saw a message pinned to the top with the title: *Permanently Closed.* Beneath was a note from the owners.

A big thank you to our loyal customers who have supported us since we opened Glad Rags five years ago. It has been a pleasure to work with you. Unfortunately, due to unforeseen circumstances, we have had to close our business, and we will no longer be able to supply your fancy dress outfits. Keep on partying, people! Love to you all, Amanda & Matt xxx.

Dan took a bottle of Prosecco from the fridge, uncorked it with a pop, and poured himself a glass of sparkling wine to celebrate. His campaign had finally succeeded. That fancy dress shop wouldn't just be unable to supply fancy dress outfits; it would no longer be able to insult customers by sending them inappropriate costumes.

He sat at the kitchen table, and his mind returned to his missing car. He supposed he would have to buy a new one as he couldn't manage without a car for long. How would he do his shopping? Asda offered a delivery service, so he could have his groceries delivered, but he preferred to choose his own produce. He considered himself to be a discerning buyer, and he couldn't trust a store employee to choose as wisely as he would himself.

How could he get a new car? He didn't have a car to drive to the car showrooms. There was public transport, he supposed, wrinkling his nose. He hadn't used that for years because he hated sitting next to people he didn't know. They could be ill and spreading germs everywhere, for all he knew. He could always book a taxi. A taxi appealed far more than taking a bus or the Metro, so he decided that was what he would do.

He would rather wait until Chris's day off so they could look at cars together. Not that Chris knew much about cars, because he didn't drive, but Dan didn't want to buy one alone.

When Chris came home that evening, Dan offered him a glass of Prosecco.

'What are we celebrating? Have the police found your car?'

'No such luck. But you know that fancy dress shop in town? The one that sent the Lone Ranger costume instead of Spider-Man. Well, I've just seen on Facebook that they've closed the business—permanently!'

'You're celebrating the downfall of a local business!' said Chris, with his hands planted on his hips. 'I don't understand how your mind works sometimes, Dan, but that's twisted. No, I don't want a glass of fizz, thank you very much.'

Dan glared at Chris as he turned away and ran up the stairs. Chris didn't know how much effort it had taken to make that happen, so how could he possibly understand how exhilarating achieving his goal had been?

43

A New Car

On Friday morning, Dan booked a taxi to take him and Chris to Scotswood Road to visit a car showroom. He couldn't wait to get a new car. How he'd managed a whole week without one, he didn't know. He'd tried ordering his groceries online, but the fresh produce was not what he would have chosen, and he sent most of it back to the shop. Then, he'd had to walk to the nearby shops to buy what he needed. There was a greengrocer's shop, a small supermarket, and a butcher's shop just a few streets away, but he couldn't return to that butcher's shop after being thrown out, so he'd had to walk even further to buy fresh meat.

They walked up and down the rows of parked cars in the yard at the car showroom until Dan saw a Mazda MX-5 and stopped in his tracks.

'I love this one!' he said.

'But it's yellow,' said Chris, pulling a face.

'I know,' said Dan. 'It's so bright and cheerful, don't you think?'

'It'll certainly stand out in a crowd.'

Dan went into the garage and asked a sales representative if he could take the car for a test drive. Within a few minutes, he pulled out onto the busy main road, his foot hard on the accelerator and the engine revving loudly.

Chris stood on the forecourt, rolling his eyes as he watched them leave, pleased that the car only had two seats, so he couldn't go with them. He didn't want to be seen in it.

'It's brilliant!' said Dan as he pulled back into the forecourt ten minutes later. 'I'll take it.'

'Thank you, Mr Howard,' said the salesman. 'If you'd like to come inside, we'll complete the paperwork.'

Dan filled out the forms and used his mobile phone to transfer the money from his bank account to the garage's account. Just like that, he was the proud owner of a very loud car, in all respects.

He walked out of the garage with a set of car keys, a pile of paperwork, and a huge grin.

On the way home, he stopped at a roadside pub for lunch to celebrate with Chris. Dan was in high spirits, delighted with his new purchase. Chris was much more subdued, and Dan suspected he might not be keen on his choice of car.

Later, when they pulled up outside their house on Somerset Road, they saw a police car parked in Dan's space.

'I wonder what this is about,' said Dan with a sense of dread.

'Your stolen car would be my best guess. That was your latest exploit, wasn't it?'

'It could be, I suppose.'

They stepped out of the car, and Police Constable Rob Marshall exited the patrol car.

'Daniel Howard,' he said, knowing full well the man he addressed was Dan.

'Yes,' Dan replied.

'Can we go inside for a moment?' He asked, nodding towards the house.

'Yes, of course.'

Dan unlocked the door, picked up the post from the doormat and dumped it on the hall table. Chris and the constable followed him into the house and sat in the lounge.

'We've located your car,' said the constable.

'Really!' said Dan. 'Oh! But I've just bought a new one. You said that there wouldn't be much chance of getting it back.'

'Where is the car?' asked Chris.

'A local resident reported a car parked out the back of his house, blocking his gateway.'

'But where?' asked Dan.

'It was found out the back of number sixty-four,' said the policeman.

'Number sixty-four, on which street?' asked Chris.

'Number sixty-four Somerset Road.'

'That's next door!' said Dan. 'I never park in the back lane. How on earth did it get there?'

'That's what we would like to know,' said the policeman. 'There's no damage to the car. No signs of forced entry. It looks like it was just—parked there.'

'What are you suggesting? You don't think I parked it there, do you?'

The policeman shrugged and waited for Dan to explain why he had reported his car had been stolen when it was on the back street near his home.

'I didn't put it there,' said Dan. 'I came back from Asda and parked right outside my house. I remember it clearly because I'd been to the supermarket and had shopping to carry in.'

The policeman shook his head slightly, and Dan knew he didn't believe him. He couldn't have parked his car out the back of the house—surely, he would have remembered that.

'I would move it right away if I were you, or it might be towed,' said the policeman. 'It's causing an obstruction, and your neighbour isn't very happy about it. He can't use his gate. I'm sure you know we take a dim view of people who waste police time.'

The constable left the house, and Chris sighed.

'I didn't park it on the back street, I swear,' said Dan. 'You believe me, don't you?'

'It's one drama after another with you, Dan. I don't know what to believe any more, and I'm not sure I can live like this any more either. I'm going out for a run, and then after dinner, there's a football match on that I want to watch—Leicester City is playing Southampton. It should be a good game.'

Chris changed into his running clothes and went out, leaving Dan alone.

Dan glanced at the pile of letters that had arrived in the post. The top one looked official, so he thought he had better open it before he went to retrieve his Mercedes. His face fell when he read it. How could he have forgotten to pay the parking fine that he'd got outside that pub when he removed the card with his phone number on it? *Where was the paperwork?* He couldn't remember what he'd done with it, but what did it matter? The date to pay at the lower rate was long gone. They were threatening to hand his case over to enforcement agents if he didn't pay the fine immediately.

He phoned the number on the letter and paid the fine in full with his debit card, but he let the man on the phone know he thought it ridiculous that he'd got a ticket when he'd only been there for a few minutes.

It was about half an hour after the policeman left before Dan took his keys from the hook and walked through the garden to move his car from the back lane. Thankfully, the car was still there.

Dan tried to edge his way between the wall and the car to get to the driver's door, but he couldn't. The gap was too narrow. How could the police think he'd parked the car there when he couldn't have got out?

Opening the passenger side door, he stepped back and covered his nose. The smell emanating from the car was disgusting. He waited for the odour to disperse somewhat before sticking his head inside and wondering if he could climb into the driver's seat from there.

Until this moment, he had considered the Mercedes to be a spacious car, but he wished it were larger still. He had to try because the only other option was to lose two or three stone in weight to reach the driver's door.

Dan tried climbing in head first, clambering across to the driver's seat, but his legs were trailing behind, and he was unable to manoeuvre them into the driver's footwell, so he backed out, bum first, and tried again with his feet first this time, and eventually slid into the seat.

Dan drove to the front of the house and parked on the street outside. Standing on the roadside, he looked at the two cars parked together and shook his head. He didn't know what to do. He loved his Mercedes and the new Mazda, but he couldn't keep them both. He had a hard decision to make. *What a dilemma!*

At dinner that evening, Dan was glad Chris was in a better mood after his run and asked him for his opinion on which car he should keep.

'The Mercedes. No question. It's a much better car.'

From that brief comment, Dan realised he had been right—Chris didn't like the Mazda. But it had been love at first sight for Dan, and he would be devastated to return it to the garage.

44

Returning The Car

The following morning, Dan drove the yellow Mazda MX-5 back to the garage on Scotswood Road and parked in front of the showroom.

'Is there something wrong with the car, Mr Howard?' asked the car salesman when Dan entered the garage.

'No, it's great!' said Dan. 'It's just that I've got my old car back, so I don't need this one any more.'

'The one that was stolen?' asked the salesman. 'Wow! You're a lucky man. I've never heard of anyone getting a car back when it's gone missing before. They're usually used for crimes and found burnt out somewhere, or taken for a joyride and found smashed up at the side of the road. Sometimes they disappear completely, and I suspect they're broken down for parts.'

'Well, I guess I must be lucky,' said Dan, feeling far from it. He handed over the keys to the yellow sports car. 'When can I expect the money to be returned to my bank account?'

'Well, if there's nothing wrong with the car, I'm afraid the payment can't be returned to you. It's not as simple as that,' said the salesman, sitting at his desk. 'You're only entitled to a refund if the car is faulty. You can trade it in for another car if you like, or if you prefer, we can buy it from you. I can work out a price.'

'I've already told you I don't need this car,' said Dan, sitting opposite him. 'I got my Mercedes back yesterday, so I don't need to trade it in either. If you buy it off me, can you give me what I paid for it yesterday?'

'Let me see,' said the salesman, looking at the documents on his desk and keying numbers into a calculator. 'You paid a little under twenty-five thousand for her. The best price we can offer you today, if you're not buying another car, would be twenty-one grand.'

'You mean it's cost me four grand to own this car for one day and drive it across the town and back?' asked Dan, frantically rubbing his hands through his thinning hair.

'Do you want some time to think about it?' asked the salesman.

'What! So you can reduce the offer even further?' said Dan petulantly. 'You must think I'm mad. I'll take it to We'll Buy Your Car and see what they'll give me for it.'

'Suit yourself,' said the salesman, shrugging his shoulders as he stood up and held open the door.

Dan stormed out of the garage, got into the Mazda, and took his phone from his pocket. He entered the vehicle's details into the We'll Buy Your Car website, waited for the online car company's offer, which came back as £22,500, and made an appointment to take it to Kingston Park, just a few miles up the road. One and a half grand more, and one more chance to drive the yellow car. Dan grinned.

He drove to Kingston Park, and when he arrived at We'll Buy

Your Car, a wiry man with a sparse beard introduced himself as Colin and examined the car.

'Can I start her up?' he said. 'Do you have the keys?'

Dan gave Colin the keys and watched him check everything from the engine to the bodywork to the boot space.

'There's one or two faults that may affect the online quotation a bit,' he said. 'Come inside and we'll have a chat.'

Dan followed Colin into his office, which was a small portable building, and they sat down. Colin asked a multitude of questions and wanted to see the paperwork for the car. Dan handed over the pile of papers from the garage.

'Wow! I've never seen a three-year-old car with eight previous owners before. Do you have the service history?'

'The what?'

'Records of its services, replacement parts, anything like that.'

'No, I've given you all I've got.'

Colin signed loudly.

'Well, Mr Howard, the original quote was for £22,500. That was based on one previous owner and a full-service history. Having eight previous owners and no service history isn't doing this car any favours, and then there's the matter of the small dent on the nearside back wheel arch and the chip in the bottom corner of the windscreen.'

Colin played on his laptop for a while and then looked up at Dan.

'The maximum price for this vehicle in this condition is eighteen grand, but the good news is that I do have some leeway on that, and I can offer you nineteen. How does that sound?'

'But—but—'

Dan was stuck for words. How could they reduce their offer by £3,500 in the time it took him to drive across the city?

'Do you want to sell it?' asked Colin. 'We can have the money in your bank account in a couple of days, or for a small fee, you could have it as soon as tomorrow.'

'I don't want to sell it at that price!'

He grabbed the keys and paperwork off the desk and rushed out to the car. He revved the engine loudly as he exited the car park.

What should he do now? Go home and consider his options. Return to Scotswood Road, take the garage's offer and accept the loss. Or call Chris for advice. No, he couldn't call Chris, not after how he had reacted the previous day when the police found the Merc.

After cruising around the city for a while, he returned to the car showroom in Scotswood.

'Welcome back, Mr Howard,' said the salesman. 'Have we changed our mind?'

When Dan saw the smug look on his face, he almost climbed back into the car and drove away, but he didn't need two cars; he had to sell it.

'Yes, I'll take your offer,' he said, tight-lipped. 'Can we sort out the paperwork as quickly as possible?'

'Of course we can. Come inside and we'll complete the transaction in no time at all.'

The salesman grinned as he held open the door for Dan to enter his office.

45

Reporting Back

'You asked me to keep an eye out for Dan Howard,' said Rob Marshall, as he put his lunch tray on the canteen table and sat down opposite Ali Hanlon. 'Did you know I was called out to Howard's place when you were on holiday?'

'No. What was that for?' she asked, pushing her empty plate to one side and reaching for her coffee mug.

'He reported his car was stolen from outside his house,' he said, unwrapping a ham salad sandwich. 'Two days later, the same neighbour who reported the cannabis plant in Howard's garden phoned to say somebody had abandoned a car out the back of his house, blocking his gateway. Guess who the car belonged to?'

'Dan Howard.'

'You got it in one,' he said, nodding and taking a bite of the sandwich.

'Insurance fraud?'

'No, I don't think so. Nobody in their right mind would park a car so close to their home and not expect it to be found. I think he must have forgotten where he'd parked it.'

'Hmm,' said Ali, trying to remember the details in Dan Howard's file. 'Don't you think it's strange this fella has flown under our radar for years when we've seen so much of him in the last few months?'

'What are you getting at?'

'I'm not sure,' she said, her hands wrapped around her warm coffee mug. 'Maybe he's having a hard time for some reason and it's a cry for help.'

'I don't know about that. He has a lovely place in Jesmond, and a partner living with him. The other guy's in a different league, to be honest.'

'Sounds like you fancy him,' said Ali.

'Not my type, but if I were that way inclined, then he'd be in with a chance,' laughed Rob. 'Seriously though, I can't imagine he has money troubles, living in a big house like that with a nearly new Mercedes parked outside.'

'I'm pleased to hear he has support at home,' she said. 'Do you think we should ask social services to check on him?'

'There's no need for that. Let's see how things go for now, shall we?'

'Alright, that's fine by me. It's not like we're looking for stuff to do. I've been busier than usual since I got back from leave—not that camping in Scotland with two demanding children was a break, I can tell you. I'm ready for a holiday after that! Anyway, let me know if you have any more run-ins with Howard. I know he rubs people up the wrong way, but I can't help thinking there's more going on here than meets the eye. Perhaps he has underlying mental health issues—or early-onset dementia. Who knows?'

'Don't worry,' said Rob. 'I'll keep an eye out for him.'

'Thanks, Rob. Oh, I forgot to ask. How did your date go the

other night?'

'It wasn't all bad, but I won't be seeing her again.'

'Why not?'

'She drank like a fish. She got through the best part of two bottles of wine by herself and didn't stop giggling all night.'

'Never mind. Better luck next time. Shit! Is that the time?' asked Ali, looking at her phone. She grabbed a bag from under the table and put her phone in it. 'I need to pick up the bairns from the childminder's and the traffic will be a nightmare at this time of day!'

Rob watched Ali run out of the canteen, wishing he could do something to help her. Since her husband left, she had been struggling to cope with a demanding job and to care for two children. He couldn't believe the stupid git had walked out on them.

After his two-year marriage to an abusive woman, Rob would do anything to have Ali for his wife, and he'd be happy to take on her two fantastic kids as well. He loved kids. He'd always wanted them, but his ex-wife didn't.

Was it still too soon to ask her out?

46

The Foul Smell

As he had failed to remove the awful smell from the Mercedes when he'd cleaned it, Dan thought he should take it to a car valet. The smell was so bad that it desperately needed cleaning. Adverts for a place near Eldon Square that offered car valets while you shopped often popped up on his Facebook feed, so he decided to take it there.

Holding his nose, he got into the Mercedes. The fishy odour was overpowering. He drove into town as quickly as possible, trying not to breathe through his nose, and hoping the smell wouldn't taint his clothes. He pulled up outside the car valet garage, and a young man approached him to assess the job.

'It stinks!' he said, wrinkling his nose in distaste. 'What have you had in here?'

'It does,' said Dan, who had tolerated the disgusting odour all the way from Jesmond. 'I have no idea why it smells this bad.'

'It will need a full valet to get rid of that. That's eighty quid for a car this size, but that includes exterior waxing and everything.'

'How long will it take?'

'We can have it ready for you in about three hours.'

'Great! See you then.'

That would give Dan plenty of time to browse in his favourite shops and go somewhere nice for lunch—maybe the new French restaurant he'd seen advertised recently.

After a successful shopping spree, Dan carried a new sweater, a new jacket, and a pair of Italian leather shoes in branded polythene bags. The Italian shoes were on sale at half price. They were a little too small for him. They were size eight, and he usually wore size nine or nine and a half, so they pinched a bit when he tried them on, but the craftsmanship was beautiful, and they were such a bargain at just over a hundred pounds for the pair. He couldn't resist them.

Then, Dan gorged himself on *confit de canard* at the new French restaurant called *Chez Moi*. He was disappointed he couldn't drink Bordeaux with his meal because he was driving home. After ten minutes of humming and harring about what drink he should have, he eventually settled for a small glass of wine. Just one small glass would be alright, wouldn't it?

He hardly recognised his car when he returned to collect it after lunch. The paintwork gleamed, and the alloys looked as good as new. He opened the door and couldn't believe how fresh it smelled inside. The rotten smell had vanished, and the only scents he could detect were leather from the seats and polish from the dashboard.

'Thank you!' said Dan, handing over his card to pay. 'You've done a wonderful job.'

'We found this under the front passenger seat,' said the man, holding out the missing parking ticket. 'I thought you might need it.'

'I've already paid it. Put it in the bin, would you?'

'And we found where the smell came from,' he said, holding a package at arm's length. 'We found this in the boot. A pack of mussels—well past its sell-by date. No wonder it smelled so bad!'

'Oh, my God!' said Dan, thinking the mussels must have fallen out of his carrier bag when he drove back home from the supermarket. *So, it wasn't the checkout operator who took them!* 'I wondered where they'd got to. Thanks again.'

Dan took the keys and drove home, absolutely delighted with his day in town.

47

Bad News

November 2019

James was bored. Incredibly bored. He was so bored that he had even considered cleaning his flat. He missed his old routine of getting up for work in the mornings, coming home and seeing Lisa in the evenings. Sitting on the sofa, he leaned forward and put his head in his hands. He wanted to scream.

If he'd lost his job because he'd done something wrong, like not showing up for work or stealing from the company, he could have lived with that, but he had done nothing wrong. He'd lost his job because of Dan Fucking Howard, who had set out to destroy Glad Rags. His only reason for doing that was that the costume he'd ordered was out of stock, and he didn't like the alternative outfit Amanda had sent him to replace it.

What the fuck!

Because of Dan Howard, Glad Rags was no more, and all three staff members were out of a job. James guessed that Matt and Amanda must have lost all the money they'd invested in the shop, too.

It was no wonder Amanda was suffering from depression. She had invested everything in that shop: her money, her time, her hopes, and her dreams. It should also have been her future, but Dan Howard came along and destroyed everything she had worked for.

Matt was resourceful. James was sure he'd find something else to do work-wise. But from what he'd said about Amanda, showing no interest in anything, it sounded like she might be heading for a nervous breakdown.

How many more lives would that bastard ruin with his vindictive internet attacks when things didn't go his way?

On the night he'd lost his job, James stayed home because he was upset. Lisa went out on the town with her friends, and she'd got off with that bloke. He wished more than anything that he'd gone out with her that night when she asked.

If he had gone, Lisa wouldn't have met her new man. She would still be his lover, and she may even have moved in with him by now, but he didn't, and he could do nothing to change that.

Tears rolled down his cheeks, and he wondered if he might be heading towards a nervous breakdown, too. He felt so alone, bored, and fucking useless.

A short while later, he dragged himself out of the house to go for a walk. He wandered around the local streets and Heaton Park for an hour or two, and when he felt a little better, he returned to his flat.

A note had been pushed through the letterbox. He picked it up and saw it had his name handwritten on it, so he unfolded the paper and read the message inside.

Hi James, Sorry I missed you. I hoped to speak to you in person. Please call me when you get home. Matt. P.S. It's important.

James went upstairs to his flat, stroked Whiskers, who was lying on the sofa, and then dialled Matt's number. Matt answered the call on the first ring.

'Hello, Matt?'

'James. Thanks for getting back to me. I'm sorry I missed you when I called at your place earlier. Are you okay?'

'Yes,' he lied.

'I'm afraid I have some terrible news.' Matt sniffed loudly at the other end of the phone. His voice forced, he said, 'I'm very sorry to have to tell you that Amanda died yesterday. She took an overdose.'

'No!' said James, shaking his head as the horrifying words sank in. 'I'm so sorry, Matt. I don't know what to say. Is there anything I can do?'

'No, I don't think so. I just wanted to let you know. I'll be in touch about the funeral when we've got the arrangements sorted.'

James heard voices in the background.

'Amanda's parents are staying with me. They're helping with all that.'

'That's good. But if there's anything I can do, please get in touch.'

'Will do,' said Matt. 'You know, Amanda thought a lot about you. She never got over having to make you redundant. It hit her very hard.'

'Thanks, Matt,' said James, silent tears running down his face. 'I thought a lot about her, too. She was a very special lady. Take care of yourself.'

He disconnected the call, his hands shaking. Going to the sofa, he sat next to the kitten, who seemed to know he was upset. She climbed onto his lap and purred loudly, rubbing her head against his hand.

Poor Amanda, and poor Matt.

The news of her death had come as a complete shock. James knew she was in a bad way after the shop closed. Matt had said as much, but James had never considered that she might take her own life.

When he'd met them, the Armstrongs were a kind, thoughtful, and hard-working couple, and they had been so good to him. They didn't deserve any of this. They should have had a long and happy life together, but now that could never happen. Matt would spend the rest of his life alone, without the woman he loved by his side.

Amanda ended her life because her business failed, and the failure of her business was due to Dan Fucking Howard.

James could not contain the scream that built up inside him this time. He yelled and threw himself down on the couch, violent sobs racking his body.

That evening, James felt empty, devoid of any emotion. It was as if they had all drained out of his body with his tears. He saw his reflection in the bathroom mirror and hardly recognised himself. His eyes were red-rimmed and swollen, his cheekbones were more prominent, and his skin was pale.

He thought he must be in a state of shock. His mind and his body seemed to be working in slow motion. He felt confused. *Was this a nightmare? Had he imagined talking with Matt? Was Amanda really dead?*

On his return to the living room, James saw Matt's note on the coffee table. He checked his phone, and it showed an outgoing call to Matt that afternoon, lasting for around three minutes. *Fuck!* It was real. Amanda was dead.

James picked up the cigarette lighter that Lisa had left at his flat, put it in his pocket, and walked out the door.

He walked through the dark streets of Newcastle until he arrived at Somerset Road about half an hour later. Dan's car was in its usual place. No longer caring if anybody saw him, James went to the front of the Mercedes and knelt on the tarmac. Taking the lighter from his pocket, he flicked it, and the yellow flame glowed in the darkness. He held the flame to the corner of the plastic number plate until it melted, and he watched in fascination as the flame spread along the bottom edge.

His eyes were fixed on the car, which had a strange orange hue surrounding it. The paintwork around the grill bubbled in the heat, and then something under the bonnet caught fire, intensifying the heat.

Standing up, he moved to the unlit side street and stood at the corner of Dan's house, watching the fire take hold.

He saw Dan and Chris run from the house towards it. Chris stopped Dan from getting any closer, saying, 'Keep back! It might explode.'

Dan stood outside his house, staring at the car and looking bewildered, while Chris called the fire service. Five minutes later, a fire engine with blue flashing lights arrived and stopped near the car, which was now well alight, with flames towering two metres above it. The windows cracked in the heat, and the leather seats emitted a sulphurous smell.

Within minutes, the firemen extinguished the fire, and water poured down the road and into the drains.

A police car pulled up, and two officers examined the skeletal remains of the car before following Dan and Chris into the house.

That is for Amanda!

48

Fire, Fire

'I don't believe it,' said Dan, running his hands through his hair. 'My car!'

'Sit down, Dan,' said Chris, helping his partner to an armchair, and he perched on the chair arm to stay close to him. He gestured for the police officers to sit on the sofa.

'You know who I am, don't you, Dan? I'm Sergeant Ali Hanlon. And you remember Police Constable Rob Marshall?'

Dan nodded and wiped his nose with the back of his hand. Chris fetched him a tissue, and Dan wiped his eyes and blew his nose.

Looking into the tissue, he said, 'My snot's black. How disgusting is that!'

'That's from the fire, Dan. It's just soot,' said the sergeant. 'Are you feeling alright?'

'No! I'm not feeling alright. My car has been burned out, right outside my house. I'm scared. What if they had set fire to the house while we were asleep?'

'I'm sorry about your car,' said the constable. 'It could have been an accident, you know, something wrong with the car.

It might be arson, but we'll have to wait for the fire officer to confirm that.'

'Of course, it's arson,' said Dan. 'I told you somebody was out to get me.'

'There's no evidence for that,' said the constable. 'We talked about CCTV when I was here before. Have you had any cameras installed since then?'

'You won't believe this,' said Dan. 'The contractors are coming tomorrow to fit two on the house, one out the front and one out the back. I booked it weeks ago, but they had a long waiting list. That's just my luck, isn't it?'

Dan turned his face into Chris's side to hide his tears, and Chris put his arm around him.

'I don't think there's anything else we can do tonight,' said Sergeant Hanlon. 'We'll be back to follow up tomorrow.'

The officers returned to the patrol car and sat for a while, watching the firemen finish cleaning up around the car and making the area safe before driving away.

'I see what you mean about his partner,' said Ali. 'He's a good-looking bloke.'

Rob laughed.

'But seriously, I thought Howard was going into shock back there—around the time he was talking about his snot,' she said. 'I almost called for an ambulance.'

'Yeah, that crossed my mind as well, but I think he's okay. He was like a child the way he was going on.'

'He's certainly an odd one. Do you think it was a targeted arson attack on his car?' she asked.

'On a Sunday night, it's more likely to be kids setting fire to it for kicks. But he was right about his luck. If the CCTV had been fitted sooner, we'd have been able to see exactly what happened.'

'If we had more resources,' she said. 'I'd have a car come round here more often, just to monitor the place, but we haven't.'

'Do you believe him? It sounds like you think somebody might be out to get him.'

'I don't know. There's a good chance it's all in his mind, but there have been a lot of incidents involving him recently. More than you'd expect.'

'Down to his bad luck again,' he said. 'Do you want to grab a takeaway before we head back to the station? There are a few good ones around here.'

'Yeah, that's a great idea,' said Ali, fastening her seat belt. 'I skipped lunch today, and I'm starving!'

49

The Yellow Car

It took Dan an entire week to recover from the attack on his car. During that time, he barely slept. Whenever he tried, nightmares about fires woke him—things he loved being on fire, being trapped in a fire, and being engulfed by flames.

He spent most of his time in bed, wearing his pyjamas and dressing gown, feeling sorry for himself, and playing on his laptop and phone.

Chris took a few days' leave from work to care for him, and he dealt with the police and the insurance company on Dan's behalf.

The fire officer claimed there was no evidence of arson, so the police didn't investigate further, and they recorded the car fire as an accident. The insurance company agreed to pay out on that basis, and they credited Dan's bank account with the funds that morning.

'We should get you a new car,' said Chris, setting a mug of coffee for Dan on the bedside table and sitting on the edge of the bed. 'Would you like to go car shopping this afternoon?'

'I don't feel like going out. I'd rather stay here.'

'We could see if that yellow car you liked is still for sale.'

At the mention of the MX-5, Dan's eyes lit up, and the corners of his mouth edged towards a smile.

'Do you think it might be?'

'I think there's a very good chance it will be,' said Chris, thinking who else in their right mind would buy a yellow sports car?

Dan climbed out of bed and removed his dressing gown.

'Okay. I'll have a shower, and I'll be down soon. Have you booked us a taxi?'

Chris chuckled and then called a local taxi firm, arranging for them to be picked up in thirty minutes.

Dan spotted the yellow car as soon as he arrived at the garage. It stood out among the white, grey and black cars that filled the monochrome yard, along with an occasional splash of blue or red. But there was only one yellow car.

'Look! It is still here,' said Dan. 'You were right.'

The men wandered over to it and looked around the car. It was just as Dan remembered it, but this time he noticed the tiny crack in the windscreen and the small dent in the bodywork.

The price displayed on the sun visor board was £24,950, which is what he paid for the car the last time he bought it.

Armed with the knowledge that it had a few minor imperfections, they went into the showroom, where the salesman, recognising them, greeted them apprehensively.

'What can I do for you, gentlemen?'

'I'd like to buy the MX-5 out there—the yellow one,' said Dan. 'As there is some minor damage to it, I would like a discount off the asking price.'

'What damage? Show me.'

They all went out to view the car, and Dan pointed out the

faults.

'I see. I can knock off five hundred quid for that.'

'Great!' said Dan, pleased he'd got the car at a discounted price. 'We'll take it.'

Dan knew he was paying far more than the garage had given him for the car when he returned it, but he wanted it. He loved this car and couldn't wait to drive it again. It had been ages since he'd been shopping, or anywhere else for that matter, and he couldn't wait to get out and about again.

After they completed the paperwork and Dan made the payment, he shook the salesman's hand and thanked him. He then grabbed the keys from the table, marched proudly to the car, and grinned as he got inside.

Revving the engine, he turned to Chris in the passenger seat and said, 'It's even better than I remembered. Thank you!'

50

Amanda's Funeral

The alarm on James's phone woke him at seven-thirty. He stretched and yawned, struggling to remember why he'd set it. He reached over the side of the bed, picked his phone up off the floor, and switched off the incessant beeping.

That was right. It was Wednesday. It was the day of Amanda's funeral.

James showered and then dressed in dark jeans and a black hoodie—the best he could do to conform to the long-established tradition of wearing black to a funeral. He didn't own a suit, never mind a black one for an event such as this.

He fed Whiskers before going downstairs, where he found a pile of letters on the doormat. Glancing through them, he saw that one was from the city council.

He opened the letter and read it.

Dear Mr Webster, Thank you for your application to work at Newcastle City Council as a Ground Maintenance Assistant. We were inundated with applications for this vacancy. As there were other candidates who more closely matched the job criteria and person specification, we will not be taking your application any further on this occasion. Yours faithfully, Miss E Moreno.

James's heart sank. This was the job that he wanted. He knew he would have enjoyed it, and the salary would have covered his monthly bills; the money situation had reached a critical level. Give them credit, though; at least they had replied. Only the council and the hospital had. He'd received nothing from the other companies, not even an acknowledgement of his application.

The other letters were junk. He took them to his flat, threw them in the bin, and placed the council letter with his job search materials.

Then James made his way to the crematorium, arriving a little later than intended, but still in plenty of time for Amanda's funeral.

He looked around at the sombre people outside, Amanda's family and friends, dressed in black and talking in hushed voices. Sedate church music emanated from the loudspeakers in the waiting area.

Amanda would have hated this.

If Amanda had arranged her own funeral, she would have had people dressed in colourful clothes, laughing and enjoying themselves, with lively music playing in the background.

Matt approached James and parked his wheelchair beside him.

'I wasn't sure you'd come,' he said. 'But I'm glad you're here.'

'Of course, I'd come,' said James, placing a hand on Matt's shoulder. 'I loved Amanda. You know that. How are you doing, Matt?'

'Pretty crap, to be honest,' he said. 'I can't believe she's gone. I know it sounds daft, but I keep expecting her to walk through the door, or to shout from the kitchen that dinner's ready, or to sit on the couch next to me when I'm watching telly and grab the remote to change the channel. When I turn over in bed and she's not there—that's the worst. I can't believe how much I miss her.' Tears welled up in his eyes, and he took a handkerchief from his pocket to wipe them. 'I can't believe she's gone, James. I don't know what I'll do without her.'

'You'll get through this, Matt. I know you will.

James hugged his friend.

Matt's mother-in-law came over and whispered, 'It's time to go inside.'

Matt's face was pale and stony as he entered the crematorium and manoeuvred his wheelchair to the front of the room, stopping next to his in-laws' seats.

James didn't know anyone else there, so he sat alone near the back and listened to the touching service commemorating Amanda's life. The stories from her childhood were funny: she ate an entire birthday cake before anyone arrived for her seventh birthday party, and at a school pantomime, she had recited everyone's lines, as well as her own. She had loved dressing up even then. From the anecdotes, he could tell everyone was so proud of her for what she'd done in her lifetime, especially for her relationship with Matt and her achievements in business.

It was apparent that Amanda had been happy and content with her life until recently.

A couple of Amanda's friends stood at the front of the room and paid tribute to the wonderful woman Amanda was, their voices breaking and tears flowing down their cheeks.

Amanda had been the most vibrant person James had ever known, and she was just thirty years of age when she died. If

Dan Howard hadn't ruined her business and, therefore, her life, he wondered what her future would have looked like.

She and Matt had a solid relationship, and James had little doubt that they would have stayed together and brought up a family. Amanda would have made a fantastic mother. He was sure the business would have continued to thrive and, in time, become a family business to support the next generation of Armstrongs—her children who would never be born now.

After the speeches, it was time for the last goodbye.

James wiped his eyes with his sleeve and watched the coffin move along the conveyor and disappear behind a curtain. Then, louder modern music started playing over the speakers. Halo by Beyoncé. Amanda had loved Beyoncé. James remembered her dancing around the shop to the Single Ladies (Put a Ring on It) track, which brought a smile to his lips.

How he wished he'd put a ring on Lisa's finger before it was too late.

The mourners filed outside, leaving donations in the collection box for a well-known mental health charity. James tried to pass inconspicuously. He didn't have money to spare for a donation, and in his current condition, he thought maybe he should be on the receiving end of the donations, rather than being expected to give them.

As he stepped outside, the bright sunshine seemed out of place for the sombre occasion. He saw a rainbow in the sky and smiled. That was Amanda up there. Bright and colourful, smiling down on the people she loved. A lump formed in his throat.

'We're going for a drink, James,' said Matt. 'Do you want to come with us?'

James fancied a drink but didn't want to drag out this day

any longer than necessary, and he couldn't afford to buy a round.

'No, but have one for me.'

He hugged Matt again before turning to leave the grounds.

'Keep in touch,' said Matt, as James walked away.

James returned to Heaton, his thoughts dominated by the death of Amanda, trying to get his head around the scarcely credible reason for her suicide. Dan Howard. He still found it hard to understand how a man who had never met Amanda could be responsible for her death. *How could that even happen?*

When he got home, Dan Howard was well and truly fixed in James's head. He switched on the television, grabbed his laptop and sat on the sofa, where he was joined by Whiskers, who stretched out beside him. As he watched the news, the screen suddenly turned black, and there was no sound. Nothing he pressed on the remote control turned it back on.

James stood up and flicked the light switch. The light did not come on. Wondering if a fuse had blown, he checked the fusebox, but everything looked fine. Then, he realised what had happened. The electricity to his flat had been disconnected. *Shit!* The electricity bill was at the bottom of the pile of unpaid bills on the kitchen worktop.

Thankfully, he'd charged his mobile phone overnight. He put it in his pocket, went out, and walked to Jesmond. When he arrived at Somerset Road, he stood at the bus stop and scrolled through the gallery on his mobile to find the photo he wanted. He scanned for available Wi-Fi connections in the area and connected his mobile to Dan's network, using the password displayed on the router image. Then, signing in as an admin with another password on the router, he changed the password for Dan's Wi-Fi network to *Vigilante*.

James waited for an email to arrive in Dan's email inbox, informing him of the password change, and when it appeared, he moved it into the spam folder. That was it. His job was done.

As he walked home, he thought back to when he lost his job and Lisa, and then when Matt and Amanda lost their business. James had wanted to make Dan suffer because he caused their suffering, but the death of Amanda had raised the ante.

51

Paranoia

Chris had gone to the gym on Saturday morning to cover a couple of classes for a colleague who was on leave, and he would be home by lunchtime. Dan wanted to go online while Chris was out of the house, but he couldn't connect his laptop to the Wi-Fi. *There must be a glitch somewhere.* Eventually, he gave up and looked for something else to do that morning instead of surfing the internet.

The kitchen cupboards hadn't been cleaned for a while. He removed everything from the shelves, and once the shelves were empty, he scrubbed them clean. Then, he sprayed them with disinfectant and gave them a final wipe.

Happy that the shelves were spotless, he cleaned the glass containers of herbs and spices, checking the use-by dates, before returning them to the shelves or putting them in the kitchen bin.

The cardboard and paper packets containing gravy powder and flour were more problematic. He couldn't wash them, so he checked the dates and then returned or tossed them. He should really have some plastic containers for things like that.

It would be much more hygienic. If only he could get online, he would order some right now.

Dan tried again, but his phone and laptop still would not connect to the wireless network. He supposed he could use the 4G connection on his phone, but he was dangerously close to exceeding his monthly limit. He didn't want to incur his phone company's extortionate additional charges.

So he turned his attention to the cutlery drawer. *How could a cutlery drawer get so dirty?* He took out the cutlery and washed it, leaving it on the drainer to dry. Then, turning up his nose, he tackled the crumbs, hair and other bits and pieces of unidentifiable stuff in the cutlery divider. He considered throwing it away and buying a new one to replace it, but, as he didn't have access to the internet to shop online, he cleaned it, leaving it in a sink full of bleach solution to kill the germs.

When the tray had soaked for half an hour, he rinsed and dried it, and put it back in the drawer, which he had vacuumed, scrubbed and disinfected. He then returned the cutlery and admired his handiwork. The drawer was immaculate.

He returned to his laptop and was so engrossed that he barely acknowledged Chris when he returned from the gym.

'I can't get the Wi-Fi to work,' said Dan after a while, his tapping getting louder on the keyboard as his frustration increased.

'Leave it for a bit,' said Chris, who was watching a football match on television. 'It's probably just a glitch.'

'That's what I thought this morning, but it's still not working,' moaned Dan. 'There are things I need to do.'

'What's so important that it won't wait for an hour or two?'

'I need to check the CCTV cameras,' said Dan. And my emails and social media accounts, he thought, but he wouldn't tell

Chris that.

'You spend so much time replaying what happened around here on those cameras,' said Chris. 'It's not normal. You may as well sit and look out the window all day and watch everything as it takes place in real-time. Maybe we should go for a run when the game's finished. It would do you good.'

Dan pulled a face.

'How about a walk, then?' asked Chris. 'Come on! It's a nice day out there.'

'It's cold,' said Dan begrudgingly, closing his laptop. 'But okay.'

'Great!'

When the match finished, Chris jumped up from his seat and took his jacket off the hook by the door. 'It'll do you good to get outside more. Switch off from all that social media stuff. It's not good for you, you know. I read an article about how spending too much time online is adversely affecting people's mental health.'

Dan put on his coat and thought it was typical that Chris was having yet another go at him. Chris had never liked how much time he spent online, and this wasn't the first time he'd mentioned mental health issues either. Chris had suggested that he might be paranoid a few times now.

His mind was in turmoil as they walked along the street towards Jesmond Dene, and he toyed with the question: was he paranoid?

'You're quiet,' said Chris. 'Is everything alright?'

'Yes, everything's fine,' said Dan defensively. 'There's nothing wrong with me, if that's what you're implying.'

'I'm not implying anything,' said Chris. 'I'm just worried about you, that's all.'

Dan continued to walk in silence, stewing over Chris's words and all the terrible things that had happened to him recently. Also, he wondered about Chris's reaction to some of those things. He hadn't been very supportive when he thought about it. In fact, Chris hadn't believed half of what he'd said, and on some occasions, he'd even implied that some things might be his fault.

'Look, Dan, if you didn't want to come for a walk, you should have said,' said Chris. 'I'd rather walk by myself than have you here with me in a bad mood like this. I hate all this negativity.'

'If that's how you feel, I'll go home,' said Dan huffily, turning around and retracing his steps, leaving Chris standing on the footpath, wondering what the hell was wrong with him.

When he got home, Dan removed his coat, sat in the lounge, and opened his laptop. Still no Wi-Fi connection. He typed his username and password from the router, but a pop-up insisted that the password he was using was incorrect. He retyped it several times, and the same thing happened repeatedly. A glitch, my arse, thought Dan.

He started a web chat with what he assumed was a bot:

Shalinka: Good afternoon. My name is Shalinka. May I take your name, please?

Dan: I'm Dan Howard. My Wi-Fi is not working today. When I try to sign in, it says my password is incorrect.

Shalinka: Thank you, Dan. Have you checked that you're using the correct password?

Dan: Yes, of course I have. I'm not bloody stupid, unlike you, asking such an ignorant question!

Shalinka: Please wait while I look into this for you.

Dan tapped his fingers on the chair arm for ages while he waited for a reply. He checked the time. It was three minutes past four. Was it too early for a glass of wine?

Two more tedious minutes passed. He left the laptop, went to the kitchen to pour a glass of Merlot, and returned to the lounge. He made himself comfortable in the armchair and then checked the chat box.

THIS CHAT HAS ENDED.

No! I was only gone a minute—no more than two. That was nothing, considering how the stupid bot kept me waiting for almost ten minutes!

Dan started a new chat and was once again connected to Shalinka. He rolled his eyes. *No surprise there.* He guessed that everyone using this chat facility would be connected to Shalinka.

Shalinka: Good afternoon. My name is Shalinka. May I take your name, please?

Dan: Dan Howard.

Shalinka: Thank you, Dan. How can I help you today?

Dan: You cut me off earlier before you solved my problem, you stupid bot.

Shalinka: What is your problem?

Dan: What's my problem? What's your problem, more like!

Shalinka: If you tell me the problem, Dan, then I may be able to help you.

Dan: I already told you once, you stupid bot. Don't you remember? My Wi-Fi is not working. It says my password is incorrect.

Shalinka: Thank you, Dan. Have you checked that you're using the correct password?

Dan: YES, I HAVE!

Shalinka: Please wait while I look into this for you.

Dan sighed and gulped his wine, not daring to take his eyes

off the screen in case he was disconnected from the web chat again. After five minutes, he received a reply.

Shalinka: Hello, Dan. Sorry for keeping you waiting. Your password was changed yesterday. Can you please confirm that you are entering your new password?

Dan: What! I never changed the password. There must be some mistake.

Shalinka: There's no mistake, Dan. I can see here that your password was changed yesterday. If you have forgotten your new password, you can reset the server by pressing a pin into the hole at the back and holding it for five seconds. This will restore it to the default passwords that are printed on the device. I hope this solves your problem.

Dan: Why would I need to do this when I DIDN'T CHANGE MY PASSWORD???!!!

'I didn't change the fucking password!' shouted Dan, banging his fists on the chair arms.

Chris opened the door to hear Dan yelling at his laptop.

'What's going on?' asked Chris, frowning when he noticed the almost empty wine glass on the side table at only twenty past four in the afternoon.

'Have you changed the Wi-Fi password? asked Dan.

'No.'

'The Wi-Fi wasn't working when I came back, so I contacted them about it,' he said. 'They said I changed my password yesterday, but I didn't!'

'Let me have a look,' said Chris, taking the laptop from Dan. He opened the email program and scrolled through the emails that Dan had received the previous day. Nothing about any passwords in there. Then he checked the spam folder, *et voilà!* An email confirming that Dan had changed the password the previous day.

'Look,' said Chris. 'There's an email here about your change of password.'

'But I didn't do it, Chris,' said Dan, his mind going back to yesterday, trying to remember what he was doing then, and wondering if perhaps he could have changed it, even though he didn't remember doing it.

'The chat box is still here,' said Chris, as he returned to the previous screen. Browsing through the conversation, his eyebrows knitted together as he read Dan's replies and saw his use of shouty capitals. 'I don't believe this,' he said. 'Before the chat ended, Shalika wrote, "For your information, I'm not a bot." Dan, this is a new low, even for you. There was a real person on the receiving end of your childish comments. How could you be so rude? The woman was just doing her job, and from what I can see, she was doing it well.'

Dan looked down and removed a bit of invisible fluff from his jumper. He was sick and tired of Chris treating him like a child. He sat in silence, stewing over Chris's harsh words.

'I see you haven't started on dinner yet,' said Chris. 'Don't make any for me. I'm going out.'

Good! I'll be able to have something I like for dinner for a change, thought Dan.

He ordered a large Texas BBQ pizza from Domino's, and while he waited for delivery, he opened his Wi-Fi account, reset his password, and waded through his social media accounts, replying to the comments on his posts.

52

Eviction

December 2019

James walked home from another depressing visit to the Jobcentre, which had been a complete waste of time. Yes, he'd come away with a couple of jobs to apply for, but did they really think he would get an assistant's job at a nail bar or a children's nursery?

He'd gone there every two weeks since the beginning of August, each time providing what little evidence he had about his earlier applications, searching for new jobs to apply for and signing the claim form—going through the motions—but it wasn't getting him anywhere.

When he entered his flat, he was startled to see the silhouette of a short, plump man standing by the window with his back to him. When the man turned to face him, James recognised his landlord, Mr Dasari.

'Mr Webster,' he said. 'I'm pleased you've decided to show up. I've been waiting here for over an hour. Are you aware that your rent is two months in arrears?'

'Yes.'

'Do you have the money to pay it?'

James shook his head and said, 'I lost my job. I'm looking for work.'

'If you can't pay me what you owe right now. I'm going to have to ask you to vacate these premises.'

'What? Just like that?'

James was at a loss for words. He had expected to get an eviction order through the post sometime in the future if he repeatedly failed to pay his rent, but he hadn't expected the owner to come to the flat and ask him to leave immediately.

'Yes, just like that,' said his landlord. 'I'll wait until you've packed your belongings. You can leave the furniture and anything you can't carry. It'll go some way to paying me back what you owe.'

'But you can't throw me out! I don't have anywhere to go.'

'I can, and I am.'

Mr Dasari stood with his arms folded. The look on his face left James in no doubt that he meant what he said. There was no room for negotiation.

Unable to believe he was being evicted from his flat, James grabbed a small rucksack and gathered his few belongings—his laptop, a change of clothes, the loose change on the kitchen top, the food from the cupboard and the milk from the fridge. He also packed a bowl from the kitchen cupboard.

He picked up Whiskers and walked out the door with his head held high, not knowing where he was going or what he would do. He may have looked calm on the outside, but on the inside, he was a combination of scared shitless and fucking livid.

What more can Dan Howard do to me?

After losing his job, his girlfriend and Amanda, losing his

home was the final straw.

53

Alone Again

Chris's off-key singing in the shower woke Dan, and he glanced at his phone. It was only seven-thirty in the morning—and it was Sunday. He tried to go back to sleep but failed miserably, so he sat up in bed, disconnected his phone from the charger on the bedside table, and browsed through his social media accounts.

An advert for personalised sweaters in a red, green, and white Christmas design caught his eye. He had bought nothing for Chris yet and thought it might be fun to have matching jumpers to wear on Christmas Day. He ordered two, one for each of them, personalised with their names.

He continued to browse the internet for more gifts and then searched for Christmas dinner ideas and table decorations. It would be their first Christmas together since Chris had moved in with him, and Dan wanted to make it a special occasion.

A few hours later, Dan wandered downstairs in his dressing gown and headed straight for the coffee maker. A cappuccino was precisely what he needed.

'You're up at last!' said Chris, sitting at the kitchen table and putting down his magazine. 'It's nearly eleven o'clock.'

'So what?' said Dan, taking a mug from the cupboard. 'I didn't have any reason to get up this morning. We have nothing planned.'

'I've been waiting for you. We need to talk.'

'For Christ's sake, Chris, let me get a cup of coffee. You know I'm not a morning person.'

'And I am,' said Chris wistfully. 'That's part of the problem. We're not compatible. We don't have anything in common.'

'That's not true!' said Dan, as the coffee maker gurgled and spluttered before pouring his coffee. 'We both like watching the soaps on TV after dinner.'

'No, you like watching the soaps on TV. I sit with you while you're watching them. That's different.'

'We both like good food,' said Dan, desperately racking his brains to think of something else they both enjoyed.

'Maybe, but our definitions of good food are very different. I like lean meat with salad and vegetables. You like carbs and sauces.'

'Where is this coming from, Chris?' asked Dan, sipping his coffee. 'Have I done something to upset you?'

'I started having doubts about us when you were getting phone messages from those guys,' said Chris. 'I know you returned at least two of their calls.'

'Have you been looking at my phone?' asked Dan, wondering what else Chris might have seen. 'How dare you spy on me!'

'Yes, I did,' said Chris. 'I needed to know where I stood with you.'

'I only rang them because—'

'I don't need to hear it,' said Chris. 'It's not just that, though. You've changed lately. I don't know how to put this, but your behaviour has been—well, just weird, and I never know if you're telling the truth.'

'I tell the truth most of the time,' said Dan, 'and I can honestly say that I've never cheated on you.'

'Do I believe that or not?' Chris shrugged. 'I don't know what to believe any more. I want an uncomplicated life, Dan, and I don't think I'll ever have that with you. I'm sorry, but I'm leaving.'

'You're what? You can't go! I love you.'

'I found a flat in Heaton. I picked up the keys yesterday, and I'm moving in today.'

'But Chris—'

'You'll not change my mind. I've been thinking about this for weeks now, and it's what I need to do.'

Chris stood up, handed Dan the torn card he'd found in his jacket pocket, smiled sadly, and then went upstairs to pack.

'This isn't what it looks like,' said Dan, shouting from the bottom of the stairs. 'I can explain.'

'You needn't bother. You'd be wasting your time and mine.'

Dan returned to the kitchen and sat at the table, his coffee mug in his hands, fighting back his tears. Why hadn't he got rid of that damned card from the pub?

He had to admit that he had been unsure about his relationship with Chris at times, but now that Chris was leaving, he felt totally gutted. He'd grown accustomed to sharing his home and life with someone special, and Chris was very special.

Chris came downstairs carrying a large sports bag and a rucksack. He nodded at Dan and walked towards the door.

'Chris!' shouted Dan, running after him. 'Please don't go!

'I'm sorry, Dan. I've made up my mind.'

Chris opened the door and stepped out of the house, and Dan

stood in the open doorway watching the man he loved walk away from him, wondering if he would ever see him again. He rubbed his eyes, which were glistening with tears, and closed the door.

Chris was gone.

Dan stood in the hall for a while, tears running down his face, wallowing in his sorrow. He wondered how he would manage without Chris. What would he do?

Bizarrely, one of the first things Dan thought about while in shock at Chris's abrupt departure was that he must cancel the order for the matching sweaters he'd placed that morning. They were no longer required because he would not be spending Christmas with Chris. But he did nothing about it. In fact, he didn't do much at all for a while.

That night, he climbed into an empty bed and cried. Chris had only been gone for twelve hours, and Dan missed him already.

Dan moped around the house for several days. His daily routine had been set to Chris's schedule: Chris having breakfast, Chris going to work, Chris returning from work, eating dinner with Chris, watching TV with Chris and then going to bed together.

Now that Chris was gone, Dan got up when he woke, ate when he wanted, which was more often than he should, and drank an inordinate amount of wine, day and night.

It was over a week before he was thinking clearly again.

He emailed the gift company and asked them to cancel and refund his order, and when they refused, he was terribly upset. Their reply said they had already knitted the sweaters with the names "Dan" and "Chris" on them. Dan could cancel his order, but he wouldn't receive a refund because the products were bespoke and could not be resold.

At last, Dan had something to distract him from his misery. He opened his laptop and wrote his standard email, threatening to leave bad reviews for the company unless they refunded his order in full. Then, he pressed send and excitedly awaited their response. He hoped they would refuse again so he could start another social media campaign against their company, as he had with the fancy-dress company. That had been so much fun.

While Chris had been living with him, he hadn't been able to do this as much as he liked. But now, he had all the time in the world to wreak havoc and vengeance on anybody who crossed him or refused to do what he asked.

Life without Chris might have its benefits, he thought.

54

Homelessness

As he drifted towards the town centre, James considered going to visit Matt in South Gosforth and asking if he could stay there for a while, just until he got something else sorted, but Matt had his own problems to deal with at the moment, and he didn't want to burden him with more.

He found a spot under the arch of a railway bridge to spend the night, thinking it would be drier there if it rained. He sat on the cold, hard tarmac and leaned back against the stone wall, cuddling Whiskers.

It was freezing. He pulled his hood up over his baseball cap and put his hands in his trouser pockets to warm them, wishing he owned a winter coat.

A young man approached him, offering to sell him drugs, but James dismissed him. He didn't see many more people that night, just a couple of dog walkers and a few drunks on their way home after a night out. Some threw coins his way as they passed.

Rats ran around near the water's edge, and he envied them. They would have a cosy nest to go home to when they finished whatever it was they were doing. He hadn't. They were entertaining to watch, but James hoped he wouldn't have to share the space with them for long. He nodded off for an hour or two, but it was difficult to sleep when his body was cold and tense.

The following morning, James woke with a start, unsure where he was. When he saw the river and bridge, the events of the previous day flooded his mind. A ten-pound note was tucked under the strap of his backpack, and he silently thanked his good Samaritan. Placing Whiskers in his bag, he went to a nearby cafe, where he charged his phone and laptop while he drank a mug of coffee and ate a bacon roll. He gave a piece of the bacon to the kitten hiding in his bag under the table, hoping she wouldn't purr too loudly and be discovered.

He stayed there as long as possible. The building was warm, and he felt his muscles relax as they warmed. He fired up his computer and checked Dan's email account, where he saw a message thread with a company called Gifts Galore. A quick internet search revealed it was an online gift store selling various personalised items.

From the emails between the shop owner and Dan, James could see that Dan had ordered matching Christmas sweaters for himself and Chris, emblazoned with their names. James pulled a face—matching personalised sweaters were just so awful, he couldn't imagine anyone wanting to wear them, but Dan had. Even Dan had changed his mind, though. He'd attempted to cancel the order, but the company refused his request because the gifts were personalised and made to order. When he could not get a refund, Dan threatened to post negative online reviews about the shop.

Déjà vu.

James shook his head. The situation was so reminiscent of what Dan had done to Amanda and Matt at Glad Rags that his stomach lurched. He saw the rest of the scenario playing out in his mind—a desperate shop owner attempting to defend himself from multiple online attacks, being forced to dismiss his staff, the subsequent closure of the business, and then the depression and desperation that followed. He couldn't allow that to happen again, not after what had happened to Amanda.

He ordered a second cup of coffee and considered his options, thinking about how he could prevent the same thing from happening again.

55

Drinking Alone

Even though Dan filled his days with unnecessary cleaning and browsing social media to distract himself from being alone, he still found time to shop at Asda and cook delicious food for himself. Now that he could eat whatever he liked, rather than having to cook healthy food for Chris, Dan decided to try some new recipes.

He gathered the ingredients for Spaghetti Carbonara with a rich cream sauce from the shelves at Asda and put them in his basket. *Yum!* His mouth watered at the thought of eating it later. He grabbed two bottles of Pinot Grigio to accompany it because he wasn't sure that one would be quite enough. It was only £5.25 per bottle, which was a very good price.

As he approached the checkout, the woman at the till saw him, looked away, and began fidgeting with the rings on her fingers. He recognised her. *Wasn't she the one who had dealt with the spilt milk incident?* That had been traumatic at the time, but it ended well enough. He wondered if she was the same woman who had misplaced the mussels for the seafood paella, although she hadn't misplaced them; he had. Knowing he should apologise, he thought better of it. It was all in the past now, and everyone knew it was best to put the past behind them.

'We have some self-service tills at the end of the row,' said the cashier. 'Would you like to try one?'

'Why would I want to use a self-service till when you're a till operator, and you're sitting here at this till ready to serve customers?' he asked. 'Anyway, it's your job to check out my shopping, not mine. Do I look like I work for Asda?'

'I'm sorry,' she said, with her head lowered. 'Most customers with hand baskets or just a few items use the self-service checkouts now.'

She scanned the items and placed them in a carrier bag.

'Stop! You can't put the wine at the top of the bag. It'll squash the stuff underneath it.'

The woman's hand froze in the air, holding a bottle of white wine in the air like a weapon.

Dan glared at her, and her face reddened.

'Put the wine bottles at the bottom of the bag where they belong.'

The shop assistant removed everything from the carrier bag and placed the two bottles of wine at the bottom and the other items on top.

'See, that wasn't so hard, was it?' said Dan, handing her his credit card.

After he paid, he picked up the bag and marched out of the shop without thanking her, wondering why people always had to be so difficult.

Chris had been difficult sometimes, yet Dan still missed him. His joy at his newfound freedom to go online whenever he wanted and eat whatever he liked was wearing off rapidly, and he missed having someone to chat with at dinner, watch TV with in the evenings and share his bed. The house was empty without Chris.

Later that day, while cleaning his already immaculate house, Dan found a white sports sock under the bed. It belonged to Chris. Dan wondered if he should return it. He could take it to the gym where Chris worked or track down his new flat in Heaton using the internet, but decided it might be considered inappropriate behaviour.

Chris seemed to think most of my behaviour was inappropriate.

Dan sighed and tucked the sock away in a drawer, which was unlike him because he didn't believe in clutter, collecting things, or storing keepsakes. But he missed Chris. He would keep it for a while, at least, perhaps until he found another guy to take Chris's place.

As he went downstairs and picked up his laptop, he considered signing up for a dating website, but he couldn't face that yet. He'd have to complete a profile page, and he didn't have a good recent photograph of himself. He didn't like to admit it, but he'd put on more than a few pounds since Chris left, and his trousers were tight at the waist.

Chris had been good for Dan and had improved his health. Dan had eaten smaller meals and drunk less wine when Chris was there, and he'd even made an effort to go jogging with him, once or twice.

Since Chris left, the recycling bin had been so full of wine bottles that Dan had considered taking them to a recycling centre to hide how much he was drinking, but what did it matter if the bin men or his neighbours knew? He didn't care what they thought.

Instead of opening a dating site on his laptop, Dan checked

his social media accounts. As he mindlessly scrolled through his Facebook feed, he spotted an advertisement for an event at a pub on the Quayside—a Christmas Party for singles on the twenty-first of December. It promised a night of music, dancing and a gourmet buffet supper.

Maybe it's time I got back out there, thought Dan, and added the event to his planner.

56

A Good Deed

'Hello, James!' said Matt, reversing his wheelchair to open the door wider. 'Come in. Excuse the mess—I wasn't expecting visitors.'

'How are you doing?' asked James as he entered the hallway and closed the door behind him. Following Matt into the living room, James moved some magazines from the sofa and put them on the side table before sitting down.

'You know me,' said Matt. 'I'm not one to complain, but one minute, I feel positive and look forward to the future, and the next, I'm a complete mess. I don't know what's going on in my head sometimes.'

'I suppose it'll take time,' said James, thinking that he had never heard Matt complain about himself before Amanda's death.

'Yes, that's what the grief counsellor said,' said Matt. 'My life is totally different from what it was a year ago. There have been so many changes—with Glad Rags struggling, we lost you as a colleague and a friend. Then we lost the business, which was Amanda's baby and our livelihood. God knows all that was bad enough, and then I lost my beautiful wife—Amanda—and I've never been so damned lonely in my life. Have you heard what's number one this week? Mariah Carey—All I Want for Christmas is You.'

Matt covered his face with his hands to hide his tears, and his shoulders heaved.

James saw a box of tissues on a shelf in the alcove and passed one to Matt, touching his shoulder as he sat down again.

When Matt raised his red-rimmed eyes to look at James, he noticed the dirty clothes, unbrushed hair, and unshaven face.

'God, I'm being so selfish, James. Never mind me. Are you alright, mate?'

'I must admit I've been better,' said James. 'I got thrown out of my flat because I couldn't pay the rent.'

'You've been evicted?' asked Matt. 'Didn't you get housing benefit to pay for your rent?'

'No,' said James. 'I didn't know I could.'

Matt shook his head sadly and said, 'When you're on the dole, you should have been able to get housing benefit, a discount on your council tax, and maybe Universal Credit. I'm sorry I never thought to tell you, but somebody at the Jobcentre should have mentioned the other benefits you could claim.'

'It doesn't matter now. It's too late.'

'When did this happen?' asked Matt.

'Last week.'

'And where have you been staying?'

'Here and there,' said James, not wanting to admit that he'd been sleeping on the streets.

'The bathroom's through there,' said Matt, who had obviously guessed as much. 'Help yourself to a shower and a shave, and there's a new toothbrush in the top drawer. If you're not in a hurry, you can put your clothes through a wash cycle. There's a dressing gown hanging up on the back of the door—you can wear that until your clothes are dry.'

James had nowhere else to be, so he said, 'Thanks, Matt. I'll take you up on that.'

After showering, James returned, wearing Matt's robe and feeling much more like himself. He sat down again and looked at his rucksack on the floor. Bending down to open it, James saw Whiskers curled up asleep inside. Lifting her out, he placed her on Matt's lap. The cat turned around, rubbed against Matt, and then curled up to sleep again.

'What's this?' asked Matt with a smile.

'This is Whiskers. She was a stray, but she's been living with me for a while. She's no bother, and she's good company.'

'You mean you brought her for me?' asked Matt, looking down at the sleeping feline. He tentatively stroked her, and she purred loudly and rubbed her head against his hand.

'I'm going away. I don't know if I'll be able to keep her. Most landlords don't allow pets.'

'I'm sorry to hear that,' said Matt. 'Where are you off to?'

'I don't know yet, but I can't stay in Newcastle. I've not been able to find a job here, and now I've lost my flat. I hope I'll have better luck somewhere else.'

'You could stay with me for a while if you want. There's a bed made up in the spare room.'

'Thanks for the offer, but I don't want to impose.'

'Thank you for Whiskers,' said Matt, smiling down at the kitten. 'I'll take good care of her, I promise. I won't feel quite so mad when I talk to myself if there's a cat in the house.'

'Thank you,' said James. 'Have you heard any more about the Paralympics?'

'The medical stuff was all sorted before Amanda died.'

'That's great. So, what's the next step?'

'They were going to send someone out to watch me play, but I haven't played for weeks. I couldn't face it.'

'Maybe you should,' said James. 'It might help to get out.'

'Aye, maybe I should,' said Matt, before blowing his nose. 'I can't sit around here feeling sorry for myself forever.'

Matt made some lunch and a pot of tea, which they ate while chatting, and he gave Whiskers some tinned salmon, promising he would buy her some cat food the next time he went to the supermarket.

When the wash cycle finished, James dressed and picked up his rucksack to leave.

'Take care of yourself, Matt.'

'Don't worry about me,' he said, following James to the door with Whiskers on his lap. 'Good luck finding a job, and let me know when you get settled.'

'Will do,' said James, although he had no intention of staying in touch with anyone once he left the city.

'Here, take this.'

Matt took a pile of banknotes from his wallet and offered them to James.

'I couldn't,' he said, thinking there must be over £200 there. 'You're not working. Don't you need it yourself?'

'Amanda had life insurance. The insurance company paid out last week.'

'I didn't think they paid out when—'

'They do if the policy was taken out more than a year ago.'

'Right. Thanks, I appreciate it,' said James, taking the money.

'And Happy Christmas,' said Matt, holding out his hand.

Noticing the surprise on James's face, he said, 'It's only a week today.'

'Merry Christmas, Matt,' replied James, shaking his hand firmly. He gently stroked the cat and said, 'Bye, Whiskers. Look after Matt for me.'

James walked away from the house smiling, knowing he'd done a good deed. Although he would miss Whiskers, he knew that having a pet would give Matt an interest, which he needed in his life, and she would keep him company when he was down. Hopefully, he wouldn't feel so alone in the house now.

57

Stalking Prey

For the next three days, James wandered around the streets of Newcastle and slept under the bridge by the river. With so much time on his hands, he went through everything that had happened in the last five months, over and over in his mind, looking at it from every angle. Each time, he came to the same conclusion. There was only one thing he could do.

James ate breakfast at the cafe on the riverside, looking out at the foggy Tyne. He switched on his laptop and accessed Dan Howard's planner. There was one event entered for the month of December—a singles Christmas party in a Quayside pub starting at eight o'clock that night.

As the party was an event for single people, James guessed Chris must have left Dan. That would explain the cancellation of the Christmas sweaters, he thought, and if he were right, Dan would probably be at the party alone.

That was James's opportunity. He knew what he had to do, but couldn't plan because there were so many unknown factors and so much that could go wrong. Even though the event was on Dan's planner for that evening, it didn't mean he would be there. He might forget about it, decide not to attend, or meet somebody there.

James would have to improvise if and when an opportunity arose.

His mood was solemn. He spent the whole day recalling Dan's actions and how they had affected him and his friends, and building up the courage to do what needed to be done. It was time for Dan to face the consequences of those actions.

That evening, James strolled through the thick fog to the Quayside, an upmarket area at the edge of the River Tyne. Dressed in a black hoodie and dark jeans, he carried his rucksack, which contained everything he owned.

Visibility was poor. The streetlights along the river's edge struggled to penetrate the dense mist and did little to light the broad pavement.

It was almost eleven o'clock. It had been dark for hours already. Despite the fog, James could see reasonably well, as his eyes were accustomed to the dark. As he approached the riverside, he heard music from the pubs, chatter, and laughter. People were partying with colleagues, fellow students, family, and friends. Colourful Christmas lights adorned the bars, restaurants, and clubs, glowing dimly through the haze.

James kept his head down as he passed a group of young men wearing furry antlers and stood in the shadows where he became invisible, but from where he could see the revellers.

He waited, his heart pounding in his chest, hoping that Dan would make an appearance and wondering if he could get away with what he was about to do.

The crowds gradually dispersed as the evening drew to an end. People kissed and hugged, promising to keep in touch.

Dan Howard was among the last to leave the pub. He looked

both ways as he stepped out of the doorway before walking to the railings at the river's edge. He held on to the top iron rail and looked down into the river below.

James wondered if he might be waiting for somebody to join him, but nobody came. Surveying the area, he saw the security guards had abandoned their posts at the doorways and that few people remained outside—an amorous couple pressed up against a wall, a guy passed out on a bench, and a student, abandoned by his mates, puking in a planter. None of them would notice him.

Dan let go of the railing and wandered along the quayside, and James followed him at a distance, wondering why Dan was walking towards Byker rather than the city centre, where he could get a taxi to take him home.

The restaurants and bars on the riverside soon gave way to industrial buildings, and apart from Dan, the path appeared deserted as far as he could see.

58

Retribution

Dan kicked himself for forgetting to book a taxi to take him home. He knew it would be impossible to get one at this time of night, especially as it was the last Saturday before Christmas. He'd had quite a bit to drink at the party, which had been a decent night, but he had missed Chris. Chris wouldn't have forgotten to book a taxi.

When he walked out of the pub, into the cold, misty night, he felt nauseous and stood by the river's edge until his stomach settled. He loved cocktails, but drinking a mixture of different alcohols and fruit juices all night had not been a good idea.

What he was doing now was not a good idea either. Chris would view it as inappropriate behaviour, but still, Dan felt a flutter of excitement at the possibility of seeing him. If he walked through Byker, an area with a reputation for being a bit rough, he would eventually reach Heaton, where Chris lived. He reckoned Chris might be out celebrating, and he might run into him. It was a long shot, he knew, but it was worth a chance. If not, he could try to get a taxi home from there. He increased his stride in anticipation of seeing Chris again.

Suddenly, he felt a hand on his shoulder, abruptly bringing him to a stop.

'What the fuck?' said Dan. 'Do I know you?'

'You tell me, Dan Howard. Do you know me?'

'How do you know my name?'

'I know a lot more about you than just your name, Dan.'

Dan stepped back and eyed James suspiciously.

'What do you want?' he asked. Taking his wallet from his pocket, he removed the banknotes and handed them to James. 'That's all the cash I've got. Take it.'

Shaking his head, James said, 'I don't want your money, Dan.'

'What do you want?' Dan was shaking now, and James saw fear in his eyes.

'Retribution.'

'Retribution? What for? I don't even know you.'

'Maybe not,' said James. 'Yet you destroyed my life.'

Dan's eyes widened.

'You don't know who I am or what you've done to me—and that concerns me greatly,' said James.

'There must be some mistake. I wouldn't hurt a fly. What is it you think I did?' asked Dan, cowering from the stranger and wondering why he was listening to him rather than running away. There was something almost hypnotic about his voice that made Dan want to listen to him. He wanted to hear what the man had to say and wanted to know how he could have destroyed the life of someone he had never met. He was spellbound.

'I lost everything because of you,' said James. 'A job that I enjoyed, the woman I love, a very dear friend, and my home.'

'But—but how?' stammered Dan. 'I don't understand. How

could I do all that when I don't even know who you are?'

'Do you remember you ordered a Spider-Man costume?'

'Yes, of course I do. How could I forget that?' Dan rolled his eyes.

James's eyes darkened, and he struggled to contain his anger. He wanted to punch this guy in the face, but he couldn't. It would spoil the plan.

'Did you own the fancy dress shop that I ordered it from?' asked Dan. 'I saw that it had closed down.'

'No. My best friends owned the shop,' said James. 'I worked there—that was until they couldn't afford to pay me any more. Let me tell you about my friends, because you destroyed their lives, too, not just mine. Matt is a veteran of the Royal Marines. He was injured while serving his country in Afghanistan and will spend the rest of his life in a wheelchair. He invested the compensation he received from the army in that shop, and he lost it all. Matt is a fighter, and he'll get over it—eventually. Amanda didn't handle it so well. She suffered from anxiety and depression when her business failed and the shop closed down, and then she committed suicide. Amanda took her own life because of what you did! You, Dan, didn't know any of us, yet you ruined all our lives. And do you know something? That got me thinking. How many lives have you wrecked without knowing it? And how many more will you destroy unless you are stopped? You must realise that actions have consequences.'

'I'm sorry,' said Dan. 'I had absolutely no idea. I promise you I won't do anything like that again. You can be sure of that.'

Despite Dan's assurances, James did not believe him. He was a serial keyboard warrior who didn't give a damn about whom he hurt.

'I know you won't do anything like that again, because I'm going to make sure you don't.'

Moving swiftly, James lifted Dan off his feet with one almighty push. Dan toppled over the railings, his hands flailing in the air as he tried to grab them, but failed. He fell into the deep, dark water of the River Tyne.

The fall seemed to happen in slow motion. Dan stretched out to grab the rails to save himself, but he was too far away. When he realised he couldn't reach them, he knew he was falling into the murky water of the Tyne and was horrified. He couldn't swim, and he knew creatures lived in the river, revolting slimy creatures, and with it being tidal, maybe even scary sea creatures. It was also full of sewage from farther up the valley. *How disgusting!*

He hit the surface of the water with a splash. The cold water shocked him and knocked the breath from his body, which smarted from the impact. He tried to scream, but he was under the water and couldn't, and he kept going down. *How deep was this river?* The descent seemed endless. He didn't dare open his eyes; he didn't want to see what was down there. Memories of the films 'Piranha' and 'Jaws' had tormented him since childhood.

He couldn't hold his breath any longer and took a deep breath, but he was still under the water. The filthy, cold water filled his lungs.

Something touched Dan's hand, and he thrashed around in a blind panic, rising through the water and eventually breaking the surface. Fighting for air, he tried to take in vital oxygen. His body fought to clear his airways, and he coughed repeatedly to clear his lungs, but they were already full of water.

He glanced up at the path to see if the stranger was still there and saw a blurry silhouette through the fog, but he couldn't be sure if it was him.

Dan's last thought was that he didn't know the guy's name.

He sank back down into the inky water, knowing he was about to die. His body was screaming at him to breathe, desperately needing air. He took another breath; the river water replaced what little air remained in his lungs. He continued to descend into the depths and, this time, didn't rise to the surface again. The pain gradually subsided as he floated into unconsciousness, and he felt relief.

James watched from above. When he didn't see Dan surface again, he walked away and disappeared into the shadows once more, knowing his job was done.

59

Identity

Standing by the riverside in Byker, with a coffee carton warming her hands, Sergeant Ali Hanlon waited for the police divers to remove a body from the water. Usually, a police presence brought out the locals en masse to find out what was happening, but as it had just turned seven o'clock on a Sunday morning, their presence had not been noticed yet. Only the dog walker who reported seeing the body floating in the water was there with her, and she had already talked to him and taken a statement. Now they waited in silence.

Ali would rather be anywhere else than here, dealing with a dead body the day before Christmas. She had two children at home, a girl and a boy, counting down the days on their Advent calendars. As a mother, she couldn't bear the thought of telling another woman that she had lost a child or a husband.

She was still reeling from the fact that her husband had chosen a woman from work over her, the mother of his children. They had been together since secondary school, and she thought they would be together forever. She never imagined that he would leave her and their children and set up home with someone else.

Police Constable Rob Marshall was striding toward her. A familiar face and a bit of moral support were just what Ali needed that morning.

'Rob, I'm glad to see you,' she said. 'I hate this kind of thing. There's nothing worse than identifying a body and having to tell the next of kin, especially at this time of year.'

'I disagree. I think it's worse if you can't identify a body and you can't tell the next of kin. Then they're left wondering what became of their loved ones for the rest of their lives.'

'I suppose so,' she said. 'If it's a local one, would you come with me?'

'Of course I will. I'll tell the family if you want.'

'Thanks, Rob, I owe you one. It's an awful thing to do, especially on Christmas Eve.'

'Any idea who it is?' asked Rob, nodding towards the river.

'A white male, quite fresh, floating face down. That's all I know so far.'

'How are things at home?' asked Rob as they waited for the divers to retrieve the body.

'I got a letter from my husband's solicitor yesterday. He wants a divorce,' she said coldly. 'He wants to marry her.'

'That's terrible news. I'm so sorry.'

'It wasn't unexpected. I just wish he'd had the nerve to tell me himself, rather than use a solicitor. It's tough when the kids ask where their dad is and when he's be coming home. I don't know what to say.'

'If there's anything I can do, let me know. And I mean it.'

'Thanks, Rob. What are you doing tomorrow?'

'I volunteered to work. I think it's only fair that officers with kids have the day off at Christmas.'

'Why don't you pop round for a drink after work? I could reheat some Christmas dinner.'

'That's the best offer I've had in a long time, and I'd love to take you up on it,' said Rob, with a smile that reached his eyes. 'Thank you.'

'Great! I'll look forward to it.'

'I think they're lifting him now,' said Rob, pointing to the river's edge. 'We'd better get over there.'

The divers hauled the body up onto the pavement, and despite there being nobody around, apart from the police officers and the dog walker who'd notified them, they screened it from public view.

Ali and Rob walked over to the body and looked down at the pallid face.

'I recognise this guy,' said Rob. 'It's Dan Howard from Jesmond.'

'I knew it,' said Ali, shaking her head sadly. 'I told you I thought he had mental health problems, didn't I? I failed him, Rob. I should have contacted social services when I mentioned it the other day.'

'Calm down, Ali. You did no such thing.'

Rob put a comforting arm around her shoulder.

'I have to admit, though,' he said, 'I thought he was a time-waster. I didn't think he'd do something like this.'

'Wait for the coroner's verdict before you say that,' said a member of the police diving team, who had heard the end of their conversation. 'It might not be suicide.'

'Do you have any reason to suspect that it wasn't suicide?' asked Ali.

The diver shook his head and frowned.

'It's always suicide at Christmas,' said Rob sadly.

The police officers watched the body being lifted onto a trolley and loaded into the back of a black van to be taken away for a postmortem, and then Ali drove Rob to Somerset Road in Jesmond.

Rob knocked loudly at Dan Howard's door, stood back and waited sombrely, ready to impart the bad news. There was no answer. He tried again, but nobody came to the door.

'I wonder where his hunky partner is?' said Rob.

The neighbour at number sixty-four stuck his head over the hedge and said, 'If you're looking for the sporty one, he moved out.'

'When was that?' asked Ali.

'Last week, or maybe the week before. Not long since.'

'I'm Sergeant Ali Hanlon and this is my colleague, Police Constable Rob Marshall. Would you mind if we asked you a few questions?' asked Ali. 'What's your name?'

'I'm Mr Backworth, John Backworth, and I don't mind at all. Come on in where it's nice and warm, and I'll put the kettle on. There's quite a chill in the air this morning.'

They went into Mr Backworth's house, and once they were all seated around a highly polished dinner table with fresh cups of tea, Rob told Mr Backworth that they had found Dan Howard's body earlier that morning.

'How well did you know Dan Howard, Mr Backworth?' asked Rob.

'I've lived next door to him since he was a bairn. They moved in as a family in the early 90s. His father died suddenly when he wasn't very old. Just in his forties, I think. His mother had cancer and died a few years ago. Dan's a very private person— he always has been. Never says more than a few words. I liked the other bloke, though. He would always stop and pass the time of day.'

'Do you know who Dan Howard's next of kin would be?'

'No, I'm afraid not,' said Mr Backworth. 'He doesn't have any brothers or sisters—or children, for that matter. He may have cousins, but I haven't seen any family visiting him.'

'Have you had any disagreements with Dan Howard?' asked Rob.

Ali raised her eyebrows, wondering why he had posed a question that had nothing to do with Howard's death.

'No, not really,' replied Mr Backworth. 'The only time there was a bit of friction was when he applied to the council for planning permission to build a conservatory. That was quite a few years ago now. He wanted to build an enormous conservatory on the back of his house, and it would have blocked the light from my garden. I wrote to the council, and they made him scale back his plans to something more acceptable. He's never once mentioned it to me, mind you, but I've always felt awkward about it.'

'Do you know anything about the plant we found in his garden a few months ago?' asked Ali, realising that Rob's line of questioning might provide them with some answers to their previous dealings with the man.

'No,' he said, shaking his head. 'But there was a gardener there one day. Nice chap. I remember seeing him because it reminded me to prune the roses on the front of the house.'

'Thank you, Mr Backworth. You've been very helpful,' said Ali.

'Thanks for the tea,' said Rob as they headed for the door.

'You're welcome. It's nice to have visitors these days, even if they do come bearing bad news.'

Rob and Ali returned to the police car.

'I would have sworn that the neighbour planted that potato in the exhaust pipe and the cannabis in the garden, but after meeting him today, I can honestly say I don't think he had anything to do with either.'

'Howard never mentioned having a gardener when I questioned him,' said Ali. 'You'd think he would have mentioned something like that under the circumstances.'

'Maybe he was protecting somebody. He could have been paying a mate cash in hand for helping, or employing an illegal immigrant.'

'Now that Howard's dead, I doubt we'll ever know exactly what's been going on here,' said Ali, starting the car.

'We should track down his partner, Chris Smith. He may be able to help with our enquiries, and he might know if Howard had any family.'

'Good thinking.'

They returned to the station, searched for Christopher Smith's whereabouts, and discovered that he'd taken up residence in a flat in Heaton.

'Come on, Rob,' said Ali, scribbling the address onto a scrap of paper. 'Let's go.'

They went to the address on Claymore Terrace and knocked on the door, which was answered by an elderly lady, who introduced herself as Mrs Green.

'We're here to see Christopher Smith. Does he live here?' asked Ali.

'He must be the new bloke that's moved in upstairs,' she said. 'I hope he hasn't been in any trouble. The last man who lived there was ever so nice.'

'Thank you. May we go up?'

'Yes, pet,' she said, opening the door wider for the police

officers to pass and then closing it after them. She hovered at the bottom of the stairs before entering her flat and giving them some privacy.

At the top of the stairs, Rob knocked at the door of the upstairs flat, and Chris opened it.

'Hey! I recognise you,' he said. 'You're the officer who came to our house when someone played that potato prank on Dan.'

'That's right, Mr Smith. I'm Police Constable Rob Marshall, and this is my colleague, Sergeant Ali Hanlon. I'm afraid we have some bad news. It's concerning Dan Howard.'

'What has he done now?' asked Chris, rolling his eyes.

'I'm afraid his body was found this morning,' said Rob. 'Dan's dead.'

Chris gasped and stumbled back towards the settee, where he sat down.

'Dan's dead?' he asked, clearly stunned by the news. 'What happened? How did he die?'

'He drowned in the River Tyne.'

Chris sat there, shaking his head. 'I can't believe it.'

'Can I make you a cup of tea or something?' asked Ali.

'No, thanks. I'll just grab a glass of water. One sec.'

Chris returned carrying a pint glass full of water and sat down on the sofa.

'Dan couldn't swim,' he said. 'I tried to get him to take lessons, but he always made excuses. If only I'd tried harder.'

'Don't blame yourself. It's not your fault,' said Rob. 'I'm sorry to ask you this, Mr Smith, but do you know what Dan's state of mind has been like lately?'

'Not really,' said Chris, sipping the water. 'I haven't seen him or heard from him since I left his place a week past Sunday, but it wasn't good then. He was drinking more than he usually did, which was a lot. It crossed my mind that he might do something stupid with the court case hanging over him and me leaving, but I couldn't stay there any longer. He'd changed. He wasn't the guy I fell in love with. God! I feel so terrible now.'

'Thank you, Mr Smith,' said Ali. 'But we shouldn't assume that Dan took his own life.'

'You mean it wasn't suicide?' asked Chris, his eyebrows raised.

'There will be a postmortem and then a coroner's inquest to determine how he died.'

'Do you know who his next of kin is?' asked Rob.

'Dan didn't have any family as far as I know,' said Chris. 'He's not mentioned anybody. On his birthday, the only birthday card he received was mine. He used my name as a contact when he renewed his passport in July. His mother was on the old one, but she died before I met Dan. He wrote a will about the same time, making me the sole beneficiary, so I suspect there was nobody else in his life. I guess he'll have changed it when I left.'

'If he had no family, why do you think he'll have changed it?' asked Ali. 'Was there a cat shelter or some other cause he supported?'

Chris laughed and said, 'I'm sorry. Dan disliked animals, and he would never donate to a cat shelter. He wasn't one to give to charity. If he changed his will, I don't know what he would have done with his money.'

'Thank you for your help, and I'm sorry for your loss,' said Rob. 'We'll be in touch soon about Dan's personal items.'

'I think we're finished here,' said Ali, turning to Rob.

The officers left Chris sitting on the settee, struggling to come to terms with Dan's death and pondering over the possibility that he might inherit Dan's estate.

As they walked to the police car, Ali was relieved that she didn't have to deal with any bereaved parents or spouses, and was glad Rob had taken the lead that day.

'If there's any foul play involved in Howard's death,' said Rob, 'the fact that Chris Smith will inherit Howard's house and everything puts him at the top of our list.'

'He seems genuine enough to me,' she said.

'Aye, to me, as well.'

Back at the station, the police officers ate lunch in the canteen.

'We should go down to the quayside after we finish here and see if there's any CCTV footage of Howard at the weekend,' said Ali, between bites of her chicken tikka sandwich.

'Is there any point before we've seen the postmortem report?' asked Rob. 'That might give us more to work with.'

'I don't think I did enough for the guy when he was alive, Rob, so I feel like I need to do something now.'

'If we see how he was behaving before he died, it might tell us if it was suicide or an accident, and if we get really lucky, we might see what happened.'

'I doubt we'll get footage of what happened, but it might give us an indication of his state of mind, and it might provide more evidence for the coroner; he's the one who has to decide what happened.'

After lunch, they took a car to the quayside and entered a bar.

'Sergeant Ali Hanlon.' She showed her ID to the barman. 'I'd like to see your CCTV footage from the weekend.'

'I'll get the manager,' said the young man, taking out his

phone and texting a message. Within a minute or two, a large middle-aged man approached them in the bar, introduced himself as the owner, and took them to his office.

'We have two cameras on the front of the building.' He pointed to the two screens on the wall above his desk. 'What date and time do you want to see?'

'We're probably looking at Saturday evening,' said Ali. 'Late, I'd guess. Perhaps start at around eleven.'

The man keyed in the details, and the recording played on the screens. Rob looked at one, and Ali at the other.

'What's wrong with them?' asked Rob. 'I can't make out anything apart from a couple of hazy street lights.'

'It's fog,' said the bar owner. 'I'd forgotten it was a real pea-souper out there on Saturday night. CCTV is useless when it's foggy. I'm afraid you're wasting your time.'

'The famous fog on the Tyne,' said Rob, thinking of the song by Lindisfarne.

'Thanks for your help,' said Ali. 'We won't trouble you any further.'

'Well, that was a waste of time,' said Rob, as they returned to the car.

'I had to try.'

When they returned to the station, Dan Howard's pathology report sat on Ali's desk.

'Blimey, that was quick!' she said, picking it up and skipping straight to the conclusion.

'The cause of death was drowning,' she said, skimming through the report. 'He'd been in the river about three days—so I was probably right with Saturday night. There were no signs of a struggle, no bruising to the body, no cuts or wounds, nothing under his fingernails. They found a wallet containing cash and bank cards in his jacket pocket—so that rules out theft. There were no drugs in his system. The only significant finding here is the high level of alcohol in his blood. There's nothing suspicious here.'

'So he was pissed,' said Rob. 'My money's on suicide.'

'Mine too. I wish I'd got in touch with social services. They might have been able to prevent this.'

Rob touched her arm and said, 'Don't be so hard on yourself. You had no way of knowing what was going on inside his head.'

60

A New Beginning

On Christmas Eve, James was sitting in a cafe near Newcastle Station when he received a text from Matt: *Hi, I hope you're doing better. Whiskers has settled in well. Did you see the news at lunchtime? The Spider-Man guy is dead, and good riddance to him. Merry Christmas, James, wherever you are. P.S. I made the team and I'm going to Tokyo!!!*

James smiled as he sent a reply: *Great news all round, mate. Merry Christmas!*

He opened Facebook, went to The Chronicle page, and scrolled through the latest news articles until he found the one he was searching for.

A man has been found dead in the River Tyne at Newcastle-upon-Tyne. The body was discovered by a man walking his dog early on Tuesday morning in the Byker area of the city. Police divers retrieved the body, which was later identified as that of Daniel Howard from Jesmond. Northumbria Police issued a statement this morning saying they believe there are no suspicious circumstances concerning the man's death, and a report has been prepared for the coroner. The inquest into Mr Howard's death will be held on January 17 at the Coroner's Court in the city.

He took the memory card from his phone, broke it with the heel of his shoe, and put it in the bin.

Then, he walked to the busy railway station with his hoodie hiding his face, and boarded a train heading south on the East Coast Main Line. The train was full of people travelling to spend Christmas with their loved ones. He kept his head lowered to avoid making conversation.

As the train pulled out of the city, James felt the tension leave his body. He sat back, looked out the window, and enjoyed the view. He passed through Durham and Darlington. The train slowed as it approached the next station and came to a stop when it reached the platform. The sign declared the station was York, which the unintelligible announcement in the carriage had failed to do.

Carrying his rucksack, James disembarked from the train and walked along the platform towards the exit, trailing behind the other travellers. At the station entrance, he stopped to survey this new city, where he intended to find a new job and a new home, and start a new life.

James had no regrets about leaving Newcastle. Lisa was happy with her new man in Gosforth. Matt had a place on the England basketball team and was heading to the Paralympic Games. Amanda was dead. That was tragic. But the man responsible for her death was dead, too.

A life for a life—perfect retribution.

The previous chapter of James's life had come to an end, and he closed the pages in his mind like a book. What had passed had passed. This was a new start for James Webster. A new city, a new year and a new beginning.

About the Author

Margaret Manchester is an international bestselling author on Amazon, celebrated for her richly woven thrillers and historical novels. Her stories bring to life the captivating landscapes and vibrant characters of northern England.

Blending her professional insights and life experiences, she crafts emotionally resonant stories that captivate readers worldwide. Her work is renowned for its authentic characters and immersive settings.

With a talent for crafting emotionally resonant tales, Margaret invites you to explore the complexities of love, identity, and societal challenges in her unforgettable works.

Margaret was awarded a postgraduate degree from the University of Durham and lives with her husband in northern England. Besides writing, she enjoys gardening, spending time with her dogs, and cooking.

You can connect with me on:
- https://www.margaretmanchester.com
- https://x.com/m_r_manchester
- https://www.facebook.com/margaretmanchesterauthor